TWISTED LIES

LISA CUTTS

For Emma and Anthony Smith, two of the world's finest people

PROLOGUE
TWELVE MONTHS AGO

It took a couple of moments to register that he really was dead – as in, completely beyond saving and not miraculously coming back to life. What kind of existence had he had in the first place? A damned miserable one, that's for sure.

The blood was already trying its best to seep into the soil, scorched by days of unbroken sunshine. The thick, black liquid ebbed towards a crack in the ground, its progress made all the harder by the dust and grit blown across the wasteland.

Burying the body would take far too long and setting fire to it would only attract attention. The safest option, surely, was to leave it here and hope for the best. It was hardly a genius plan – but then neither had been meeting an unhinged individual in a lonely, isolated spot and not letting anyone know.

Still, it was better to live to see another day, which was more than could be said for the man on the ground with a pair of secateurs through his eye socket.

When it came down to it, the choice wasn't all that difficult.

CHAPTER ONE

I'm not sure when it first dawned on me that I'd wanted to kill my husband for some time.

If I close my eyes and wish really hard, perhaps he'll stop breathing and die of his own accord without any intervention from me. Something quick and painless. Wait, no, I'd like him to suffer. Really suffer, with a searing pain straight through his heart. Just like he did to me. Just like he's currently doing to me.

My pain was emotional – it still is. I blink rapidly. It's less a fluttering of my eyelashes at him, that's the last thing I want; more to bat away the tears that prick the corners of my eyes.

'Avril,' he says. 'Are you listening to me?' There's annoyance in his voice.

How bloody dare you? I want to scream. You've done this to me and now you're perturbed because I wasn't hanging on your every boring, condescending word. Instead, I nod like a child wanting to be praised.

'What did I just say?' He leans forward in his Marks and Spencer's café seat, his saggy face almost the same shade of alabaster as the table. He pushes the metal teapot so that it's exactly square on to the edge of the garishly bleached surface, all the while staring me in the eye.

'Was it something about how you left me for your secretary?' I say, tone as nonchalant as I can manage, which isn't by very much at all.

I watch as my husband of fifteen years drums his fingers on the table. Another thing I hate. I used to let him touch me with those hands. They're very soft, but then he never did an actual day's proper graft in his life. His entire existence has been spent poncing about in an office, tapping his hairy digits on a keyboard.

Even though the shop-regulated air temperature is a mildly pleasant one and nowhere close to giving me goosebumps, I shudder.

I hear a sigh as he throws himself back in his seat. I tear my gaze from his hirsute knuckles and glare back at him.

'You always get like this whenever I mention Caitlin,' he says, his mouth turning down. It seems a staged move, and one designed to make me feel as though he truly is sorry. Not that he seems to have felt all that anguished when he stuck his cock in her.

'Besides, Caitlin isn't a secretary,' he continues, a slow shake of his head to emphasise what a simpleton I am. 'She's so much more. She's an executive associate assistant. She's a—'

'What exactly do you want to speak to me about?' I've had enough now and I'm itching to get home. When I say home, I, of course, mean the two-up, two-down tiny cottage I've been renting for the past month. It's charming, although I'm not looking forward to the winter. It has so many draughts letting June's soft breezes in, I dread to think how cold I'm likely to be once autumn is a dim and distant memory.

'We should start to talk about a divorce,' he says. The

attempt to appear genuinely remorseful helps gravity drag his jowls closer to the ground.

'I need to get a lawyer,' I say, knowing this was coming, yet feeling my insides turn to ice. I swear I can't feel my fingers or toes.

'No, no,' he says, 'a lawyer would only make everything complicated, slow and not to mention expensive. We can sort this out ourselves. It'll be so much easier that way.'

Christ, this fool doesn't know me at all. I'm hardly likely to fumble along without legal help now, am I?

'You're in a bit of shock,' he says, stretching across the table amid the used crockery that looks as if it's been arranged by a psychopath. Everything is angled precisely and lined up like instruments in an operating theatre. 'I'll give you a day or two and we'll talk again.'

With that, he pushes his chair back and stands up in one movement, goes to turn away and then waggles his fingers at me before heading for the escalator.

Such an abrupt end to a fifteen-year marriage which would be made all the worse without the prospect of shopping for a dine-in meal deal. I push my own chair back and head to the food hall.

Forty minutes later, having bought my dinner and a very nice bottle of Rioja, I clamber off the bus at the top of Wicked Lane. I don't much like the name but it's a beautiful short stroll from the bus stop to my cottage. I don't have a car because, many years before Caitlin wiggled into our lives, we decided that two cars were an extravagance, and I could take the Mazda MX-5 whenever I felt like it. Except, I couldn't take it whenever I wanted to now, could I? Because it was twenty miles away in Bearsted.

I should have known then that he was having a mid-life crisis, the stupid, self-obsessed—

I jump back as a black Honda Civic races towards me. The pavements are narrow, country pavements, not designed for much, and certainly not a great barrier between pedestrians and passing vehicles. Especially so when the traffic is hurtling towards me at an alarming velocity. I try to catch a glimpse of the driver, but other than the car's speed not really allowing for much in the way of idle perusing, the glare of the sun catches the window as it shoots past me.

It's not a car I recognise from the short time I've lived here, although I haven't taken all that much notice of my neighbours. I've been too busy falling to pieces. That's always been one of my specialities – making a total mess and hoping other people will help me out of it. They usually do, yet there's always a price to pay. Sometimes I pay the price, and on other occasions, they do.

I struggle back towards my humble home, the paper bag handles cutting into my skin as the ever-heavier goodies weigh me down. The wine makes it worth it. Another bonus of being red, despite the warmth of the late afternoon – I don't have to wait for it to chill.

Happy thirteen per cent alcohol content thoughts filling my head, I meander along the pavement towards the small row of six former farm labourer cottages, and then I stop dead.

There on the ground is a shape, a person – an unmoving figure with blood seeping from his head.

For a second, I freeze, unsure what to do. Should I run towards him and help? Make my way to my nearest neighbour and ask that someone does something, or should I summon medical assistance myself?

This isn't the first time I've seen a man on the floor with blood leaking out of his head, so I run towards him. He isn't moving or responding to me shouting, 'Oi, are you okay?'

I place my bag down carefully so as to avoid breaking the bottle – I'm not made of money. Besides, what's the point of wasting good Rioja on what could turn out to be a corpse?

I hear him groan and I crouch down, partly relieved he's not dead, yet a tiny bit on edge as to how I deal with him. I really don't want to kneel in the blood. It's hell to get out of linen and this is one of the most heat-friendly things I brought with me in my escape from the less than perfect marriage.

His brown eyes flicker open and he tries to focus. 'I need an ambulance,' he says, attempting to sit up and failing spectacularly.

'Give me a second and I'll call one,' I say, once again a little bit pleased that he's alive. My first aid skills are a touch on the rusty side. Besides, it'll be the first time in years I've had to administer CPR and he has something of the unwashed about him. I'm not sure if he's cut his lip or whether he has a cold sore. No, if he's talking, he's breathing.

He looks at me again, a hard stare. On the verge of asking him what he's looking at, I remember that I'm supposed to be helping him. I pull my mobile phone from my pocket and stand up in a vain attempt to get a better signal.

The satellite is hundreds of miles away in the earth's orbit, yet somehow the extra three feet or so is going to save the day.

I let the call connect, ask for an ambulance and tell the operator where we are. Then the questions start.

'Er, I suppose he's around thirty-five, not had a shave for a while,' I say.

Through the blood dribbling down his face, he narrows his eyes and gives the tiniest of sighs.

'His name? Hang on,' I say. 'What's your—'

'John,' he says, 'John Smith.'

'Oh, it's John Smith.'

The operator repeats it back with less incredulity than I'm sure I would have managed. As I hold the phone to my ear, I try to take in what sort of person John is. I'm usually good at this – the exception being my husband. I peg this guy as reasonably fit, casually dressed in supermarket jeans and a T-shirt, unbranded trainers and a close-cropped light brown haircut. The lack of hair is also making the blood look plentiful, unless, of course, that's only because there *is* a lot of blood.

I'm aware that the operator is saying something to me. 'Hang on,' I tell him, 'I'll ask John.'

John looks round – it could be bewilderment due to his head injury, but then again, it could be because his name isn't John.

'John,' I all but shout, 'can you tell me what happened?'

'My head's bleeding,' he says with a tone that suggests I'm the moron.

'Yes, I can see that,' I say. 'How did the injury occur? Did someone hit you? Did you fall?'

I watch him open his mouth to say something. No longer narrowing his eyes, now he opens them wide with shock. He can't believe what he's seeing. I glance over my shoulder at whatever it is he's looking at and it's my turn to stare.

The black Honda Civic is on its way back in the direction of my home. I still can't make out the driver and, as I move towards the edge of the pavement to get a better look, John cries out in agony.

I spin my head back round so suddenly I think I've given myself whiplash. I doubt that it is in any way possible from watching a car hurtle past, but I've always had a knack for ridiculous stunts.

'What is it?' I ask John, all the while trying to answer the

999 operator's seemingly endless questions, while trying my best to see if I can get a glimpse of the driver's face.

'My head hurts. It's bleeding.'

'It's good that he's conscious,' says the operator. 'Can you find out how the injury happened?'

'They need to know how you hit your head,' I say.

John looks at the now empty country road, a single narrow expanse of concrete pathway separating us from the tall, green hedgerow and a farmer's field beyond. A similar set up on the other side of the road leaves me with a niggling feeling: I'm completely alone with this unbranded trainer-wearing man who has a slightly thuggish air about him, now that I'm able to get a better look at him. He's avoided answering how he got his injuries and there's not a soul around. My cottage is one of only six. I know that my neighbours on one side of me are out at work, two have been empty since I moved in and I've only met one of the other two occupants.

I'm alone.

I feel the panic start to rise, and I wonder if I can get to the bottle of Rioja and smash it over his head before he can attack me.

'The paramedics will be with you in seconds,' says the operator. 'They're turning into the top of the road now.'

Now I know I've got company, I can't believe how easily I was about to freak out – not to mention waste a perfectly good Marks and Spencer's wine. If it came to it, I'm sure I wouldn't bash him over the head. I don't have to worry about it though, as the sound of the ambulance racing towards us, blue lights flashing, sirens silenced, helps me regain my composure.

'Well, I'll leave you to it,' I say, 'especially as I know nothing, saw nothing and you still haven't told me how you got hurt.'

John gives me a look of complete contempt before rolling onto his side to watch the paramedic team leap from the ambulance, one coming straight over whilst her colleague busies herself fetching equipment via the vehicle's back doors.

It's not the first time a man has looked at me with such disdain moments before rolling over, so I move towards my shopping bag to head off home.

'Afternoon,' calls the cheerful paramedic. 'This must be John.' She steps towards his prone figure, her movements smacking of wearied efficiency.

'I found him like this,' I call out, reunited with my paper bag and waiting for no one. 'I don't know what happened, he didn't get round to telling me. Your control room has my name and phone number, so, bye and good luck.'

I stroll away to a momentary silence where I picture the paramedic staring at the back of my head as I make my way home. Then I hear her talking to John and snapping on a pair of latex gloves. Even with my back turned, that's a sound I instantly recognise.

CHAPTER TWO

I hurry home, the shopping bag hitting the side of my leg every few steps I take. Yes, I'm rushing to get away from *John Smith* and his blood-encrusted cranium, but I'm also grateful for the first time since moving here that this home is my new sanctuary.

As I all but gallop around the bend in the road, safe in the knowledge that the paramedics and their charge can no longer see me and I can't hear what they're doing, I feel my face break into a rare smile as my modest home comes into view.

It's a little rough around the edges but the plain, white-painted façade and sash windows comfort me. The entire row of humble abodes smack of a bygone era and fill me with warmth. No doubt this soppy feeling is entirely down to the happy summer holidays I enjoyed as a child staying at my great auntie Ivy's cottage on the outskirts of Faversham. The building itself was certainly nothing to write home about – and I definitely wouldn't have penned a letter to my hideously miserable parents, not without someone holding a gun to my Cabbage Patch doll's head. What gives me so many wonderful memories was the warmth of my great auntie Ivy and how she loved having me to stay.

Anyway, I take a deep breath and forge on towards home. Someone once told me that the front of a house was designed to look like a face with the windows as eyes and the door as a mouth.

If that's true, then my cottage has a very startled look. Its mouth is hanging wide open. Its expression is one of violation.

I rush towards the open front door, initial thoughts of protecting my property and confronting anyone who dares to force their way into my home. Then, one foot on the crumbling concrete step, hand reaching for my weapon of choice – the bottle – I freeze. Is that a noise? Is someone upstairs? If there is someone here, what am I realistically going to do about it?

Heart pounding, sweat pooling in the small of my back and my breathing coming harder and faster than I really like in any given situation, save for those that involve sex or me being very much in charge – or a combination of the two – I pause.

This won't end well if I rush in.

I take a step back, place my shopping on the front lawn and glance around. I'm already fully aware that there aren't many people nearby at the best of times. After all, if I was going to burgle a house, I'd pick the arse-end of nowhere.

The noise of a car coming along the road instantly calms my nerves, until I'm gripped again by panic that it could be an accomplice. Even the daftest of thieves would have enough brains to make sure they could get away with the goods. There's nowhere to hide a car along this stretch with high hedges directly opposite the cottages and each cottage having either a scratch of lawn or room for a car. If this is the getaway driver, would I be better off pretending I don't even live here?

Indecision keeps me rooted to the spot until I see the same black Honda Civic heading along the row of cottages back towards me, this time being driven worryingly slowly.

The driver stops the car at the curtilage of the first cottage and, as if an afterthought, swings the car into the tight driveway.

I'm unsure what to do now. Since I moved in, I'd thought that that particular place was empty; I'd seen no sign of life nor any vehicle at the front. Not even the wheelie bins had moved. I didn't know this neighbour, and there was nothing to indicate they may be a good person.

I have a clear view across to the driver's door as it's swung open and someone steps out. It's not what I'm expecting.

Call me sexist, but the aggressive way the car was being driven and the confident handling of how it was pulled into the driveway, I expected to see a man staring back at me. Instead, a woman looks my way, late forties, dark brown wavy hair draped over one shoulder, eyes covered by a pair of aviators. Against the height of the car's roof, I can tell she's around five eight, five nine, slim but curvy and, dare I say it, pretty sexy.

'You all right?' she calls, turning her head slightly in the direction of my home. I clock that her chin stops shy of giving her face a triangular shape, and she's striking.

I can't tell if she's looking at me or not until she starts to walk towards me. She barely moves her head as she begins to stride purposefully across the front gardens of the property that stands between my house and hers. With ease, she steps over the low boundary brick wall, her black ankle boots crunching on the gravel.

'I'm, I'm not sure,' I say, feeling slightly stupid now. Surely if anyone was inside, they would hear what was going on and either barrel through the front door or try to make good their escape through the kitchen door and out through the jungle-esque back garden.

She stands a few feet from me, takes off her sunglasses and gives me a cool blue-eyed stare.

'What's happened?' she asks, glancing down at my bag of

shopping. 'I'm assuming that's not an online delivery dropped on that feeble excuse for a lawn.'

'At least I haven't paved mine over to park my car on it,' I say, indignant that she's having a pop at my garden – and when I say my garden, I obviously mean the one that I've been renting for a month and have little to no responsibility for the upkeep of.

Her head swings round to look at the driveway where her car's parked. 'You're very touchy about it. I was only saying it's an eyesore.'

'I...I.'

She steps past me to the front door.

'You live alone, I'm guessing,' she says, tucking the aviators into the back pocket of her mid-thigh denim skirt. 'Anyone else here who shouldn't be? Your entire demeanour and the panicked look on your face is telling me that something's definitely wrong here.'

On the cusp of asking her what on earth she thinks she's doing making these snap judgements about me, I decide to wait and see what she does. There is something reassuring about her presence, and not because I was alone until a few moments ago, still with no idea why my front door is wide open.

'I don't know what's happened, I've only this minute got home.'

'Don't suppose you've any kind of weapon to hand?' she asks over her shoulder.

'Just my sharp wit and intellect,' I say, trying out a smile.

She raises an eyebrow. Her forehead shows the faintest of lines. 'I'll take that as a no.'

With that, before I get a say in what she's doing, she's inside the house. I watch her cover the distance of the short hallway to the kitchen, her head cocking to the left where the dresser and grocery cupboards are. She bolts out of sight for the briefest of times and springs back into view with the largest kitchen knife I own in her right hand. The glint of steel mesmerises me as she takes two purposeful steps back towards me.

I think I actually gulp. There's a fixed look on her face that I'd only seen once or twice before, and that had never ended well.

She stops beside the living room door on her right-hand side, gives me a wink and kicks the door open, charging inside.

Should this be the moment I call the police? I find I have the phone in my hand but I can't bring myself to do it. Whoever this budget Gal Gadot is, I think I like her.

It's seconds before she's out of the living room and in the hallway. Her footsteps are almost silent on the wooden stairs, although I hear her crash from bathroom to bedroom, slamming the wardrobe open and shut.

'Hey, staring woman,' she calls down the stairs. 'It's all clear up here in the rooms. Does this loft open?'

'Er, no, no, it doesn't,' I call back. I step inside the front door. Her hair has fallen forward as she leans around the banister to speak to me.

'Then I'd say you're all set, unless there's a basement somewhere you're keeping quiet about.'

'Thanks,' I say, wondering how I could possibly have gone a whole month without noticing my vigilante neighbour. 'Can I make you a cup of tea or anything, to say thanks? Besides, it always pays to get to know who's living a door or two from your own home.'

She walks back down the stairs towards me, her sunglasses now perched on the top of her head, knife by her side, as if this is the most natural thing in the world.

'You should still probably call the police anyway,' she says. 'Coming home to find the front door insecure is certainly something to worry about. You need to make sure nothing's been taken.'

For a moment, I'm off my guard. I blurt out, 'You've only this minute pulled up outside your house and I never said anything about the front door being open.'

She steps towards me again. 'I never said I was your neighbour, either.'

We're inches apart now.

When she speaks, I can feel her breath on the side of my face. 'You were outside your own home, looking like fair game, as I've already told you. I'd say the situation was obvious; even so, it's amazing the assumptions we make. It can be dangerous, you know. You should be more careful who you let into your house.'

I feel her hand come up, the one with the knife. She holds it level with my face.

'You'd better take this too,' she says, holding it by the blade.

I watch my trembling fingers grab the black handle and fight the urge to rush after her as she walks back outside into the sunshine.

CHAPTER THREE

I wait for the police. I'm apparently not a priority as the intruders have long since gone. I can't find anything missing but the instructions were to leave things alone as much as possible. I mostly sit idle with my hands in my lap until the first hour is up. Then I remember the wine and the rest of the discarded shopping.

I take a peek out of the front door, running a wary eye towards the next-door-but-one neighbours. It was the house I'd thought was empty until she turned up, charged through my house with my kitchen knife in her hand and left as quickly as she arrived.

My dine-in meal and other goodies are still where I left them. Mercifully, the sun moved round enough to place the food in the shade. Deliveroo or Just Eat are approximately fifteen miles or twenty years away from my tiny corner of England. I'm faced with a choice of a sun-kissed, slightly on the turn Italian feast for one or a boiled egg and a crust of white bread.

At least the wine's lived to tell the tale.

I take the bag inside, put the food in the fridge and gloat at the tiniest of celebrations in my day – the wine is screw top so I don't have to open a drawer to get the corkscrew out. Last night's wine glass is still on the draining board, residue of a rather tasty Malbec clinging to the sides. I try to picture exactly what the burglar got up to: did they break in, sniff my knicker drawer and leave without taking anything, but pause in their clandestine mission to lick my dirty wine glass? It's not that likely, but I wash and dry it anyway, before pouring myself a generous glug.

I hold the glass up to the light, swirling it to admire the colour and release some of the aroma. Don't be surprised – I'm not a complete monster. As I lose myself in admiring the Rioja's legs, my eyes are drawn to something in the garden, something I knew wasn't there this morning before I left to meet Adrian, the boring, cheating tosser.

A single red ribbon is dangling from a branch of the crab apple tree at the bottom of the garden. There isn't much in the rectangular thirty by forty-five-foot space barring a few fruit trees, some weeds and a once-loved vegetable patch. Through the foliage, dandelions and daisies, I can't help but notice the red thin of material hanging directly in my eyeline. Whether it's been deliberately placed there or the wind has blown it onto the branch, it's hard to tell.

The first issue I have with it finding its own way into the tree is that there has hardly been any breeze today. The second is the significance of a red ribbon.

I realise I'm holding my breath and I haven't even had a chance to fully process this when I'm jolted by a rapping on the front door.

I gather my wits about me and go to let the police in.

Two police officers, who couldn't instil less confidence in me if they tried, ask a few questions as they wander from room to room. They pay attention when I mention my mystery caller and tell me to leave the knife in the kitchen for the CSI. I'm told that I should expect her within the hour, unless something more sinister happens to send her spiralling in another direction to a poor unfortunate. Other than take the knife away for fingerprints, no one seems to know exactly what the CSI will do when she gets here. I suppose it's something to do with the very bad press the police have of late when it comes to attending burglaries and car crime. I take it for what it no doubt is, a PR exercise.

At least the police knock on my neighbours' doors before they leave. It's completely pointless as no one's home. Still, they do their duty. Box ticked.

I can't rest. Everything about today is weird. I find myself back in the kitchen, my attention drawn again to the ribbon in the tree. I hadn't mentioned it to the police officers and I have no intention of telling the CSI about it. I'll wait until I know I'll be alone and then go and get it. I understand now that the purpose of breaking into my home wasn't to steal anything from me. It was about leaving something behind as a warning. I had no option but to let the police come in once I'd called them, or that would have been even more suspicious. The staged break-in was to get my attention, and it certainly did that all right.

I go through the motions when the CSI arrives, greeting her warmly and offering her a cup of tea. She's young and pleasant enough. She tries to make small talk, quickly realising that she's wasting her time. I watch her for a short while as she unpacks her box of goodies, gets her paperwork in order and begins by taking a couple of photographs of the knife.

I've already explained to the police about my earlier visitor and how she came to have my kitchen knife in her hand. This young CSI – Sally, I think she said her name was – was clearly told about it. The knife is the first thing she peers at from under her blonde fringe, her face a mask of concentration. I find myself watching her as she examines the knife.

'I'll need to take this with me,' she says, her focus still on the knife. 'Can you tell me where it's usually kept?'

'The woman I've already told your colleagues about, came into the kitchen and went over to this side of the room.' I notice Sally nodding as I speak. 'When I left this morning, it would have been stuck to this metallic knifeboard, the one with the other four knives on it.'

To give Sally her due, she looks with more interest at the remaining four knives than I could have mustered. She takes a couple more photos, puts on some latex gloves – I've not seen or heard a pair snapped on in years, and now twice in one day – and she seals my kitchen knife inside a long, solid-looking plastic tube.

Once she's dusted the door handles, drawers and some other parts of the ground floor that either she knows from experience may wield some fingerprint identification return, or simply to make more mess, I give her the tour upstairs. I've already explained twice now that nothing seems to have been moved or taken from the bedroom or bathroom. Perhaps Sally is remodelling her own tiny doll's house of a home and wants some tips on how to squeeze her life into a cupboard-sized space.

After we traipse downstairs, she picks up her gear and tells me that someone will be in touch if anything turns up.

Once I'm finally alone again and know I won't be disturbed, I let myself into the garden; the garden I swore to the police and the CSI that no one else could possibly have been in as the only key was with me on my keyring all day.

I really should try to lie less.

I grab the ribbon from the tree and stuff it into my pocket. Unlike the police, I don't have to worry about preserving it for forensic evidence. I know who left this here, only I'm not entirely sure why this is happening now, or how they found me.

I'll need to get to the bottom of this if I'm to survive this whole sorry mess and walk away from Adrian unscathed. It was never part of the plan for me to linger longer than was strictly necessary, and anyone would agree with me that fifteen years is, indeed, taking playing the long game to the extreme.

I got lazy and comfortable, that was the problem. It won't happen again.

The garden is a secluded spot, trees along the perimeter of the fields beyond and fences of six foot high on each side. The only possible way to spy on me would be from the upstairs back windows of one of the other five cottages. Another reason I took this place was the seclusion. It was also as much as I could afford to spend without having to ask my wayward husband for money. If I had to, I'd ask him, although only as a last resort.

The hairs on the back of my neck stand up and I have the oddest feeling that I'm being watched. I very much doubt I am though, as I've heard no signs of my neighbours returning home. One side – the side that my Honda-driving intruder made it her business to walk across the lawn of – is a couple that drive to Faversham train station and park for the duration of their commuting day. They won't be home for another hour or so. The other side is empty and next to that lives a man of around sixty who I have only spoken to once. He didn't seem the friendliest and told me that he spends most of his time at his partner's in Joss Bay or his daughter's in Westgate Upon Sea. He muttered something about hating being this far inland, forcing me to give him the nickname Uncle Albert and wondering why his beard wasn't longer.

I can't see anyone watching me from the back of the other cottages, so I chalk this one up to my nerves getting the better of me and go back inside. I close the door, locking it for good measure, and pull down the window blind. I don't have a basement complete with secrets and keepsakes I hide away from prying eyes, but I do have a full-size larder with a loose panel. I feel around in the gloom and ease the plywood board away from the recess alongside the door. My fingers grip the edge of a small cardboard box, large enough to keep the few things I hold dear and inconspicuous enough that no one would glance twice if I inadvertently left it in plain view. Hiding it away does add an air of intrigue, although living alone, the only chance of anyone discovering it would be if they were prying.

I shuffle round with the box in my grasp, my back against the cool of the solid brick wall, and take off the lid.

Some time ago, I lined it with pink tissue paper and folded the contents neatly inside. The effect is like opening a small gift box, only no one would really want this one. I poke my forefinger in amongst the hoard and when I'm satisfied that I've reacquainted myself with each and every memory, I take the red ribbon from my pocket and carefully place it between the baby's booties and my passport, the one with my real name inside the cover.

CHAPTER FOUR

It doesn't take long before I shake myself out of my melancholy and get back to reality. No one is coming to help me with this, and even if they were, would I trust them? The answer is categorically, no. Once I decide to stop feeling sorry for myself, I shove the box back in its hiding place, replace the panel, and when I'm satisfied that everything is in order, I stand up and turn my attention to the rest of my evening. There's a microwavable meal that's waiting for me to extricate it from the fridge, stab away at its plastic cover and introduce it to the world's laziest method of cooking food. Still, it's cheaper than heating the oven and I'm saving the planet at the same time.

At first, over the gratifying noise of the blade piercing the lasagne's taut wrapper, I don't realise that someone is knocking on the front door. I'm not sure how long they've been there but now there's a frantic banging. This isn't the done thing in the Kent countryside unless there's an emergency or the person knocking has lost their patience at being ignored.

I hurry along the hallway and reach for the door latch. I'd be stupid to open the door wide to my friendly neighbourhood burglar or the denim-skirted woman who dropped in and rapidly disappeared, so I hesitate. 'Who is it?' I call out.

'Police.' It's a woman's voice; firm, authoritative. 'Avril Benham? It's DC Katie George and DC Dan Sanders. Can we speak to you, please?'

We? Then I hear my neighbours going out through their front door. It would be hard not to as the doors are so close together. They often come home from work and go out for a run together or take their bikes out for a ride through the country lanes. Sad pair of sods. On the plus side, neither of them has ever struck me as morally corrupt, so I'm sure they'll wade in if the callers at the door aren't really the police.

I open the door and peer down at a young woman, mousy blonde hair scraped back from her face, dressed in a white cotton shirt, dark green trousers and the world's ugliest brogues. She's clutching a black folder to her chest as if she's about to ask me questions for a pointless door-to-door survey. A man with red hair, freckles and an air of mild interest stands behind her. His shoes and shirt are very similar to his colleague's, only the colour of his trousers prevent them from looking as if they're wearing CID uniforms. Each of them waves an ID badge at me from lanyards around their necks.

My neighbours have paused on their driveway to bend and stretch – and have a nose at what's going on – all the while, both nodding and smiling at me.

'If you're here about my burglary,' I say, 'there's not much else to tell you.'

DC Katie George glances across at my neighbours again. 'No, we're here about something else.'

My heart starts to pound so loudly I can hear it in my ears. It shuts out the sound of the sparrows chattering in the hedgerow opposite and the grunting and noisy breathing coming from the two eavesdroppers limbering up a stone's throw away.

'Could we come in?' says DC George, taking a step forward.

They can't know already, can they?

I hesitate briefly before giving them the most genuine smile I think I can pull off and stand back to let them into my home.

DC George walks past me, a waft of something soft and floral as she makes her way along the hallway and into the kitchen. Her colleague gestures that I follow her and obligingly, I do.

I hear the soft click of the front door as I trail behind DC George, watching her as she runs an eye over the garden. Is she paying particular attention to the crab apple tree and its earlier red ribbon, or is that a figment of my imagination?

'Do you want to sit down?' I ask.

She glances at the tiny kitchen table and its two fold-out chairs, a small bunch of plastic hydrangea mopheads poking out of the top of an empty Douwe Egberts jar completes the scene of sadness. 'Thanks, but I'm okay standing,' says DC George.

'What can I help you with?' My palms feel sweaty and more for something to do with my hands than anything else, I put my meal for one back in the fridge.

'It's about the incident earlier today,' says DC George.

'I've already said that there's nothing more I can tell you about the burglary.'

'No, that's not why we're here,' says the other officer who's moved around the kitchen so that the three of us are now in a triangle formation. His voice is soft with a slight West Country accent to it.

I'm confused, but I think that plays to my advantage. I stare at him, open-mouthed and speechless.

'Dan's referring to much earlier on today when you called the paramedics for the injured man in the street,' says DC George, a tuft of hair falling across her cheek. 'We understand that you've had quite the day. How are you feeling?'

Care and compassion I'm not expecting, that's if it's genuine. I have never trusted the police, and for good reason. These two don't appear to be capable of much in the way of skulduggery, especially DC Sanders. He seems to be more interested in checking out the cheap lino flooring.

'I'm holding up, thank you,' I say to DC George, with a scowl in her colleague's direction. 'You're right; it's been one of those days. I was about to have something to eat and perhaps turn in for a very early night.' I'd like them to take the hint.

'We were following up your first telephone call,' says DC Sanders. 'You've been very unlucky having to call the emergency services twice in one day.' He shifts from foot to foot as if he's the one with something to hide.

'Is there anything else about the man or his injuries that you can tell us?' says DC George.

The young detective phrases it simply enough, an inviting smile to accompany the words, yet there's a fluttering to her eyelashes I hadn't noticed before. Perhaps DC George isn't ready for high stakes poker just yet. There's also a good chance it's my paranoia muscling in again.

'No, no there's not,' I say, aware I'm wringing my hands. These two are making me feel guilty and I haven't done anything wrong. Well, not today at least. 'He told me that his name was John Smith. I came across him lying on the pavement as I was walking home from the bus stop. He didn't tell me what had happened, despite me asking him.'

'He has a nasty head injury,' says DC George with a new intensity to her stare. 'He's been stabbed in the head.'

I inhale sharply. It's partly genuine surprise, with a smidge thrown in for effect. 'I hope he's not accusing me of—'

'Absolutely not,' says DC George, this time her expression is broken with pursed lips and an earnest shake of her head. She wants me to fully understand that I'm not being implicated for the slash on his skull, calling an ambulance and then trotting home for a lonesome meal for one. 'We've been to see him at the hospital – they're duty bound to let us know about something as serious as this – and he's remaining very tight-lipped about the whole thing. He reckons he has no idea who did this to him.'

'We'd expect him to at least have got a look at the person who plunged a knife into his head in an almost deserted part of the countryside,' says DC Sanders. He raises his eyebrows as if he's encouraging me to speak.

It's extremely tempting to tell them about the Honda that made John Smith appear so terrified, especially as I have a description of the person driving it from when she entered my home. And yet, I hesitate over giving them this connection between the two events. It makes no logical sense. I don't owe the Honda driver anything and I've handed over the knife with her fingerprints on it to CSI Sally. Yet, at the same time, I'm not sure if she was here for anything untoward as far as I'm concerned. Possibly she was here by chance.

I realise that I've not said anything for an unnaturally long pause with two detectives in my kitchen asking me about my first emergency services call of the day.

'Sorry,' I say with an apologetic shrug, 'I saw John on the ground, called the ambulance and didn't see another person until the ambulance crew arrived.' Not strictly a lie – I couldn't see the driver with the sunlight glancing off the windows.

'Here's my number,' says DC George leaning forward and pressing a small, cheap rectangle of card into my clammy hand. 'Don't hesitate to call me if you think of anything else. If I don't answer straight away because I'm off duty or unable to answer, I'll call you back as soon as I can.'

'Thanks. Of course.' I study the line of words and phone number printed on the card below the blue and red police logo.

'It goes without saying,' says DC Sanders, his accent a little stronger now, 'that if it's an emergency, you should dial nine nine nine.'

I open my mouth to ask him if I'm in danger. Then I clamp it firmly shut. As soon as I came back to Kent, I made myself a target for everyone with a grudge against me.

CHAPTER FIVE

I have a fitful night's sleep, broken at times by my overactive brain wondering if the local police will discover who I really am. At other times it is due to the bottle of wine I'd finished off, which has given me a pounding headache. Try as I might to get back to sleep, it's futile. In the end, I get up and put the kettle on.

The day is warm and the house feels claustrophobic; I don't want to stay alone in here any longer. There are few places I can get to directly via the local buses, but I know I can't feel hemmed in all day. I rush to shower and get dressed, grab my purse, phone and keys and check the back door before charging through the front door. I pause only to double lock it before I head up the road towards the bus stop. Whatever bus comes along first is the one I'm getting on. Slim pickings on a weekday morning after the rush hour, if you can call what passes for a rush hour around here busy. It isn't desolate – nowhere in the southeast is – but it's not what I would call vibrant. It's pleasant enough in a way, or it was until I knew that I'd been followed here.

I hurry to the bus stop, feeling both vulnerable on my own

and pleased there's no one else waiting, meaning I can avoid any kind of small talk. I try to work out the times from the sun scorched timetable pinned behind a Perspex cover. Unable to fathom from the faint print whether I've missed one by minutes or will have to wait another hour, I see a double-decker rolling towards me like a pauper's mirage. I give a sigh as I fumble for my purse. One of the indignities of having a past that includes disposing of dead bodies and fleeing in the night, is that you sometimes have to take public transport.

As it gets closer, I see the bottom deck is almost full – mostly with old people making the most of the first off-peak bus of the day. I wave my hand, unsure whether the bus will actually stop otherwise. I'm not familiar with bus etiquette but find that flapping an arm usually does the job. With a weary air lacking all emotion, the middle-aged balding driver pulls over and lets me on.

I get my ticket and not wanting to sit with the Werther's Originals gang, I mount the stairs hoping the top deck isn't full of weirdos. There are a lot of them about. Even being in a rural setting doesn't mean it's possible to get away from them; there's less of them, but then there's less of everything so they stick out like a sore thumb. It's easier to be unhinged in a city than a village. Unless you're rich, and then you usually own the village so there's little anyone can do about your state of mind.

The bus driver doesn't hang around to make sure I'm sitting comfortably but accelerates away as I'm halfway up the stairs. I stumble my way to one of the first empty seats I come to across the aisle, settle in against the window and marvel at the view. Mostly, it's green fields, trees and the odd house dotted along the route. And then I see her again.

At least, I assume it's her. A black Honda Civic overtakes the bus as we approach a long straight of road, it pulls in neatly ahead of the bus and races away into the distance. It could be any black Honda Civic, but the confident and cocky way it's being driven, I know it's her. I crane my neck to get a better view, but she disappears from sight in the direction of Faversham.

A strange feeling comes over me, it's the start of butterflies in my stomach at seeing her again, albeit briefly and technically, it's only her car I catch a glimpse of. Assuming that she is in it, I find myself momentarily breathless at the thought that she's still around. There's every chance she's dangerous, but that only makes it all the more intriguing.

I sit back in my seat, willing the bus to get me to my destination. I'd only chosen Faversham because that's where the bus is heading. There are a dozen or so other passengers scattered throughout the top deck, most of them fiddling with their phones or with completely blank expressions as earbuds deliver music or podcasts or audiobooks to their brains. No one looks anywhere near as excited as I feel at the car that tore past us.

After what seems like an eternity, but was more like ten minutes, we pull up close to Faversham town centre. It's bustling already; market day certainly brings in the crowds. The place has become another area of the county for developers to cram hundreds of identikit houses with non-existent gardens onto plots of land. No infrastructure to support it means the roads are getting busier than ever before, parking is difficult, so most people are already in a bad mood before they've even got out of their cars and stepped foot in the town. I stop to read a plaque that tells me the market was mentioned in the *Domesday Book*. Bet they didn't say anything about the lack of parking.

I wander to the market itself, picking up knick-knacks,

giving them the once over before putting them down and smiling politely at the stallholders. It's not that I don't need anything to make my house a home, it's that I'm not likely to be around for long enough to give it a proper make over.

As I move from the Guildhall in the Market Place and along Charter Street, I idly peruse the goods on sale, lingering over the bakery stall and cheese-based goods for longer than the artwork and pet food stands. The waft of freshly baked bread is making me hungry. The stallholders glance at me and the other shoppers from time to time, but focus most of their attention on filling their trestle tables and shelves and catching up with their fellow market traders.

I realise that I'm now ravenous at the same time I notice something out of the corner of my eye. At first, I'm not sure if it's low blood sugar, what with the onslaught of carbs all around me and my growling stomach thinking my throat's been cut. My head snaps to my left. There outside the bookshop on the corner of the marketplace, is my mystery caller from yesterday.

Her hair has the same casual over-the-shoulder look, her face has the same bemused, slightly mocking expression, and everything about her demeanour says unperturbed. With her aviators on, I can't tell whether she's watching me or merely looking this way. I'm in a crowd, but not hard to spot. I'm the one staring directly at her with my mouth hanging open slightly. And I'm holding a kangaroo doorstop.

I drop the kangaroo and push my way through the throng. The crowd has trebled in size. I'm really not sure how long I was looking at amusing doorstops, but a couple of coachloads of shoppers must have arrived whilst my back was turned. I can't see her now, but that doesn't stop me elbowing some old people out of the way. A man in a wheelchair rolls into my path and I contemplate grabbing the chair and spinning him in the other direction. That probably wouldn't go down too well. Besides, she's gone.

With a sigh, I stand with my hands on my hips, do a complete three-sixty in case she somehow managed to get behind me, and come back round to face the bookshop. Perhaps she went inside.

Tales On Market Street is a glass-fronted bookstore on the corner of the marketplace. Its welcoming exterior allows me to peek inside and satisfy myself that she hasn't disappeared inside the shop. As I scan the crowd again, I feel my phone vibrating in my pocket and fish it out, still with my eye on the people milling past.

The number is withheld; I answer it with a cautious, 'Hello.'

'Hello, Avril. It's DC Katie George. I have an update for you.'

I'm still slowly turning on the spot like an overweight jewellery box ballerina, desperate to find out where my mystery visitor has gone. The last thing I'm interested in is the latest on *John Smith's* battered bonce.

'Hi, I'm in the middle of something right now, to be honest with you, detective.' I put my free hand up to shield my eyes from the sun that's burst through the clouds.

'An update on your burglary,' she says, immediately grabbing my attention. I move over to the bookshop and loiter by the window. 'We've had a result back on the fingerprints.'

'That was quick.' My mind now kicked it up a gear or two. I'm not sure how fast the police establish someone's identity from fingerprints for something as routine as a break-in. 'I thought that kind of thing was only so rapid for a very serious crime or on TV police dramas to stop everyone getting bored and switching channels.'

'Well, we made this a priority.' DC George pauses. I can't interpret it as either a dramatic interlude or whether she's stalling for time. 'Rural breaks are on the increase and a woman living alone moved it up the queue.'

'Okay. Where were the fingerprints?' I think I know what's coming.

'On the knife.' She lets that sink in.

'It's not that helpful,' I say. 'I told *you* that the woman who came to my help held the knife.'

'Yes, you did.' DC George is trying to keep her tone light without venturing into the territory of speaking to me as if I'm a massive great simpleton. 'Do you understand that if we've had a hit on the prints, it means she's somewhere on the system?'

Standing in broad daylight in Faversham surrounded by hordes of shoppers, I suddenly feel alone as goosebumps prickle my skin. They've found me.

'Who is it?' I say, my voice barely a whisper.

'Her name's Rena Hargreaves. It probably means nothing to you.'

It doesn't, but that hardly accounts for much.

'I'm outside your house,' says DC George. 'I wanted to make sure you're safe and well. She's... she's a worrying individual with a bit of a past.'

I shrink back against the glass and move away from the market to where the street is a little quieter. 'Is she violent?' I close my eyes; not sure I really want to know the answer to that.

DC George takes a deep breath. 'The thing is, Rena is very well known to us because she was a police officer. That's one of the reasons we have her fingerprints on record.'

'A police officer?' My voice is higher than it should be. 'And what do you mean by "one of the reasons"?'

'The other more concerning part is that she's served a custodial sentence.'

'For those amongst us who speak English, do you mean she's been to prison?' I say this a little louder than I intended – hardly surprising given the circumstances – and a couple of people look my way. I move over to a doorway and stand in the tucked back alcove situated a welcome few feet back from the pavement.

'Yes, she has. We don't think she's necessarily dangerous, but it's best that you have no further contact with her and let us know if she shows up again.'

'You don't think she's dangerous?' I all but hiss into the mouthpiece. 'This is very little comfort to me, DC George. The woman came into my house and grabbed a knife.'

'She hasn't been violent in the past,' says DC George.

'Then what did she go to prison for?' I ask, my fingers gripping the phone so tightly I'm starting to lose feeling in my hand.

'It was for perverting the course of justice,' says DC George. 'Basically, Rena lied about something and two people died. I can't really go into too much detail.'

'You can't go into details? This is something else.' I realise that I've put a hand up to my head and I'm literally tearing my hair out. I take a deep breath. 'Why is she interested in me?'

DC George is making the noises of the uncertain – something I clearly don't have time for. After a pause and some umming, she says, 'We don't know it's you, it's probably a coincidence she showed up when she did. I can't stress enough how she's never been violent in the past. Only... if she should come back, would you let us know straight away.'

I know little about the workings of the police, but I hazard a guess that Rena Hargreaves is very far removed from her previous employers and all they stood for. She's spent time behind bars and now she's shown up at my door.

I have a very bad feeling about this.

CHAPTER SIX

I listen to Katie blither on about my safety and welfare and go through her checklist of whether I wanted an alarm if I felt unsafe. The mere fact that she's offering me one in the first place ratchets up the fear factor, all the while, my mind is whirring into gear so fast I can't follow my own thought processes.

When I can't take any more, I end the call and stand in the doorway, wondering what my options are. I know that I have to do something, waiting for things to happen is a sure-fire way to get myself killed. The way I see it, Rena is probably coming for me, and if that is the case, why hadn't she done me in when she was alone with me in my house armed with my largest kitchen knife? If someone had paid her to find me and end my days, that would have been her chance.

I tap my mobile against my chin as I consider this. She's either toying with me or I've got it all wrong, and it's as Katie explained, only a coincidence. Only, why now? Why the day my house is broken into, and someone left a very personal message for me? I decide to do what only a fool would do and go and look for her.

With a quick glance left and right before leaving the refuge of the doorway, I step onto the pavement and turn away from the market. I don't really have her pegged as a kangaroo doorstop, alpaca wool scarf type of shopper. I think I'm going to have more luck finding her in one of the coffee shops or restaurants, and even if I fail, I can have lunch. My stomach growls to remind me how hungry I am. Excitement always does that to me.

It's not long before I cover most of Faversham's town centre and find myself back where I started. There's no sign of her and I don't know which of the car parks she would have picked to park in, so there's no point in me trying to track down her car. If she has driven off, I'd only be wasting valuable eating time. My recce took me past some decent looking food places, so I double back and head towards Guildhall and along Middle Row to one of the cafés I'd spotted.

It's started to fill up and there are only two tables left, one at the back and one in the window. I opt for the one with the best view in case Rena happens to walk by. I'd rather be forewarned, although the butterflies in my stomach tell me I'm nervous, I dismiss it as hunger pangs. I'm only lying to myself.

The server comes over to take my order. He's around eighteen or so, an attempt at stubble on his chin, good looking in a nerdy way. After his mumbled greeting, I glance down at the wipe clean menu and order a black coffee with a full English breakfast with extra hash browns. He's standing between me and the door, head bent forward as he writes my order down. The people on the next table get up to go, causing a momentary distraction as they move their chairs, clatter the crockery and loudly discuss their plans for the rest of the day. It's such a melee, I don't realise at first that, as they wander onto the pavement, someone slips inside the café.

Then she's standing in front of me, sunglasses perched on the top of her head, one hand on her hip. Her eyes bore into me, then she softens her expression and says, 'Mind if I sit down?'

Before I have a chance to answer, the server's back with my coffee. 'I'll have a cappuccino,' she says, taking her eyes off me for a beat to melt the young man with a winning smile. It's certainly the most cheerful he's looked since I got here.

Rena slides herself into the seat opposite me, but not before I have a chance to admire her very tight black trousers and black, women's England rugby T-shirt.

Now it's my turn to be disarmed with the intensity of her charm. The edges of her blue eyes crinkle as she smiles, her look turning to one of delight as my two thousand calorie breakfast is put on the table, a knife and fork beside it.

'I admire someone who eats what they fancy.' There's no judgement or mockery in her tone. 'In fact, I'd have to go so far as to say that you impress me.'

For some reason, I'm flattered by this ridiculous playground compliment, for reasons unknown to my sanity. The only interaction I've had with her resulted in her tearing through my house with a knife and now she's followed me when I was supposed to be seeking her out. I convince myself that I'm more intrigued than scared and pick up my knife and fork.

'The police called me earlier,' I say, slicing through a piece of bacon. 'There's clearly more to you than meets the eye.' I pause as Rena's cappuccino is placed in front of her, with more care than my coffee was banged down, I notice.

'You're an absolute love,' she says to the young man whose face attempts a smile but doesn't quite make it there. 'Thing is, Avril, I could say the same about you.' I'm not sure how to respond to her words, let alone the wink she sends my way.

'I never told you my name,' I say, fork poised inches from my fried egg. This is always the best bit – breaking the yoke, now she's spoiling it.

'Well, you'll find I used to be a detective.' Rena's hand shoots out and she grabs one of my hash browns and plunges it straight into the egg. I think about piercing her skin with my fork. I've done worse for less than egg violation.

I lower my cutlery and lean across the table. 'Why did you get kicked out of the police and end up inside?'

Rena's face is impassive. She blinks twice and bites into the hash brown. It's so hot she looks alarmed and chews rapidly all the while waving her free hand in front of her mouth in a vain attempt to cool down the food. Eventually she says, 'It was only a matter of time before you found out. Don't forget that I told *you* to call the police, and I knew full well that my prints were on the knife. I'm not so stupid that I'd have done that by mistake now, would I?'

'I don't know.' My head is starting to hurt; it's been a busy couple of days. 'You might have messed up and that's why you followed me to Faversham, to find out what I know.'

A sly smile creeps over Rena's face. 'And what exactly makes you think that I followed you here? Perhaps you followed *me*?'

'I, I don't have a car,' I say, realising that my bluff hasn't paid off. She'd have noticed the lack of vehicle outside my house when she dropped by for a quick ransack. 'I can't keep tabs on where you are and appear in the same part of the county by using public transport, can I?'

I watch her break the rest of the hash brown in two, allow it to cool for a second or so, then put the smaller piece in her mouth. 'I reckon that you like having me around, despite what you think you know about me.' She's talking out of the side of her mouth, attempting to keep the food from escaping onto the table. It's a little off-putting.

'I only know that you went to prison and some people died.' The smell of the greasy food inches from my nose is making me feel a little queasy. On the other hand, it could be the talk of prison.

Rena pauses mid chew, gives me a look that could mean anything, and shrugs. A tiny piece of the hash brown falls to the table as her shoulders drop. We both stare at it before she flicks it to the floor. 'Two people did die, but it's important you know that I didn't kill them. They'd have been dead no matter what I'd done or not done.'

For the first time she appears rattled, not exactly scared or even remorseful, more awkward about what I've said. Perhaps it's embarrassment, yet still, she doesn't offer any further explanation.

'I happened to be driving past your house yesterday and thought I could help you,' says Rena, her focus on the potato product pinched between her forefinger and thumb. 'Today, I chanced across you as you sat down in this rather authentically charming café, so thought I'd say hi. That's all. See you around, Avril.'

Rena shoves the last of the hash brown into her mouth, takes a gulp of her cappuccino, pushes back her chair and in two strides, she's at the door. As I watch her march off along the street until she's out of my eyeline, I can't understand why I'm sorry I've upset her. After all, she is the one who has a discredited police career and the weight of two deaths around her neck. I know very little about her – and what I do know is far from positive – yet I can't work out why I'm even contemplating running after her and asking her to come back. She's wrecked a perfectly good breakfast, if nothing else, as well as leaving me more than intrigued about the darker parts of her life.

All I can hope is that our paths cross again before too long.

CHAPTER SEVEN

The rest of my morning is uneventful, boring even, after the thrill of seeing Rena. Yes, she's probably dangerous – despite Katie's thoughts to the contrary – she may even cut my throat in the night, but I like the idea of bumping into her again. When I say bump into her, I really mean me on the verge of stalking her by walking the length and breadth of Faversham on market day to track her down.

I wander around the town aimlessly, meandering from shop to shop, browsing, but my heart's not in it. I stop at one of the market stalls and buy a chicken and leek pie, for no other reason than it was there in front of me, and I still haven't got much in the way of food in the house. With my second minimum effort meal in as many days, I head back to the bus stop to join the other sad sods who, despite their left-wing protestations that increased public transport is one of the ways to tackle global warming, would still rather be on their own in a car, leaving whenever they fancied and not at the mercy of the driver's schedule.

After being bounced around in far too close a proximity to the great unwashed, I get off the bus and trudge back along the same lane where John Smith had spun me a line about his name, shortly before the ambulance turned up so he could lie all over again to the paramedics. It was bad enough he didn't want to tell me the truth, but those poor women had a job to do. Still, not my problem.

Glad to be home, I push the door open and cross the threshold, glad to see that no one had thought my empty house was fair game today. I glance down at the mail on the floor, a couple of interesting looking envelopes along with a flyer and a mailshot addressed to the occupier.

I step over the post and close the door behind me. For a couple of seconds I stand with my back pressed against it, listening. Other than the hum of the fridge-freezer and a few birds chattering away in the distance, I can't hear anything else. It doesn't stop me going from room to room, ensuring there are no surprises or unsolicited gifts. I go unarmed; I'm not expecting any more danger today. There's a stillness to the place that I hadn't felt yesterday, although that could have been Rena marauding through the house.

Satisfied that I'm quite alone – a peek out of the window into the back garden to make sure nothing's out of place – I return to pick up my shopping and the correspondence lying on the floor.

My head is already telling me to put the kettle on and get on with the business of trying to fill the rest of the day, when I suddenly stop and stare at the envelope in my hand. I drop it onto the kitchen table as if an electric current has surged through me. It's a white handwritten envelope addressed to me, a local postmark on the stamp. It doesn't look familiar, yet I know there's something wrong. Few people know I live here, and those that do wouldn't write to me. Who writes letters anymore?

I wipe my hands down the front of my dress. I'm unsure

whether this is because my hands are clammy or because touching the envelope makes them feel that way. I pull out a chair and plonk myself down.

'Stop being so stupid,' I mutter to myself, then grab it with both hands and tear it open. I can feel it's a card of some sort. It's not my birthday for some months and it's too late for a *welcome to your new home where hardly another human being knows you're living* card. My breath catches as I pull out a condolence card.

Sorry for your loss is printed in embossed silver letters with a dove taking flight underneath the wording. The envelope has my name on it, so there's no mistaking it was meant for me. I open it. Other than the usual banal twenty or so words of waffle, there's nothing inside except for a clumsily drawn smiley face. And it's winking.

This isn't good at all.

CHAPTER EIGHT

THEN

For some hours I had laid awake on my lumpy mattress in the tiny flat, but I was too petrified to move. I could hear all sorts of noises and none of them were pleasant. Each grunt and moan left me with a renewed feeling of dread. The walls were paper thin, the temperature freezing and, not for the first time, I wanted to go home. The only thing stopping me, apart from being too petrified to move – if I could hear them, they could hear me – was the indignity of returning to my parents with my tail between my legs, and listening to them tell me, 'We told you so!' No, I'd rather feel scared, vulnerable and alone than go back and bear witness to their sanctimonious waffle. At least, that was what I thought until my fourth evening here and Heather told me that she was bringing someone back to the flat. Naively I'd imagined it was another of her old school mates. Or possibly even a boy she was seeing but had forgotten to mention when she asked me, almost begged me, to move in with her.

I suppose the need to get away from my parents grew along with my lack of tolerance of their constant nagging and criticism of everything I did. It was suffocating, as were the chintz and gold edged teacups. As a child and now as a teenager, I had never taken negative feedback or outright judgement very well at all. In fact, the only truly happy times had been when I was at my great auntie Ivy's run-down and cosy cottage. I had adored her and everything about the warmth and love she radiated. If I'd have been less selfish, I would have moved in with her for good. She was getting old and I overheard my parents talking about her soon needing care around the clock. I didn't want to do it. I was eighteen and didn't want to lift an old lady in and out of bed and take her to the toilet. I never claimed to be virtuous.

As I felt my teeth chattering and could see my breath in the glow of the dim bedside lamp, I wondered how much of the situation I'd found myself in was entirely my own doing. I preferred to blame my parents for it: if they'd have been more palatable, I'd still be at home in my warm bedroom with its John Lewis soft furnishings, wrapped up in my duck down duvet. Damn me and my determination to be told absolutely nothing about life. If I was anything at all, I was stubborn. I'd been prepared to fester in Heather's two-bedroom flat perched above the kebab shop, the place smelling of grease and frost on the inside of the windows, rather than admit I was wrong and ask to go home.

The problem wasn't merely the temperature, location and lack of any kind of home comforts. Now I had sweaty, leering men to contend with. I'd seen two of them coming up the stairs behind me when I came back from getting a pint of milk at the corner shop. We had no food at Heather's, only a handful of teabags and not even a drop of semi-skimmed between us. I told her I'd nip out and get some and her reply came out hushed, delivered like a warning. 'Be quick, they'll be here soon.'

The look she was sporting was one of apprehension and

tinged, I thought, with guilt. 'You said that you had someone coming over this evening, Heather. Now it's "they"?' I kept my voice steady, not wanting to start a row and not wanting to appear freaked out. She had been living by herself for eighteen months and on the surface, she was doing all right. I had a shiny pink bedroom at my parents' boring suburban home, she lived by herself in a flat and hung around playing pool and drinking in pubs with older men. I wanted what she had, only I hadn't really thought through the part about the older men.

We stood facing each other until Heather looked at the cheap alarm clock on the living room floor. 'I told them eight o'clock,' she said. 'They'll probably bring vodka and, well...'

I didn't want to know what the 'and, well' was, so I rushed for the door with the few coins I had in my pocket, keen to make my escape and get back with the milk before these men arrived. If they got here first, I didn't know that I'd want to come in and I didn't fancy a night sitting in the park on the swings or by the bins at the back of the Co-op. It was bloody freezing. Truth be told, I hadn't a clue what I should do. I was reluctant to go out, freaked out at the thought of staying and I didn't feel as though I had anywhere else that I could go.

My feet took me to the corner shop, and back up the urine-soaked concrete stairs to our security lacking flat as fast as they could manage. My soft-soled shoes on the steps did nothing to block out the growling coming from the men behind me. It was the sort of noise I used to think was only associated with wild horny animals. I suppose I'd not met the kind of gargoyles Heather invited to her home. When I referred to it as her home, I, of course, meant our home.

I legged it up the flight of steps to the door, and through it to relative safety, in remarkable timing. Pretty ironic as I didn't linger long enough to actually put the kettle on. And now here I was, cowering in my own bed. Bed was probably a far too generous description. It was a stained mattress on the floor with a thin and threadbare sheet laid over it, a hard pillow lacking a pillowcase and an eiderdown that I'm sure could crawl across the floor of its own accord. What had I done?

CHAPTER NINE

Loud banging snaps me from the memory of Heather's rancid flat and its stream of sexually depraved visitors, back to Faversham, back to my kitchen table where I look down to see that I'm still clutching the condolence card. I was so lost in thought that, for the briefest of moments, I can't place where the banging is coming from. Then, when I realise it's the front door, I spring from my chair and rush along the hallway.

Still not entirely sure that I should open the door without checking who it is, especially after that day's postal delivery, I hesitate as a woman's voice calls out, 'Avril, are you okay? It's Fiona from next door.'

I'm temporarily lost for words. I would have absolutely no idea who Fiona was if she hadn't added the bit about being the next-door neighbour. I haven't bothered to learn her name and I'm mildly surprised that she made the effort to learn mine. Still, with all the running and other self-improvement, I suppose she feels it makes her a better human being knowing details about people, such as first names.

I open the door and find her dressed in a striking summer dress that was designed to never see an iron. Her face has a smug middle-class look about it that says I sponsor an unfortunate child somewhere poor and recycle everything.

'Oh, hi,' she says, an indiscreet attempt to peer over my shoulder. 'I wanted to check on you because, well, you know... the police are back.'

It's my turn to gawp over her shoulder. 'Where? I can't see them. Did you get burgled too?'

'Me?' Her voice is a squeak and she looks horrified at the thought. 'Heavens, no. Thankfully it's something further along the road.' Fiona inclines her head towards the other end of the row of cottages from where we're standing. I step outside, forcing her to move backwards as I look to where she's staring.

'There's no one there,' I say. What's up with this idiot neighbour and why isn't she at work. 'Why are you home during the day?'

My question catches her off-guard and she stumbles over her words. 'I, er, we're having some furniture delivered. I need to wait in.'

'So what did the police want?'

'I don't know,' she says. 'I missed them.'

'I'll level with you, you're doing my head in. You knocked to tell me that the police are here, and it turns out they aren't, and now you have to wait in but didn't open the door because you were busy.'

Fiona gives a small laugh that she probably imagines is charming. It isn't.

'I heard a car pull up and looked out because I hoped it was the delivery van, instead it was a Ford Fiesta. When I saw it was those two detectives back again, I thought they'd come for you, Avril.'

I blink rapidly at her words and know that my face gives me away as I watch her reaction. 'Why would they come for me?' I ask with my tone as neutral as I can manage.

She does her tinkly laugh again. 'Not for you, but to see you. After your break-in. Then I saw that they were knocking on doors at the far end of our row. I was doing the neighbourly thing and making sure that everyone's okay.'

'Thanks, I couldn't be better.' I step back inside the door, ready to slam it and hope this annoying woman leaves me alone. 'Hope your furniture arrives soon.'

All I want to do is get inside and give myself a chance to work out who sent me the condolence card. I have a good idea, although I know that would be very unlikely. Who knows I'm here? I thought I'd covered my tracks better than that. My fingers grasp the door, ready to slam it shut.

'I wonder if you'll come with me?' says Fiona. She rapidly chews the inside of her lip. Strange, I had her down as a vegan, but she seems to be trying to eat her own face.

'Come where with you?' I'm now a little more than suspicious that Fiona has an ulterior motive for knocking on my door, one that has nothing to do with my safety. My paranoia elbows its way past repulsion that I should come to her rescue. Is she trying to set me up for something?

'I thought we should find out if the rest of the street's all right,' she says, fiddling with her ponytail. 'We're both obviously fine, but perhaps someone in one of the other houses needs our help.'

'Our help? Help that the police can't manage?' I've hardly spoken to Fiona since I moved in and now she's asking me to become some sort of street pastor with her.

Fiona's face takes on a harder expression, one that tells me she's not taking no for an answer and won't bugger off and leave me alone until I do what she wants. Glad that my lease is up in a few months, I grab my keys from inside the door and give her a sigh of epic proportions.

With a slam, I'm ready to go and make nice with the

neighbours so I can get back to stewing over who seems to be trying to put the wind up me. I wait for Fiona, ready to let her lead the way in her fitted summer dress that oozes not so much as a penny change from £200. I have the Primark equivalent, except it wraps itself around my thighs like cling film on a turkey leg. 'Which house did they knock at?' I say, as I silently, yet begrudgingly, admire her effortless elegance.

'It was Nigel's,' she says, pointing two doors down to Uncle Albert's house. This is turning into a complete waste of time. The man's hardly ever there and not the friendliest when I've been unfortunate enough to exchange a couple of words.

'All right, then,' I say, aware I'm huffing. 'Let's find out what's happened.'

We trudge along the narrow pavement towards Nigel's house, not a word exchanged between us. A couple of times Fiona opens her mouth to say something and glances back at me as she leads the way. My raised eyebrows and pursed lips no doubt stop her from sprouting whatever nonsense she was about to utter. Fortunately it's only a short distance, so I only have to bite my tongue for no longer than a few seconds.

An unashamedly muddy four-door Ford Fiesta is parked at the far end of the row, tucked back beside the edge of the last property. It looks as though it's travelled hundreds of miles of filthy country roads since it's seen a wash. The discreet parking spot means it's not visible from my house or any of the others without heading in this direction. Even then, it looks like a car parked next to a house. Absolutely nothing unusual in that.

It starts me thinking that it wouldn't be impossible to hide a vehicle – or a person – out here. There's more than one reason I've let Fiona walk ahead of me; it gives me a little longer to run things through my mind. For such a small cluster of cottages with few inhabitants, there seems to be an awful lot going on. I'll have to make some discreet enquiries as to whether it's always been this eventful or am I simply unlucky enough to attract trouble.

As we approach Nigel's house, he presses his face against the window like a dog that wants to see what the neighbours are up to while his owners are out. Only he lacks the cuteness and warmth of a canine. He stares first at Fiona and then at me before tearing himself away. I hear the noise of his front door opening and I will Fiona to keep going. I'm not sure why I said yes to this nonsense. I've got things to sit by myself and fret over.

At the sight of Nigel appearing on his driveway, Fiona stops short, forcing me to do the same. He's wearing an open necked checked shirt and some sort of corduroy trousers without any sense of irony. All he's missing is a cravat to go with the haughty expression on his face, and he'd be the epitome of the rural middle classes.

Nigel glances at me before addressing his question to Fiona. 'Have the police been to yours too?'

'Hello, Nigel. They knocked but I was otherwise engaged. Avril, here,' she makes a gesture that could be mistaken for scattering seeds, 'only went and got herself burgled!'

'Careless,' says Nigel. He narrows his rheumy eyes at me and tuts. 'You're lucky you caught me in. I was on my way to Canterbury to visit my father.'

'We don't want to hold you up,' says Fiona. She moves closer to him and for a second, I think she is going to put a hand on his arm. Nigel clearly thinks so too. His face hardens and he gives an all-over shudder. I saw it, and I'm standing some feet away from the two of them, Fiona couldn't have missed it. Credit to her, she carries on unperturbed.

'The last thing we wanted was to leave you out of the loop,' says Fiona, hands now back in her pockets – my dress doesn't have pockets, and if it did, weighing the material down with so much as a tissue, let alone my sausage fingers, would probably stretch it way beyond its original proportions.

'This area has gone to the dogs,' says Nigel, once more his attention on me. 'If things work out for me, it won't be my problem. I'll be away from here soon.'

I am about to tell this irritating man that I don't care very much for his insults when I hear a noise from the front door of the cottage I thought was unoccupied.

'I thought that place was empty,' I mutter, more to myself than Fiona and Nigel.

'Don't be ridiculous,' says Nigel, a sharp tone to his voice that does nothing to make me warm to him. 'That's Joan Fielding's place. Has been for years. She rarely goes out, so I fetch her shopping and often pop in and see her, have a cup of tea. Keep her appraised of local events and tragedies.'

He squints his hazel eyes at me as he says the last word. I open my mouth to give him one of my best insults but before I get the first word out, someone calls my name.

I glance up and see DC Katie George on the front step of Joan Fielding's cottage. Her expression appears neutral; no hint of a smile or a frown. Something about the way she handles herself makes her seem older than she was when we met after my burglary. I had her down as a bit wet behind the ears, someone who was used to going about their job efficiently, while not actually being that switched on. Perhaps I had underestimated her; even the way she is standing means business.

Katie holds up a hand and beckons me with her index finger.

I step between Nigel and Fiona, they move back.

'Do you need us, officer?' says Fiona.

'No, I have to speak to Avril, but not you two,' says Katie. She raises her voice, assertive, yet an even tone.

Ridiculously I feel special. Not that it would be that difficult to feel superior to the daft pair of bookends who are now gawping in the direction of Joan Fielding's cottage.

I've barely taken two steps along the pavement when two police cars drive into everyone's view. Both vehicles have their blue lights flashing, but mercifully, the sirens are silent. The lack of noise does little to lessen the mounting sense of urgency. Two cars adorned with Kent Police's badge and lurid yellow and blue markings, plus a plain-clothes detective in an otherwise seemingly unoccupied house? This is about more than a burglary. Unless it's a burglary gone wrong.

'Rena Hargreaves?' asks Katie as she comes to a stop at the end of Joan Fielding's pathway, a line of baby blue forget-me-nots on either side of her. 'Did she come back? Have you seen her since she was here?'

'That's a lot of questions.' I try to look past her shoulder, to catch a peek inside the house I thought was empty. It's dark in there. The curtains might have been closed to keep out the sunlight, along with prying eyes. Then again, perhaps it's to keep something inside.

A chill passes down my spine at the same moment I see the sweat bead above Katie's top lip. Her hand comes up to wipe it away.

'Has she been back, Avril? It's important.'

I turn, briefly distracted by four police officers piling out of cars, punctuated by the sounds of the air traffic from their radios and equipment being dragged from car boots and backseats. A garbled conversation starts between them about crime scenes and crime scene tape, all the while Katie continues to stare at me.

She tries again. 'It really is important.'

'No, Rena didn't come back here. What's happened?' Once again I'm drawn past the open front door, my mind racing ahead, trying to join the dots, fill in the gaps. 'Where's the woman who lives there? Joan something.'

'That's why there are so many police officers here,' says Katie as more vehicles draw to a stop in the road. I don't even have to look to know that each and every one of them will contain an employee of the local constabulary.

'We had an anonymous call about your neighbour. When we got here, Joan's property was insecure.' Katie takes a breath, either giving herself a minute to harvest the right tone and pitch, or else to prepare me for the worst. 'We found Joan's body. Someone's stabbed her to death in her bed.'

The next few hours are a whirlwind of police activity; cars and vans pull up, a large vehicle the size of a mobile library adorned with the words Mobile Incident Unit sits at the far end of the row of cottages, its engine idling besides Joan's cottage. The noise is distracting me from clearing my mind and coming to terms with what's happened over the last day or so.

Katie's revelation is a lot to take in. It's not every day that a detective constable breaks the news to you that one of your neighbours was found murdered in their bed, and it's not every day that you come home to find your own front door wide open. Add to that a visit from a disgraced former police officer who armed herself with my favourite kitchen knife shortly before Joan Fielding was being stabbed in her sleep, and my nerves are shot.

I stand at the front room window, my fingers playing with the neck of my grey T-shirt and my temples throbbing at the chug of the mobile incident unit's diesel engine. The detectives plod up and down my road, knocking on doors, asking their questions, trying to solve the crime that the local and national news will undoubtedly report as a 'shocking incident that has left local people in total disbelief at the horror in their close-knit community' or other similarly empty words.

It suddenly feels warm and stuffy in the house and I want to get away from here. How suspicious would that look? The police have already taken my fingerprints to eliminate me from my own crime scene. There's no point in me running, not now. It'll bump me to the top of their list of suspects. No, I'll have to be cleverer than that.

Katie is in my eyeline, her grey trouser suit now covered by a thin white paper one. It makes her appear as though she's got hold of the dressing-up box. Her mousy blonde hair scrunched up beneath a white paper cap completes the look.

Something catches her attention and she walks briskly across the pavement, past the boundary of my garden and towards Fiona who is holding two mugs in a *come-and-get-it* way.

'She's made them coffee,' I say to my empty home. 'Why didn't I think of that?'

Not to be put off, I dash towards the kitchen and start opening drawers and cupboards until I find it. The pure joy of finding an unopened, still in date, packet of Jaffa Cakes is almost too much. It's the closest I've come to an orgasm for longer than I care to remember.

I hold back from ripping into them – these are for my new besties. Fiona and Katie, here I come.

Not wanting to dawdle, firstly because I'm on a time-sensitive mission here, and secondly, in case the chocolate melts, I open the front door and am delighted to see Fiona and Katie chatting amiably only feet away from the garden path.

With as much sincerity as I can muster, I hold out the peace offering and wait until they turn their attention my way. I watch Fiona, whose expression tells me that she wants to know why

I've interrupted their cosy chat. Is that mild annoyance I see pass over her sharp cheekbones, her straight nose and cat-like eyes?

'Sorry to butt in,' I say, waving the biscuits – or cakes, depending on your viewpoint – at the two of them. 'Thought you might fancy a snack?'

Katie spends a second or two perusing the other officers, looks back at the packet in my hands, and says, 'Oh, go on then.'

It's a stroke of genius on my part that I didn't open the wrapper inside, as neither of them can manage it with a mug in one hand. It gives me the briefest of chances as I fumble to tear it apart. 'That coffee smells wonderful, Fi. I don't suppose you've made a pot?'

I steal another look at her. Now her mouth makes a cat's arsehole shape, which is nice company for her feline eyes.

Fiona remembers her manners and tells us, 'I'll be back in a jiffy, and I'll be certainly tucking into a Jaffy!' I resist rolling my eyes; I don't want to come across as too unpleasant. I want Katie to find me approachable and trustworthy. As much as a detective can when she is in the midst of investigating a murder two doors down from my home.

Katie reaches over and takes the first Jaffa Cake. 'I'm so hungry,' she confides. 'I don't want my detective inspector to see me eating this. She'll tell me it's unprofessional, which of course, it is.'

The cake – or biscuit – is gone in two bites. I hold out the packet again, thrusting it inches away from her nose when I think she's going to refuse. I need her to keep filling her face so that I can talk before Fiona comes back.

As soon as her hand waivers over the packet, I say, 'Weird that Rena Hargreaves was here, parked on Joan's driveway, and then the very next day, Joan's found dead.'

I give a slow nod of my head, as if I honestly can't believe this turn of events.

Katie holds the Jaffa Cake, concentrates very hard on it and says, 'Yes, I couldn't agree more.'

I hadn't in all honestly expected her to make any kind of comment. As if reading my thoughts, or possibly merely regretting what she's said, she adds, 'Must be low blood sugar, or something. Please forget I said that.'

'Absolutely, absolutely. You poor thing. Pop in later and I'll make you something more substantial to eat. It's cruel that you can't even get yourself some lunch.'

I hear a noise from behind me and know that Fiona is coming, her heels clipping on the concrete.

'Rena does give off a sinister vibe, you know,' I say, exposing more chocolate, sponge and orange delicacy. Katie looks down and bites her lip. I keep talking. 'Perhaps it's what I now know about her, only I've got this feeling...'

'Here we go, Avril.' Fiona hands me a huge blue Denby mug, forcing me to stop being a temptress of sugary goodness and switch my focus to the steaming drink. It's the last thing I need on such a warm day, but it's here now, so I take a tentative sip. I have to admit, it's very fine coffee. Not that I expected anything else from Fiona The Middle Class Goddess.

I am about to suggest that we move into the cool of my front room when a shout rings out from the edge of the scene cordon. All three of us turn to the source of the bellowing. A large, mumsy-looking woman wearing a mid-calf, deep purple dress waves her hand at us. It's one exaggerated, deliberate move, as if she is directing traffic and really won't tolerate any kind of failing to comply with her instructions. Her greying messy hair does little to accentuate a face that has lost its battle with gravity. Katie mumbles her apologies at us, that she has to go, her face now a shade of crab-stick pink.

I watch her as she rushes off, her paper suit-covered shoulders up to her ears. I assume she is Katie's DI, and from the expression on her jowly face, she is very unhappy about something.

CHAPTER ELEVEN

I watch the exchange between Katie and her detective inspector. There is much gesticulating and scowling, even an amusing moment where the DI – head and shoulders taller than Katie – tries to duck down so her face is obscured. She clearly has me down as some sort of lip-reading specialist. The fact she isn't trying to keep her voice down all that much makes it even more ludicrous. I hear something about a car and the words 'woods nearby'.

Aware that Fiona is watching me, I concentrate hard, narrowing my eyes and tilting my left ear towards the detectives. Now I'm behaving like the world's worst spy; I have no idea what's got hold of my sanity today. Perhaps it's a combination of the warm weather and a strong coffee I really didn't want, then again, it could be the news about my murdered neighbour.

Then the ill-muted verbal exchange is no longer my focus. Instead, it's the police officers and crime scene examiner who are walking back and forth from Joan's house to the CSI's van. Each person is clutching carefully packaged items in brown bags, the words 'Police Evidence' plainly visible on the sides. CSI Sally leans towards the back of her van, some of the exhibit bags slip from her hand, and there it is – a flash of red through the see-through window that runs the length of the bag. The late morning sun glints on the cellophane panel, momentarily making me doubt what I see. No, I'm not wrong about this. Inside one of the bags is a long length of red ribbon.

'Are you okay? Avril, I said are you okay? You've gone very pale.'

I hear yet don't comprehend what Fiona is asking me. I turn my attention back to her and blink rapidly. It really is bright out here. I think I'm getting a headache.

'Shall I help you back inside?' Fiona is still talking to me and then tries to grapple for her Denby mug. I stare at her hands; her long slender fingers try to uncurl mine which have turned white as I hold on for dear life. I give little resistance when I understand what's happening and with a satisfied sigh, she removes the item from my grip. She holds all three of her precious mugs in one of her piano-player's hands and gently pushes me towards my front door.

'Yes, yes,' I murmur. Now I want to be inside on my own. I need to think calmly and I need a plan. The last thing I want is to fall to pieces with my neighbour witnessing me have some sort of melt down. 'Honestly, I think that it's all got a bit much for me, that's all.'

Once I'm in the safety of my own hallway, I turn to Fiona and give her a reassuring smile. 'Thank you, but I'll be fine now. Just need to get out of the sun and into the cool, I think.'

I take a step back and start to close the door. She appears a bit surprised, and I suppose there is always the chance that she expected me to invite her in. In the time I've lived here, which admittedly isn't that long, I've never been inside her house, and she hasn't crossed over the threshold here. Today won't be the day that changes.

I push the door and the soft click of the lock sounds

reassuringly pleasing, then I glide the bolt across and lock myself in. I'm going nowhere for the rest of the day.

I move from room to room checking the windows are closed and secure. Once I'm satisfied that if someone tries to get inside, it will involve them making a lot of noise, I draw the curtains in each room before I leave. The whole place is much darker, but I like that. I've always felt safer when it's night-time; it gives me somewhere to hide.

Even though it will be hours until the daylight fades, it doesn't stop me from wanting to take a shower, remove the grime of the day and get ready for bed. I do my best thinking when I'm in my cotton pyjamas; tartan slippers to match. I may even go crazy and take my make-up off properly for the first time in three days.

I find a clean glass, fill it with water from the tap and climb the stairs to the bathroom. The bathroom is at the back of the house. It's functional enough, despite it being on the tiny size, and everything works. When I moved in, I thought that hot and cold running water, plus a flushing toilet, were the least of my worries.

I take a sip of the water, set it down beside the sink and reach across for the luxury branded cleanser I splurged on. Something catches my eye through the frosted window and I freeze.

There is movement in the garden. I try my best to quell the rising panic – it's probably the police. But shouldn't they knock and ask me first? Or, at the very least, tell me they have a warrant. Both Katie and her DI know that I'm at home.

With trembling fingers, I turn the catch and push open the window. A figure moves quickly across the rough lawn towards the overgrown border.

'Why are you in my garden?' I shout.

Nigel, my neighbour, looks up at me. His expression instantly switches from startled to disgusted as if I should have the nerve to challenge him clumsily stamping about in my weed patch.

'Isn't it obvious?' he says, one hand against his forehead. 'As I was about to head out to Canterbury, my pet weasel got out. The decent thing would be for you to come and help me look.'

Anyone else, I would be inclined to think that perhaps it was a ruse to get his loafers onto my property. I had no fear of Nigel indulging in such skulduggery.

'Did it break out of your corduroy trousers?' I ask, hoping that the answer is yes. Even before he answers, I can tell that my question angered him. It is a combination of the scowl on his face as he drops his hands to his sides, clenches his fists and makes a hilarious hopping motion.

With a sigh, I pull the window closed and return downstairs to see what I can do to help Nigel and his AWOL weasel. Now there's something I didn't expect to find myself doing.

By the time I get through the back door and into the garden, Nigel has forced the padlock off the shed door.

'You've broken that!' I say, livid that this man has the audacity to come into my garden, damage my property and cause me palpitations at the thought of who could be watching me. 'I'm going to have to replace that.'

Nigel looks down at the lock in his hands, and then back up at me. 'Rubbish. It was already broken. See.'

He thrusts the item towards me, the two pieces of metal appearing tiny in his enormous palms. 'Someone's cut clean through this steel shackle. How on earth would I manage that with my bare hands?'

He has a point. Even, though his hands are like a bunch of bananas – what's with my neighbours and their unfeasibly large hands – he couldn't have snapped it in two. On closer inspection I can make out a clean slice through the metal that should have been secured around the door clasp on my dilapidated shed. This isn't good at all. I know it wasn't like that the previous day.

My headache's back and I don't feel at all well.

'Are you all right?' says Nigel. 'You've gone a very strange colour.'

I'm about to quip that I couldn't be a stranger colour than his terrible trousers when I feel my legs about to buckle.

Before I slump to the ground, my neighbour leaps forward and catches me. He's incredibly strong and fast for a man I had pegged as well past his prime. Fortunately, my brain is telling my mouth to stop working and concentrate on staying upright. I don't have the energy to chat and stand, so I keep quiet.

'Let me help you get back inside,' says Nigel. He moves to one side of me and somehow grabs both of my elbows and guides me towards the house. I know that my feet are in contact with the daisy-strewn lawn, but they don't feel as if they are. I glide inside the kitchen where I flop onto a chair.

I close my eyes in an attempt to block out the day. When I open them again, Nigel is bent over at the waist, his face inches from mine, staring straight at me.

'Don't be startled, young lady. I'm trying to see if you're having some sort of a fit or an episode.'

'Are you a doctor?'

'No, no, but I had to shoot a few horses in my time. Only when it was necessary, you understand.'

Perhaps I did fall and hit my head after all. What's he talking about?

Nigel gets me a glass of tap water and gives me instructions to sip it slowly.

'What was that about shooting horses?' I ask. 'And are you comparing me to a lame one? And why do you have a gun?'

He waves my questions away and glances around the room. 'Bit of a mess in here, but that's what I expected. It's something from my previous life working in veterinary care. When I say shoot, of course, I mean euthanise to end their severe suffering. Just trying to be economical with my words because you look like death warmed up and I wasn't sure if you were going to keel over on me.'

I sip the tepid water and blink slowly several times. I'd like Nigel to leave now, and my head is foggy trying to remember what he's doing in my kitchen in the first place.

'You were looking for a weasel,' I say. 'Why do you have a weasel?'

'Right at this particular moment, it seems that I don't.' He crosses his arms and brings one hand up so that his index finger is propping up his bottom lip. 'Mmm. Nothing wrong with your short-term memory. Good, good.'

If Nigel's happy, I'm happy. I need to get him out of here and away from me so that I can think and form some sort of a plan. I grip the glass with one hand and point a shaky finger – it's not all an act – towards the window. 'That looked like something running across the lawn, back towards your house.' It's a complete lie, but let's be honest, he isn't going to find the creature standing in my kitchen. I am about to tell him that it's about to scale the fence when I realise that I don't know if weasels can climb. I wouldn't want to find out with one hanging on to the end of my nightie.

Nigel takes a stride towards the window. 'Well, I'll be. You're right! Thank you, young lady.'

And he's gone. He makes it through the back door and across the unkempt lawn to where a rodent-like thing seems to recognise him and races towards him as Nigel calls, 'Willy!' and the two meet head on, or rather, foot and head on. I watch as Nigel bends down and Willy the Weasel scurries up his arm and is immediately cradled to his chest.

If today isn't the most bizarre of days.

CHAPTER TWELVE

It's a relief to get away from everyone and everything, especially weird neighbours and their absurd pets. A murder a few doors from where I live is enough to contend with, let alone the reoccurring thoughts that play on my mind and keep me awake even on my Rioja-fuelled nights. Tonight I made the decision to leave the booze alone, afraid it would make my pounding headache all the worse. My brain feels like a cartoon one, pulsing away in my cranium as I make my way upstairs to bed.

I doubt that I'll slip into an easy sleep, but I'll give it my best go. I've used some lavender spray on the pillow, tried some calming breathing exercises, and even had a camomile tea. Despite the taste reminding me of the time I capsized on the one and only attempt I had at canoeing. I took in water like a whale with a punctured lung, but I still got back in the damned canoe and paddled like my life depended on it.

Something must have worked as it isn't long before I slide into a fitful sleep, all the while convinced I have company that is intent on doing me harm. My mind tries to block out the absurdity of such thoughts, at the same time as my senses tell me a different story.

As I reach that cosy dreamy point where the day melts away and another better world is within my reach, I'm jolted awake as something lands across my mouth. My eyes instinctively open and I try to sit up but I'm pinned to the mattress. I try my best to remain calm, and think rationally, and, of course, instantly fail. My breathing is fast and hard and I claw at the hand clamped across my face and the other on my chest.

'Avril, shush,' says a voice, one I recognise. 'It's Rena. Don't shout or scream. Please.'

I nod, unsure if she can see me in the fading light, convinced she can feel the movement of my head against the pillow. The sun has long gone down, but the moon is high and visible through the bedroom window. I know that I didn't pull the curtains back, and I definitely shut the window before I crawled into bed.

'Okay, I'll take my hand away. You have to keep quiet.'

I feel her fingers loosen their grip; it's more of a caress. It doesn't stop me feeling totally petrified. I've been warned about this woman – she's been to prison and so far, up until the point she entered my home in the dead of night, has given me no explanation as to why she was banged up. As my heart stops pounding, I remember that if I'd been caught for the crimes I'd committed, we could have been cellmates. Undoubtedly Rena would still have got out before me.

'You have to listen to me,' she says, 'what you've been told isn't true. Well, not all of it, anyway.' I see her look away and I get a chance to study her profile. The moonlight gives her an edge, one I hadn't the chance to previously appreciate. Her chin and jaw make her seem tough but the downturn of her lips and the glistening of her eyes give her a vulnerability that I'd missed. Perhaps I had judged too quickly, been swayed by the words of Katie, a police officer I know just as well as Rena. Should I take the word of a detective over that of a former, and now disgraced, police officer, who is at this moment sitting on the edge of my mattress, having broken into my house and woken me up with one of her hands on my mouth and the other on my chest? I'm caught in the moment and think I'll give Rena the benefit of the doubt.

'I won't make a sound,' I say, words escaping through her fingers.

Slowly, Rena releases a breath and whispers, 'I believe you.'

I inch my way up the pillow until my head is resting against the wall. We stare at each other for a second until she breaks the spell and says, 'I could do with a drink.' She holds out her hand and without thinking or questioning, I take it and she pulls me upwards at the same time she stands towering over me.

I glance down at her feet. 'You're wearing high-heeled boots,' I say. 'It's the middle of the night, you've broken into my house – not to mention it's about twenty-five degrees – and you're dressed up to the nines.'

She grins. 'I like to make the effort. Let's go and raid your drinks cupboard.'

With that, she steps towards the door as I call after her, 'You won't find much in this house: I've drunk most of it.'

'Didn't I tell you how resourceful I was?' she says from the landing. 'Give me five minutes.'

I hear her run down the stairs and open the front door, followed by complete silence. If she has already managed to get past the police officers at the cordon around Joan's house once, then I suppose a second or third time isn't going to be a problem for her.

Unsure what to do in my own home, I stand in the bedroom, glance down at my pyjamas and think that perhaps I should get dressed. I have a feeling that this will be a long night. Besides, if

Rena has gone out the front door, she's probably left it open and anyone could wander in. I grab a pair of cutoff jeans and a T-shirt from the chair, tear off my nightwear and get changed. I feel a tiny bit more in control now that I'm dressed, albeit I didn't think I had time to add underwear into the mix.

By the time I get to the top of the stairs, Rena is back through the door, a bottle of vodka in her hand. 'I take it you've got ice?'

Without waiting for an answer, she strolls through to the kitchen.

I almost fall down the stairs in my haste to get to the front door and push it closed, before I pull the chain across for good measure. Why am I so worried about making sure no one knows she's here? I could have called the police while she was gone. What's stopping me?

Instead, I join her in the kitchen. There are two large glass tumblers on the sink and Rena is busy poking around in the freezer.

'The ice is in the small drawer at the top,' I find myself saying instead of *What the hell are you doing in my house in the middle of the night.* 'Where did you get the vodka?' Because that's clearly the most pressing issue here.

Rena pulls a small plastic tray from the freezer and gives me an enquiring look. 'Had you down as a bag of ice, girl. I didn't have you pegged for one of these.' She waves the tray and then proceeds to add half a dozen cubes to each glass. As she's now preoccupied with unscrewing the Grey Goose vodka, I pad across behind her and close the freezer.

The sound of the ice cracking as she adds generous measures of liquid is satisfying. She hands me a glass and I resist the urge to say that I wanted lemonade with mine. *What* is wrong with me? Why can't I speak up?

I take a greedy gulp and instantly regret it. It looks more thirst quenching than it actually is, what with all the alcohol. I feel it numb my mouth, followed by a burning sensation as it slides down my throat.

'You don't appear to be enjoying that.' There's a faint smile on her lips as she takes a long drink of hers and immediately reaches back to the countertop for the bottle. I shake my head as she holds it out to me, so she shrugs and tops up her own.

'What is going on, Rena? You have to give me an explanation. And where did you get a bottle of vodka from in the middle of the night? Especially with the police still guarding the murder scene only doors away?'

And then I find myself trailing behind her into my living room.

Rena throws herself onto my armchair, legs stretched out in front of her, glass propped on her thigh. Her expression is hard to read. I'd like to say that it's one of contemplation, but then it could be that she's merely wondering whether she should have brought the bottle with her. She sighs and holds her drink up to me. 'Cheers, Avril. You could have completely freaked out then when I came into your room. You look very vulnerable when you're fast asleep.'

'Don't most people? And for the final time of asking, what are you doing here?' I swirl my drink, the sound of the ice clinking against the side of the tumbler the only sound in the room.

I wait.

'I wanted you to know the truth about me.' There's another pause. 'I was a police officer for eighteen years when I did something spectacularly stupid. I was rightly punished for it, although the stigma of going to prison has been much lengthier than the sentence the judge gave me.'

Her voice begins to crack a little; she shifts her head back against the chair which stops me from seeing her expression in the dimness of the room. A table lamp in the far corner – switched on by Rena, I guess – is the only source of light.

'How long did you get?' I quietly ask.

'I served eight months. What an eight months that was. And when I was done, most of my friends either didn't want too much to do with me, or else avoided me altogether. I can't really say that I blame them. Perverting the course of justice ranks pretty low on the sliding scale of naughtiness.' She gives a chuckle, then shakes her head, her hair fanning out behind her on the back of the chair. 'I don't have much left in the way of family either, so it's been lonely, but I've got by.'

Rena takes another drink and sighs. 'I worked with a colleague who was what we used to call in the police, "a good old boy". It has a few connotations, some meaning old school, gets the job done, a bit of ducking and diving going on, but they're usually the type that the management unofficially like as they're thief-takers and produce good results, even if it's a little unorthodox. Their contemporaries want to work with them because they're fun to be around and make decisions, and again, get results. Win-win. Except, I owed this one a favour, and he called it in.'

This time, I take a gulp of my drink, all but draining the glass.

When Rena goes to get up, I hold out my hand. 'I'll get it.'

I rush off to retrieve the dwindling Grey Goose and rush back, not wanting to break the spell.

I need not have worried. As my backside hits the sofa seat, she begins again. 'We were friends, good friends. There was even a little dalliance, if you know what I mean.' She looks up and then back down again, her face still hard to read in the gloom.

'What was the favour?'

'I'd arranged a couple of things that I needed time off work for and I had no cover. As ever, we were running at minimum staffing – nothing new there – but on this occasion, I had to get away and I had no other way but to tell a few fibs and take the time off, despite being told I couldn't have leave. Lewis covered for me and told a couple more fibs to explain my absence.'

'That doesn't sound like a huge deal to me,' I say. Her head snaps up and I know that I've hit a nerve. 'But I don't know the workings of how policing operates,' I hastily add.

Rena nods. 'You're right. From day one in the police, everyone will tell you that if you mess up – and you will mess up – as long as you admit what you've done and don't cover it up, criminal charges aside, there's a good chance you'll get your knuckles rapped and you'll be out of the crap. The absolute worst thing anyone can do is lie. So, what did we both do? We lied.'

'Over some annual leave? That's why you went to prison.'

'Don't be so fucking stupid.' She spits the words out; I jolt back in my seat. It would appear that vodka doesn't bring out the best in Rena. I'll have to remember that. There are a few reasons that I don't want to get on the wrong side of her, but getting a beating is most definitely high on the list of things to avoid.

'Sorry,' I mumble. It seems to calm her and she continues.

'Lewis covered for me, so in return he asked that I went to the exhibit store and retrieve dashcam footage so he could have a look at it. Of course, I wasn't happy at all. He was basically asking me to commit a criminal offence, and while I didn't exactly have an unblemished record, I'd never done anything of the sort before. I loved my job, despite the piss-poor management and grief it brought with it, and the last thing I wanted to do was jeopardise it.

'Yet, that's exactly what I found myself doing. He was very persuasive and said that I'd be helping him out more than I could ever know. All I had to do was get the footage, he'd look at it and know once and for all.'

'Know what?'

Rena arches an eyebrow at me. 'The story he gave me was that his younger sister was in an abusive relationship and while fleeing for her life from her drunk husband, her car had clipped the wing mirrors of a couple of cars along Ashford Road, just the other side of Maidstone. He said that he wanted to make sure it was her driving and not the dead-beat husband, and that his sister wasn't, once again, covering for him.'

I don't like where this story is going. I can't believe that Rena would be taken in with a ruse like this. From the moment I saw her, I had her down as a confident and together person, so for her to risk so much to comply with the instructions of a man she had a fling with doesn't make sense.

'What was on the dashcam footage?' I ask, cradling my empty glass.

'It wasn't his sister knocking a couple of wing mirrors askew, that's for sure.' Rena holds her own glass between thumb and forefinger and examines it. 'Turns out it was two young lads on a night out who decided it was a good idea to drag a teenage girl into an alley and rape her.'

I hear a gasp before I realise it's me who made the noise. All the unpleasant things I've done, had done to me, and witnessed in my life, yet this still comes like a physical blow. 'But you didn't know.'

'Doesn't matter, does it? These two loathsome shits actually got away with it because a couple of their mates said she willingly went with them and she was too out of it to remember. The town CCTV shows her holding hands with one of them before they disappeared around the corner from the main High Street. The dashcam was the only other recording.'

'I don't get why Lewis was so desperate for you to remove the dashcam.'

Rena leans forward so I can see her pale skin and the dark circles under her eyes.

'Because the two young men were Lewis's sons.'

CHAPTER THIRTEEN

It was some time before Rena stopped throwing vodka down her neck at an alarming rate. In fact, it was pretty much the time that she poured the last drop into her glass. Against my better – not to mention, saner – judgement, I offered her the sofa. As I wake up, my breath undoubtedly still reeking of last night's drinking session, I savour the relief of being alone in my house. Quite what I was thinking, asking her to stay, is beyond me. Beyond me now that I'm stone-cold sober.

I put my hand up to my clammy forehead and muster the enthusiasm to get out of bed.

Once I've brushed my teeth, showered and put on clean clothes that don't have Grey Goose in the weave, I feel marginally better.

I'm on my third coffee when I hear a knock at the door. My first thought is that Rena's back, but then I remember that requesting entry isn't really her style. I peek through the front window and stare straight into DC Katie George's eyes.

She gives a tight smile and gives me a nod. Something seems off with her; I can tell even in the two seconds I spend at the window before walking to the door.

'Hi,' I say, stepping back in case my breath is still flammable. 'Everything okay?'

'Not exactly. Are you on your own?'

It's not a particularly strange question, yet it makes me a little uneasy. Does Katie know more than I think she does? She can't know that Rena broke in here in the middle of the night, and if she did, surely she would have got here sooner. Despite my hangover, I've been up a fair while and had time to wash the glasses, put them away and hide the empty bottle deep in the recycling bin.

'Yes, home alone. Can I get you a coffee?'

Katie moves into the hallway and waits for me to move out of the way before she follows me towards the kitchen, and accepts my offer of a drink.

We make small talk about the garden, the weather and property prices while the kettle boils merrily away and I make her a drink and finish my own, now cooling coffee.

'Please, have a seat,' I say as she hesitates at the kitchen chairs. 'Is everything okay?' I may as well get to it. We're both busy people and Katie looks like she has something a little on the delicate side to say to me.

The young police officer settles herself in the chair, pulls her coffee cup across the table towards her and gazes at it. She bites her lip and then turns her attention to me. 'You know that your neighbour Joan Fielding was murdered.' I nod. 'Well, there's a bit more of an update.'

'Right,' I say slowly. 'You said she'd been stabbed?'

Suddenly Katie appears more alert, as if a switch was flicked and she is back to professional police officer mode. 'She was stabbed. A number of times.'

'Oh,' is all I find to say. I fight to stop myself turning my head to my metallic knifeboard, the very same one Rena had reached for within moments of being in my house under the guise of protecting me. My mouth goes dry. Perhaps the vodka is about to put in a reappearance.

I act as normal as possible. I sit at the table opposite the detective and contort my face in what I hope is an expression that says *wow, I've only just thought about this.* 'You don't suppose there's any chance Rena stabbed her?' I study Katie's face for any sign that I'm on the right track.

I'm disappointed when she shrugs and pulls a genuine look of not having the slightest idea. This is going to be more difficult than I'd imagined. Usually I can get the measure of someone, although it would be fair to point out that I hadn't exactly got to grips with how much of a useless, faithless git my husband was when I first met him. Katie is proving to be hard to read. Is she telling it to me straight or does police training have an acting class. I can almost picture the fresh-faced newbies being coached on how to come across sincere when delivering a death message and how to engage in good cop, bad cop, in an interrogation.

Then I'm aware she's talking to me and I've drifted off. 'I can see you're in shock. Do you want me to call someone?'

I shake my head and she carries on. 'There was more than one stab wound to Mrs Fielding, and the post-mortem showed that stabbing was the cause of death. It's sometimes not always clear, you know? Someone might have killed her and then tried to cover it up, to detract us from the real cause of death.'

'Why? If she was pushed down the stairs, for example, why then stab her repeatedly?' My brain forgets it's my mouth's gatekeeper. I push my lips together to stop myself from straying any further into dangerous territory.

A muscle twitches centimetres above Katie's left eye; she sits up a little straighter. 'I didn't say repeatedly, just more than once.'

'Well, that's repeatedly, surely?' I pick up my coffee cup and go to take a sip. 'It's cold. I'll make another.' It gives me a chance to turn my back and gather my thoughts. If Rena stabbed her, then she can't have used my knife unless, by some amazing coincidence, I have the same set as Joan Fielding or the identical one that Rena brought with her, stabbed Joan with, entered my house and swapped them over. That's completely improbable.

With the kettle boiling, I have no option but to face Katie again. 'So, are you going to arrest Rena for murder?'

'We have to find her first. Any idea where she might be?'

I prod myself in the chest with my finger. 'Me? Why do you think I know where she is?'

'When did you last see her?'

The kettle reaches boiling so I concentrate on making a drink. 'The last time you asked me whether she'd been back here, I told you the truth. However, what I didn't tell you was that I'd seen her in Faversham.'

I step towards the fridge and avoid Katie's eye.

'What did she say to you?'

'I was having a spot of late breakfast and she came into the café and spoke to me. She told me that she went to prison for something but that she hadn't killed anyone and the two people who died would have died anyway.' I sound as if I'm defending her and that was most certainly not my intention. I struggle with my reluctance to throw her under the bus. I owe Rena nothing, yet I like her.

As I move back towards my seat, I hear Katie give the tiniest of sighs.

We stare at one another and finally she says, 'It depends on whose version you want to believe. Rena took some footage from the property store and then destroyed it. It was never found and we really didn't get to the bottom of why she took it. All I can tell you is that she stole, she lied and by getting rid of the evidence, a drunk-driver wasn't brought to justice, and went on to mow down a father and his eight-year-old son on their way home from a football match.'

There's a distinct pinch in my temple from the combination of the lack of fresh air, the bad night's sleep and enough caffeine to make the most ardent of coffee drinkers think about a nice herbal tea.

'Are you saying that the driver was Rena?'

'No.' Katie gets a notebook from her bag and scrawls something inside. I can't see what's she's writing from where I'm sat. 'The driver was a woman called Celia Matthews, and she was drunk. She had a habit of going to her local pub – somewhere she could have easily walked to – and then after six or seven drinks, she would drive home. An anonymous call alerted us to what she was doing, but the usual with not enough patrols around at the time when she was apparently three sheets to the wind and behind the wheel, meant we had to take action before someone was killed.'

My mind is trying to catch up with the bombardment of information. Something isn't right, only I can't get to grips with what's bothering me.

'If the police think someone's driving regularly when they're drunk, surely you can't just hope for the best,' I say, more to clarify matters to myself than to get an answer.

'You wouldn't be wrong.' Katie's face is the perfect picture of sadness. 'We're obliged to do everything we can to prevent anyone getting hurt, or in this case, dying. Only, we didn't.'

'I still don't understand why Rena would take the footage and protect this woman,' I say. 'Are they related or friends?'

'No, not exactly. As far as we know, they never met.'

'Then why take the footage from the police station?'

'Because Celia Matthews is the wife of one of Rena's colleagues. She's married to a close friend of hers – Lewis Matthews.'

CHAPTER FOURTEEN

The grunts and shrieks kept coming from the front room as I cowered on my mattress. I had pushed a chest of drawers across the door; it was the only substantial furniture I had. I knew it wouldn't be heavy enough to stop two hairy-arsed men if they decided to push on through, especially as it was virtually empty. I had so little and no prospect of any money coming my way soon. Heather kept encouraging me to join her in her enterprise, but I didn't fancy earning money on my back. And from what she told me, laying back and thinking of England was not what her discerning clientele were after.

I sat for ages, my spine imprinted on the wall and my knees pulled up under my chin. I hadn't eaten properly in days and my already slight frame was bordering on skinny. As my stomach growled and I eyed up the warming pint of milk sat on the stained carpet, I wondered if it was time to go home and have a hot meal. My mum might not have been up for any parent of the year awards, but she made a mean lamb hotpot. The very thought made me salivate.

I reached across, grabbed the milk and tore open the carton. In my haste, some spilled down my navy-blue T-shirt –

obviously – and the liquid momentarily fooled my brain into thinking something more substantial was heading to my stomach.

Any satisfaction was short-lived by the noise of my bedroom door banging open against the flimsy chest of drawers. It rocked precariously; I held my breath.

'Melissa.' The top of Heather's head bobbed up and down in the small gap between the door and the frame. 'Why can't I get in? Have you barricaded yourself into the room?'

I put the milk down and crawled across the filthy carpet towards her. I didn't have the energy to stand up.

'What are you doing on the floor?' Heather tried to squeeze into the room, the plywood chest of drawers didn't put up much of a fight. Before I knew it, she was inside. 'Are you all right?'

I nodded. 'Have they gone?' I hitch my thumb in the direction of the living room. And that was the point I saw the bruising around her throat and jawline. I stared up at her, the finger marks clear in the harsh light of a bare 100 watt bulb suspended from the ceiling.

For some inexplicable reason, Heather looked ashamed. I would take her expression of guilt with me to my grave. 'Things got a little carried away,' she said as she put a hand up to her neck, winced and dropped it back down again.

'So, the two men, they've got injuries too?' By now, I'd found the strength to get up and I faced her full-on. All I got in reply was a shrug, and I could tell that caused her some discomfort.

'Listen, I came to ask you how you felt about popping out to the chippie with me. How about a couple of large portions of chips? My treat, obviously.'

What I wanted to do was tell her that I didn't want her money, money that she'd earned doing who knew what. And I certainly hoped that whatever it was she had endured brought in more money than a few quid for two lousy bags of chips.

Instead, my stomach growled again and I found myself following her out of the room and to the front door.

I convinced myself that I could almost smell the salt and vinegar. It was another trick of my mind and preferable to the stench of sweaty bodies leaking out of the living room.

CHAPTER FIFTEEN

Rena recognises that she should really get herself together. Except she didn't think it would be so difficult to motivate herself. When she had a life, a career and respect from her friends and colleagues, nothing seemed impossible. Life was hard, it always is, but at least it was fair. Now, all she has is sofa surfing to get away from a grotty one-bedroom flat she pays cash for to a dubious contact.

This particular sofa isn't one she wanted to spend a night on, but curiosity more than anything got the better of her. Rena doesn't want to use up all of her favours, and this is the home of someone who really owes her. And she'll make sure that she milks it for all it's worth.

Since her release from prison, Rena has worked hard to make sure that everyone essential to her plan is aware that she is out and about and very much looking for payback. It's much better to be the person about to strike than the ones who have no idea when or where they'll find out how vengeful she can be.

The thought makes her smile as she rolls over on the Sophie Conran four-seater, her face now inches from the Cornish blue stripes. 'About four grands' worth of bloody furniture,' she mutters to herself. The rest of the twenty-five-foot long living room is strewn with equally expensive pieces and the décor is to a high standard. The wood panelling on one wall is painted a soft grey and the made to measure curtains are worth more than her Honda Civic.

Rena purses her lips at the thought of her car now a burnt out lump of metal, its days numbered as it rots away in the corner of a scrapyard somewhere. She loved that car. Not the fastest, definitely not the flashiest, but a reliable and solid ride.

With a glance at her watch, she knows that she will have time for a coffee before anyone disturbs her; she would much rather slip out of the door without bothering anyone, leaving her the option of further nights on the comfiest couch this side of the Thames.

The coffee pods next to the Nespresso machine catch her eye, so she chooses one rather than wait for the kettle to boil. It'll be quicker and better than the instant Kenco she knows is in the cupboard above the toaster. For a moment she thinks about a quick slice of toast before she hits the road, then thinks better of it. A coffee is simple to consume and get away, whereas toast will create mess and take too long. No, the drink will do before she resigns herself to going home and concentrating on her next move. It's a lot harder to get anywhere without a car.

Her fingers grip the mug, the aroma wafts towards her and she takes a sip. The caffeine does its job as it floods her system and she feels a surge of enthusiasm for the day. Prison was a setback, but it won't stop her. She has work to do and Avril Benham strikes her as exactly the right person to help her achieve her goals.

Rena peers out of the double glass doors that overlook a beautifully landscaped garden, complete with a pond in the far left corner and a spacious covered seating area in the right-hand corner. It's expertly designed and maintained to a standard that

Monty Don and his team would be proud of. It's the sort of home Rena could have had, if her weakness for the wrong type of man hadn't been her undoing. Quite why she was so inclined to let them make a fool of her, she didn't understand. Still, that is behind her, and from now on she has little to lose, so it's no holds barred.

The thought warms her from the inside, a bit like the coffee, only this feeling comes from a natural stimulant – adrenalin.

A second coffee is tempting, but her rule is to get out while the going's good – ever since she went to prison – and so, with a final look around the sleek kitchen tops and a final peek in the drawer beside the hob, she grabs the two twenty pound notes she finds there and lets herself out into the street.

CHAPTER SIXTEEN

I spend another half an hour or so with DC Katie George at my kitchen table, willing her to drink her coffee and get out. I need to find Rena. She can explain some of this to me. I'm sure she can. Katie is still talking about whether I think that the former police officer might come back here and would I prefer the police to put me up somewhere for my own safety. As she waffles on about the budget only going so far, therefore it is going to be a local hotel rather than any sort of a safe house or a grand premises in rural Oxfordshire, I should set my expectations a little lower, I make out that I'm listening. All the while I'm on the edge of my seat for other reasons.

Rena can answer a lot of questions and, for some reason, I feel better when she's around. And it's not only because I can keep tabs on her when she's in my company.

Weirdly, the woman who marched through my house and armed herself with one of my kitchen knives and then woke me in the middle of the night with her hand over my mouth, is a reassuring presence.

'So, if you're okay with that, I'll leave you to it,' says Katie. She puts her notebook back in her bag and stands up.

'Yes, yes, absolutely.' I'm not really sure what I've just agreed to, but with luck it's nothing that will come back and bite me.

'I'll be here at seven pm to pick you up,' adds Katie with a smile.

'Er, remind me again what exactly you need. If you don't mind.' I add the last bit because frankly she looks really pissed off.

'We'd like you come to Ashford police station and be interviewed on video – well, DVD, not video as we don't have video tapes and nothing to play them on if we did.'

I doubt Katie has ever known the joy of going to the video shop on a Friday night and picking out a film only to be told all three copies of the movie of the week have already been taken, so that's your evening down the pan.

'Of course,' I feel I need to add. 'I'm sorry. I still get a bit overwhelmed with everything that's gone on over the last couple of days. Not to mention poor Joan Fielding. Have you managed to speak to her family?'

'Someone has been in touch with them.' She fiddles with her shoulder strap. It's clear that she's reluctant to say more. 'Seven pm?' The last is more of a question than a statement of fact.

'I'll be ready,' I say, not entirely sure how I'm going to start to find Rena. A quick check of my watch tells me that I've got around six hours. Surely that's plenty of time.

***

Once Katie drives away in her police-issued standard unmarked Nissan Juke, I rush upstairs to grab my handbag, mobile phone and anything else I think I may need for my own home-made episode of *The Hunted*. I grab the bag from the chair in the corner of the bedroom. I reach for both black handles, but I only manage one, so as I swing the small leather bag towards me, the contents all but spill out over the floor. While cursing myself for not doing up the zip or at least taking more care, a small piece of white paper inside the main compartment catches my eye.

I sit down on the bed, the bag on my lap, and pluck out the piece of paper. It's been torn from a notebook and in handwriting that I don't recognise someone has written:

Rena – 23A The Annex, Squires Close, Hill Hole
This message will self-destruct in five minutes 😊

The smiley face was a little crude and I didn't take very kindly to Rena using my Estee Lauder eyeliner to write down her address. Especially as it was my Double Wear Waterproof Kohl Noir one. Now I'd have to shoplift another one. Don't judge – I'm not made of money.

Rena clearly wants to talk to me, and I'm about to pay her a home visit.

CHAPTER SEVENTEEN

The journey to Hill Hole isn't a straightforward one. It's the less salubrious part of Swale Borough Council's domain and has earned itself the predictable nickname of Hell Hole. The hilarious folk of Kent can surely do better than that.

I have to take a bus into the town centre and then another out again in the direction of Goodnestone, a place I find hard to pronounce. Fortunately I'm not going that far so don't have to try and let the bus driver in on my secret of not being able to say it properly. He didn't look the type to find it amusing.

It would have been much easier if Rena had simply tagged her phone number on the end of the message, saving me several quid and possibly a wasted journey. I have already got used to her making things far more difficult for me than she needs to. I've decided to find it charming.

Once I'm off the bus (having thanked the driver – I may be light-fingered but I'm polite) I take my mobile out of my handbag and add her address into a street map app. It doesn't take me long to walk the half mile to a depressing looking road, with MOT testing centres, timber yards and second-hand electrical units on one side, and tatty looking houses on the other. Like so much of south-east England, even the tiniest scrap of land has a disproportionate amount of dwellings squeezed in, and this was no exception.

I glance to my left and a once seemingly mundane cul-de-sac is teaming with life. Six or seven cars and two vans are parked on the pavements making walking along them out of the question. A few people are out in front gardens – if they qualify as gardens – and a couple of the cars are jacked up on bricks while young men in shorts and jeans, their tattooed chests on display for all to see, work on the vehicles. Two teenagers are racing up and down on electric scooters and another two practicing juvenile delinquents both flip me the finger as I run an eye over them.

Just my luck to get the only street in Great Britain where the kids didn't get the news headline that they never go outside and spend all day in their bedrooms playing *Call of Duty* instead.

I walk with purpose, not wanting to alert anyone to the fact that I don't know where I'm going or that I have any apprehension at all about strolling along this badly tarmacked road. To avoid making myself a target, I tuck my mobile phone into the pocket of my linen trousers and hold the handles of my bag that little bit tighter.

Other than the two lads of nine or ten trying out mime for those who love expletives, virtually no one else takes any notice of me. I concentrate on the sign that promises to point me in the direction of The Annex and with my head held high and purpose in my stride, I seek out 23A.

My first thought is that it isn't too bad. Then my sense of smell locates the overflowing communal bin. Foxes, or possibly the feral children, have ripped open black rubbish sacks dumped outside the bin store and rotten food, dirty nappies and plastic containers are strewn all over the ground. The stench is tinged with the distinct aroma of marijuana which could be coming from any number of properties. Many have their windows open, presumably to rejoice in this olfactory heaven, so it could be anyone enjoying a little bit of me time with their Class B friend.

The Annex turns out to be a small block of flats over three floors, four flats to each floor. Either I'm lucky and it's going to be on the ground floor, or else it's up two flights of stairs for me.

Someone has kindly removed the need for me to ring the buzzer by propping the door open, and another charitable soul has used a red felt-tip to write 'A to D' on the wall inside the entrance with a very wonky arrow leading along the concrete corridor floor. It's the best bit of luck I've had so far today. Perhaps this will go smoothly too and Rena will let me know exactly what it is I've been pondering all morning.

The corridor itself is only about fifteen feet long and is well lit from the sunlight behind me. It leads to another internal fire door, this one is closed, but beyond that it's too dark to see. I take out my mobile phone and turn on the torch. As I reach the second door I can see the four flat doors, one is boarded up, a second has the pane of glass missing and the other two appear intact. Flat A is one of those that has so far escaped damage.

I put my hand up to knock, about to turn off the torch, when the phone starts to ring. DC Katie George can't seem to get enough of me.

I step back into the shadows, unsure whether the noise of the call will carry through to Rena's flat, and I don't want her to know I'm about to speak to a police officer. More to stop the noise than anything else, I answer the call and hiss, 'Yes.'

'Avril?' says Katie.

I move further back from the door. 'What? I'm about to head to a friend's.'

'Look, I'm sorry to disturb you again, especially as we're

meeting in a few hours, but there's something I think you should be aware of.'

There's a noise from the flat. Someone is walking towards the door.

'It's about Rena Hargreaves and Joan Fielding.'

'Yeah.' I've pushed myself back against the internal door and I reach behind to grab the handle. At the same time as I miss the mark, the flat door opens and Rena stares straight at me.

'We've found out that there's a connection between Rena and Joan.' I hear Katie's words in my ear as I focus on Rena's piercing eyes. 'Joan Fielding was one of the jury members on Rena's trial for perverting the course of justice.'

Rena takes a step towards me and she's holding a baseball bat.

CHAPTER EIGHTEEN

My instinct is to turn and run, but I'm frozen to the spot. If this is my body's chance to show me its primordial choice of fight or flight, it's clear I won't do either. Panic grips me and I can't speak. I'm on the phone to a police officer but I'm silent and still.

Rena puts a finger up to her lips and then beckons me inside. She gives a furtive glance towards the communal hallway and lowers the bat.

'Er, I have to go now,' I say to Katie who's asking me for the second time if I can still hear her. 'I'll ring you later.' I end the call and follow Rena inside her flat.

It's a modest space, to say the least, with a small bedroom off the hallway – the door is open so I can see a double bed squeezed in at one end, and the wardrobe is also visible from the doorway as I make my way past. There is another door that I presume leads to the bathroom. She stops in the middle of the living room/kitchen, hands on her hips. She's still holding the baseball bat but it's by her side, grazing her fuchsia denim clad thigh.

I look around the room long enough to show interest, yet not for so long that I appear nosy. Imagine a very tiny, messy, badly decorated and mostly barren version of Monica Geller's apartment on the *Friends'* set. A kitchen has been installed along one wall and a rickety table with one stool stands in front of the fridge that's cheerfully humming away to itself. A two-seater sofa that could have been found in any one of a number of rubbish tips is positioned against the opposite wall. There is no television, bookcase, coffee table, or in fact, any sign of anyone trying to make this homely.

'So this is where you live.' I try to speak without any hint of judgement to my voice. My house is hardly palatial, but at least I have scatter cushions and curtains. An old quilt cover has been nailed above the window and is currently tied back with a cord from a dressing gown. Sunlight floods into the room, despite the filth on the glass trying its best to keep it at bay.

'This is where I live,' says Rena, her frown complimenting the edge to her tone. 'What an absolute shithole. A shithole in Hell Hole.'

'Why...' I don't know how to finish the question. We're both standing facing each other, only a baseball bat's length between us. I don't want to sit down. The place smells funky and I know it's not coming from Rena. Whatever her living conditions and money issues, I smelt the floral fragrance of Prada eau de parfum as I followed her from the front door.

'Why what?' asks Rena, gently bouncing the wooden bat against her thigh. At last she realises what she's doing and reaches behind her to rest the bat against one of three kitchen cupboards. 'Why am I living in this place? It's what a cheesy estate agent would call "bijoux with potential". You know, somewhere you can really make your own.'

For the first time since I met her, she is giving off vibes of despondency, and I don't like it one little bit. In the few interactions I've had with Rena, she came across as strong and dependable. A murderer possibly, but a bloody reliable one.

'Come on,' I say. 'Sit down and I'll put the kettle on. We can talk about this.'

Rena nods and plonks herself on the stool, her back to me, her elbows on the table and her head in her hands.

I take a moment to study her straight back, her head tipped forwards as her fingers grab at her hair. There are one or two grey hairs, and it looks recently cut. Her white vest top shows off her toned arms and I can't help wonder if she had always kept herself in check or whether it was from use of the prison gym.

The kettle sounds as though it's about to boil so I switch my focus to finding cups and teabags. I open the undercounter fridge and find some milk that's a little on the turn but does at least have the good manners not to curdle as I pour it into the mugs.

'I had you down as a coffee drinker,' I say, more for something to break the silence than because I'm all that fascinated about her choice of hot beverage.

Rena lifts her head up. 'What?'

'The other day in the café in Faversham, you ordered a cappuccino.'

She gives a small bark of a laugh. 'How interesting that you remembered that.'

Then she turns on the stool, leans back against the table and stares at me. It's a look that tells me she is well and truly back and anything that just happened, any weakness I might have noticed, should be forgotten. Her dark hair has fallen forwards over her shoulders and there is a sheen to it that tells me she is definitely not skimping on the self-care. Her skin glows and there's a sparkle in her eyes. I feel like I'm the prey and she's biding her time. This is why I want to be in her company: she's a force to be reckoned with and I don't want to miss any of the action.

There is still the matter of a woman getting stabbed to death in her bed, her body found not long after Rena appeared at my door, grabbed a knife and took it upon herself to search my potentially burgled home. And now it turns out that the murder victim was in part responsible for Rena's time in prison.

Yet I'm still standing here holding out a mug of tea to her.

CHAPTER NINETEEN

I lost count of the amount of times I pleaded with Heather not to have men at the flat. *Our* flat. I could see what it was doing to her, and their mere presence petrified me. Heather wasn't looking too good on it either. Her once glowing skin was often peppered with the smallest of marks, bruises just below the surface, but bruises nonetheless. Some mornings she emerged from the bathroom a little unsteady on her feet, holding her side, or limping, or unable to stand completely upright.

Two days before I finally gave in to what I had known all along was inevitable, she made her way towards me where I sat on one of the only two kitchen chairs we owned. Her expression was a picture of defeat.

Heather pulled out the other chair and gingerly sat down opposite me.

'Things have to change,' she said.

I put down my tea, the colour of a terracotta plant pot because we were almost out of milk again. 'I'm glad you're coming to your senses.'

She gave a harsh laugh. 'No, I don't mean *I* won't be doing this anymore to keep a roof over *our* heads.' She leaned across the table; I could see her bloodshot eyes as she stared me down, willing me to disagree.

'What... what are you suggesting?' Even to my own ears, I knew that I sounded as panicked as I felt.

'You've been here, what, three weeks?' asked Heather, tapping her bitten nails on the plastic tablecloth. I nodded, not liking where this was headed. 'So, if you want to stay here, you have to pay me rent.'

'But, I–' The words catch in my throat. 'I don't have any money, I don't have a job.' She held up a hand to silence me.

'I'm offering you a job.' She held her brown and yellow mottled chin high, raised an eyebrow and waited for me to say something. The finger marks around her jawline didn't give me any right to argue. It was either find some money – and I didn't relish the idea of Heather's line of 'work' – or I had to go home.

I found myself nodding, agreeing to something that I had no intention of carrying out. By the time Heather knew that, I'd be long gone. As soon as I'd freshened up under the lukewarm spray that passed for a shower and put on some clean clothes, I was going to see my parents and find out if I could come home. That had to be better than sleeping on a lumpy mattress above a kebab shop waiting for some blubbery, clammy man to heave himself on top of me, all so I could continue to live in a flat that smelt of doner kebab.

***

The bus 'home' took me most of the way. The journey was uneventful, the weather miserable. I got off at the stop nearest to my parents' and stepped off the bus into a deluge. I hadn't thought to bring an umbrella and the collar of my raincoat only served to stop the water running down the back of my neck. It didn't stop my hair getting completely soaked in the five minutes it took to reach my parents' house. It was a route I had walked thousands of times when I had taken the bus to school, and for the briefest of stints at a Saturday job. I didn't use the time to check whether anything had changed in the few weeks I'd been gone. Instead, all I concerned myself with was getting to my destination without looking like a drowned rat.

I turned into Snelling Avenue, the street I had grown up in, where I'd learnt to ride a bike, climb a tree and have my first kiss with Connor Masters. Connor and his family used to live next door, but they were long gone. Mrs Patterson who lived the other side was still there, a remnant of a bygone era where adults called each other by their married status and surnames. Despite the miserable weather and the recent cold snap, Mrs Patterson's front garden was still full of autumnal colour.

I stopped at the front door and put my hand up to knock. A quick glance to Mrs Patterson's beautiful borders made me think that perhaps I should have bought my mum some flowers. Then I remembered that I couldn't afford rent or food, so flowers were a bit of a luxury. Not to mention one that would probably be unappreciated.

With only another couple of seconds' hesitation, I rapped the door knocker and waited.

My mum opened the door and her expression of surprise was instantly replaced by one of annoyance. 'Hello, love,' she said, her face forcing itself into a smile. 'Well, come in, you're getting soaked. You look like a drowned rat!' This remark seemed to please her. It was okay if I thought of myself as such, but I took offence to her doing it.

I wandered behind her, shedding my drenched coat as I went.

'Don't drip all over the hallway,' she called without looking back at me. 'Take it off by the mat and then straight through the kitchen to the lean-to. You know the drill.'

I clenched my teeth; I said nothing. Not yet anyway.

Once we were ensconced at the kitchen table with its six chairs and not a plastic tablecloth with cigarette burns in sight, my mum fixed her gaze on me and said, 'So, what's happened?'

'Happened?' I said, momentarily avoiding her eyes as I picked up my Wedgewood teacup. I took a tentative sip. It actually tasted like tea and not tepid pond water; a rare treat compared with the last few weeks.

'Your father and I said that we expected you to come back browbeaten and remorseful after a fortnight, three weeks if you managed to find a way to sustain yourself. That it's taken you almost a month is something neither of us had taken bets on.' She looked smug and I felt my hackles go up.

'Bets?' I spat the word at her.

There was the flutter of the eyelashes I had grown to despise, the faux abashed look, as if I was the one in the wrong and she was merely defending her right to be so sodding rude.

'We had a sweepstake. I said a fortnight and he said three weeks. I owe him a Toby Carvery.' She giggled. 'And you know that I hate carvery, but a bet's a bet.'

I gripped the tiny teacup with such ferocity, I thought it might crumble in my trembling hands. How could she? How could they?

I breathed in through my nose and out through my mouth, just the way the therapist had taught me. Fortunately it was one of those times that it worked to calm me down.

'All I wanted to do was come and pay you a visit,' I said. I willed the hurt gone from my voice. Whether I succeeded, I couldn't tell; the red mist was dispersing.

'And it's very nice to see you, dear.' My mum leaned across and placed a hand over my clenched fist. 'So tense. Are you getting enough roughage?'

Of all the things I came here to talk about, bowel

movements was not one of them. Still, at least she cared enough to worry about my digestive system.

'I'm eating just fine,' I lied. 'I wanted to come and say hello and see if you and dad are okay. Is that all right?' I concentrated on sipping my tea, as I battled to stop the scowl raging all over my forehead.

My mum sighed and pushed her chair back. She went to the corner of the room where her large black shoulder bag was neatly stored next to a regency striped Chatsworth chair. She picked up the bag and removed a large black purse, opened the clasp and pulled out two ten pound notes. 'It's all the cash I have on me,' she said, as she held the money out towards me.

'You think I came here for money?'

'Well, didn't you?' Her perfectly plucked eyebrows are raised. It struck me then how much my mother reminded me of Margaret Thatcher – not necessarily the political views, though they were probably closely shared – but the clothing, hair, the oversized accessories. It was all there.

I had tried, I really had, and now all that remained was to take the money and get out of there.

It was the penultimate time I ever saw my mother.

CHAPTER TWENTY

Rena stares at my hand as I hold the steaming mug towards her.

She hesitates and says, 'I'm having trouble wondering why you're being so nice to me. What's in it for you?'

'Perhaps I want to help you.' I see her eyes narrow and a muscle twitches in her cheek. I put one of the mugs down and move over to the pitiful sofa. 'I'm hardly riding high on the crest of a wave, as you know.'

I sit with my drink perched on my knee and wait for her to speak. I get that she's struggling with many aspects of why she's found herself in this predicament. She doesn't only have my sympathy, she has my understanding too.

'I started out with very little in life,' I say when it's evident she's going to let me take the lead on this. 'I built a reasonable existence for myself and got married. I thought that was it for me, until the bastard porked his secretary and told me it was best I moved out.'

'Yeah, you mentioned he was charm personified.' Rena picks up her mug and brings it over so she's standing in front of me. 'Sorry he was such a knobber.'

'And I'm sorry I married such a knobber. I thought I was

doing the right thing at the time, marrying a stable – boring – but nonetheless, solid and predictable man. So predictable, he had sex with his secretary. My point, though, is that like you, I've moved on and I have to work out what to do next. It's the same for you.'

Rena remains impassive as I talk. What I would like to say is that we've both been caught up in the crimes committed by other people and none of this is our doing. Except I know that will sound trite and give too much away. The importance of revealing my past at the opportune moment can't be underestimated.

For the briefest of times, I bask in the glory of being the one with the information, the one with the upper hand. I like Rena far more than I really should for someone who's been one step ahead of me and turning up when I least expected it.

I take a sip of my tea and calculate my next move.

Then I see her face sharpen. The change is barely perceptible, yet it's there. Something's changed and I don't like it one little bit.

Rena pulls a stool towards her and perches on the edge, crosses one long leg over the other. 'Except that's not really quite right, is it, Avril?' There's something about the way she says my name that sends a chill down my spine. 'Shall we stop playing games?'

I have the weirdest feeling I know what's coming next, although I've no idea *how* she could know. I hold my breath.

'You know, I wasn't always in the main CID office.' She nods as if affirming her own understanding of the facts. 'I moved around, worked in Child Protection for a bit, Tactical Operations – kicking down doors and the likes – and even had the briefest of attachments to Traffic.' She shivers at the word. 'But my favourite place in all of the policing world was

Intelligence.' She leans towards me. 'The reason being is that I got to know things. Lots of things.'

I don't like how this has taken a turn. My attempt at nonchalance is a poor one. 'You don't say,' is all I can muster before I take another sip of my rapidly cooling drink.

'You've hit the nail on the head once more, *Avril*,' she says, adding a conspiratorial wink for pantomime effect. 'I don't say. So how about you tell me what resulted in you crossing paths with Kent Police's Intelligence Unit?' She sits back with a triumphant smirk.

I won't be able to keep everything from her, especially not if I want to stick to my own agenda. As in the face of any predator, it's best if I don't show any sign of weakness. I meet her stare with one of my own.

First, I let out a dramatic sigh, shift in my seat and then I put my mug on the floor. There is no danger of it damaging the carpet any more than the last couple of decades' worth of stains and matting have already caused. Besides, it gives me a few more moments to gather myself.

'It's like this, Rena – I know that you were accused of doing something that wasn't necessarily your fault. You might have taken the footage, but you did it for good reason, to help someone out. That someone lied to you and the consequences meant the thing you helped to cover up – the pissed up woman driving her car into stationary vehicles – meant she carried on getting behind the wheel of a car while inebriated. *You* didn't buy her drinks, *you* didn't encourage her and you most certainly couldn't have known she would kill those two people. It's about time you stopped beating yourself up for circumstances that were beyond your control. Lewis is the one at fault here, as well as his drink-driving wife.'

Rena jiggles her foot up and down as I speak, otherwise she is motionless.

'My turn,' she says at last. 'Your tale of woe isn't quite so simple: you and your friend Heather Knight bit off more than you could chew.' She smiles at my reaction to my former friend's name. 'As I said, I liked working in Intelligence. Knowledge is power.'

With only those three words, I feel a shift in the dynamics. The last thing I want is Rena to have the upper hand, yet right now, I can't help but feel she has it.

All I know about her is what she's chosen to tell me or the scant details passed on by DC Katie George, and I'd guess that my police officer pal is only telling me the bare minimum. Rena continues.

'So, when things got really bad and your mate's *misdemeanours*, shall we say, and means of keeping a roof over both of your heads by selling herself for money became too much, you did the only thing you could think of. You went to the police and saved your own skin in exchange for hers. Have I got that right, Avril? Oh no, wait.' She clicks her fingers and concentrates as if she's trying to remember something. 'It was Melissa Collins back then, wasn't it?'

CHAPTER TWENTY-ONE

THEN

I made it as far as the front door, my mum with her massive handbag in her hand watching me as I went. She called after me, 'Melissa, stop being so dramatic. You do this every time.'

I paused with my hand on the door handle. 'Do what, Mum? What do I do every time?' But she continued to look at me with disapproval all over her carefully made-up face. 'How about I leave every time you're patronising and condescending? How about I continually disappoint you because I didn't want to be a bloody doctor or a lawyer or a teacher or whatever other perfect job you had lined up for me to tell your friends at the Tennis Club?' I was furious with her, and even more angry with myself for letting her get to me. This wasn't how this was supposed to go. I wanted – no, I had wanted – to come back and live here, only not now. She would have won, and I couldn't stomach that, no matter the alternative.

And that was what I told myself as I walked back to the bus stop, still wet and miserable, but at least I had twenty quid to my name now.

I repeatedly shoved my hand into my pocket where the two banknotes were, my fingers caressing their edges as I dreamed about how I would spend the money. I really should have gone back and split it with Heather, offered her a takeaway or bought some food. We had virtually nothing in the flat, yet I didn't want to. I had earned this money. Not in the traditional sense, but in doing something I really didn't want to do in order to get my hands on it. That was a job, wasn't it? The only time I had ever been employed, other than a stint at babysitting a neighbour's toddler, was an even shorter stint at Woolworth's on the record counter. How was I supposed to know that I couldn't help myself to the pick 'n' mix? The entire Saturday job was miserable from the scratchy polyester uniform to the surly supervisor who grassed me up for scoffing raspberry ruffles by the handful. The worst part about being fired was when he leaned across to snatch my name badge (it was handwritten as I wasn't there long enough for the embossed one to arrive) and he expelled sour breath all over me. His pockmarked cheeks and vein-ridden nose were inches from my face. No amount of chocolate covered cream fondant was worth that.

I should have learned from my mistakes with the pick 'n' mix, yet here I was on the bus back to a flat I hated living in, about to stoop much lower than selling top twenty vinyl singles, all to pay the rent and put food on the table.

At least it had stopped raining.

Two and a half hours after I walked out of the flat door, I walked back in. This time with a carrier bag of essentials from the corner shop and a feeling of impending doom.

Before I shut the door behind me, I heard laughter from the front room. A man's deep bark of a laugh rang out and the lighter, more false laughter of a woman. 'Is that you, Melissa?' called Heather.

I stood with my back against the front door, eyes up to the ceiling, carrier bag clutched to my chest and said, 'Yes, just going to the kitchen. Won't be long.'

I hadn't even made it along the short corridor before she was out of the living room and at my side. Heather grabbed my arm and pulled me out of earshot of her visitor.

'You remember what we spoke about?' Her voice was the same but her eyes told a different story. They had a glazed look about them and the vodka fumes were coming off her in waves. I nodded, still cradling the blue plastic bag of groceries. 'Good. You need to get yourself cleaned up and presentable and in here with us in ten minutes. Gary's expecting you.'

I blinked in rapid succession and tried not to show both my fear and revulsion. I wasn't sure which was the stronger of the two. 'Okay,' I said, aware that she was holding on to my arm with a vice-like grip I hadn't realised she possessed. 'What does Gary expect me to do?'

Heather gave a short bleat of laughter, leaned towards my ear and said, 'Use your imagination, sweetheart.'

Perhaps it was the use of the word sweetheart, but that was undoubtedly the low point for me. I was fed up with people taking advantage and manipulating me into their world, when really it should have been about me. I didn't ask for any of this. All I wanted was to carve out a life and have a safe space to call my own. Was that so much to ask?

With little more than a gesture of acquiescence, I trotted along to the bathroom and got ready for what I knew was going to be a long and unpleasant night.

CHAPTER TWENTY-TWO

I'm not completely surprised when Rena uses my real name, the one my parents gave me and I used for the first eighteen years of my life. Even so, it feels odd that someone is calling me Melissa for the first time in very many years. I continue to act as if it's not a big deal, or at least, I try to act as if it's not a big deal. Of course it is. This fascinating, yet frightening, woman has found me out. I had kept this from friends, colleagues, even my husband of fifteen years hadn't known my actual name. And now, here was Rena Hargreaves, disgraced police officer, ex-con, murder suspect, with all of my long-forgotten personal information at her fingertips.

'Well, you've certainly got me there.' I uncross and cross my legs. 'I always thought that what happened in Kent Police stayed in Kent Police. Seems not.'

Rena shrugs. 'I'd say it does as long as they don't turn on one another and make other people's lives a living hell.'

'As long as you're not bitter about it.' I sound her out with a placatory smile. There's no reaction. 'Thing I'm having a problem with is how you know all this about me and coincidentally happen to drive past a burgled house some years after this insider knowledge is shared with you, and you happen to bump into me.' I point at myself in case there's any chance she's misunderstood who I'm on about.

A dark, sly grin takes hold of her face.

'You know as well as I do that it was no coincidence.' As Rena talks, the grin is still there, giving her a manic, almost possessed look. 'I needed to find you and work out what makes you tick. Even put the wind up you a bit.' She glances down and gazes into her tea. When she looks at me again, her features have softened. 'I need your help.'

This surprises me and I toy with the idea of telling her, yet I'm still uncertain whether any form of honesty will give her further advantage over me. As I open my mouth to speak, I see a movement out of the corner of my eye. There is a loud thud, immediately followed by the noise of glass shattering, and tiny fragments explode all over the living room. My natural instinct is to duck and cover my face at the same time. I hear, rather than see, Rena jump up from her stool and crunch across the shards of glass that are now embedded in the carpet and glistening over every surface.

'You bastard!' she shouts. 'I'll find you.'

At this, I chance a look in her direction and as I peek out through my fingers, I see a flash of fury on her face as she turns and speeds towards the front door. 'Rena, wait.' I scramble to join her, cutting my hand on a shard of glass that's landed on the sofa next to me.

Rena isn't slowing down for anyone, least of all me. I gather momentum to ensure I'm not left behind as she goes through the front door, back down the hallway and to the street. She stops for a second. She scans the communal car park, the neighbouring driveways and front gardens, but there's no one at all.

Out of breath and panicked, I stop beside her. 'Do you know who it was?' I ask.

Rena nods. 'His name is John Smith.'

'You're kidding me? White bloke, fit-looking, thirty-five or so with short cropped brown hair.' Rena isn't registering the merest hint of curiosity at how I know this man.

'Yes,' is all she says.

'When I met him, he was lying on the ground with a fair amount of claret leaking out of his head and your car was making off into the distance. Care to elaborate?'

'No.'

I find myself chasing after her again as she takes off towards the street. What is it with this woman and her rapid exits?

'I think that you should explain,' I say, as I take hold of her arm. Rena shoots me a withering stare and I immediately let go of her. 'Whoa, there's no need to be so defensive. I just think that a lot's happened since the day we met, so perhaps you could give me an explanation.'

Rena chews her lip and eventually says, 'Come on then. Let's find a pub. I'll worry about the flat later.'

Again I find myself running to keep up with her as she strides off towards the cul-de-sac which is now devoid of children and their electric scooters. A few heads turn our way as we rush across the street towards the dual carriageway. Yet, again, no one really acknowledges our existence.

At last, three or four streets later, I catch up with Rena when she suddenly turns into what I think is a closed-up shop at first glance. As she pulls open the solid wooden door, I'm hit by a smell long forgotten. Remember the old pubs that reeked of stale cigarette smoke and urinals? It is a proper blast from the past.

We walk along a short corridor that is giving off Working

Men's Club vibes, but as we walk into the main bar area, the ten or so men who simultaneously gawp in our direction give off little indication they have a job between them. What I take to be stolen or prohibited goods are stuffed back into rucksacks, holdalls and pockets, and we are eyed warily.

Rena takes no notice of the drop in temperature and pushes her way to the bar where most of the missing link are congregating. She nods at a couple of them and the woman behind the bar; she is around fifty years old, with hair pulled back so tight it smooths out the crow's feet. Her mouth is a slash of red lipstick, tiny puckers along her top lip telling the world that she smokes heavily.

'Hi, Rena. Usual?' the woman says before turning her attention to me. She shoots me a mean look.

'Please, Sadie.' Sadie moves across to the chiller cabinet, pauses and waits with her hand on the door until I speak.

'Er, I'll have a bottle of, umm, Budweiser.' I don't even particularly like Budweiser but I sense I shouldn't keep her waiting. I get the impression that one wrong word and I'll be out on my ear.

Rena slaps a couple of coins down in exchange for her Peroni and my Budweiser, which seems remarkably cheap, and we take a seat as far away from everyone else as we can manage. It doesn't escape my notice that she picks the side of the table facing the throng at the bar. I don't particularly like having my back to them, but at least they can go about selling their contraband without fearing I'm watching. Not for the first time, I wonder whether everyone in here knows that Rena was a police officer. Perhaps that's why they take very little notice of her. If they know about her fall from grace, there's little chance of her being a threat.

I find myself staring at a chipboard wall, a few posters

attached to it with yellowing Sellotape. It seems that this fine drinking establishment is home to karaoke, quiz nights and the occasional band. Good luck with trying to entertain this crowd. Bottle-throwing is probably actively encouraged by the landlord.

I take a sip of my weak beer; at least it's cold. 'So, do you want to tell me what the drama is with John Smith and why he's just lobbed a brick at your window?'

Rena picks at the label on her bottle and holds it up to the light before she takes a sip. 'John was someone I was reunited with not long after I got out of prison, and thought would be a useful ally. As things transpired, he was far removed from that. If anything, he brought more trouble my way than he was supposed to keep from me. Hence, I opened the door to you today with a baseball bat and why I'm not totally surprised that he broke my window.'

'Shouldn't you have called someone to get that fixed?' I ask, remembering the reach of the tiny beads of glass all over her living room.

This was met with a shrug. 'Nah, the place is a total toilet. No one's going to break in and steal any of the crap I've got. Besides, the window wasn't completely broken, merely smashed.'

'As long as you're fine about it.' For the briefest of moments, I think about asking her if she wants to stay at my house. Then I remember that the police want to speak to her about a murder, and she's already let herself into my house – twice if I count the time she walked in when I was in the doorway, and the other when I was fast asleep. If she wants to get in, she certainly will. And, of course, she's probably very dangerous.

Neither of us say very much, so the beers don't last long. 'Want another?' I ask. When she nods, I feel I have to add, 'Fine, but you have to tell me what this is all about. You have until the end of the next drink and then, if I'm not convinced or you don't let me know what's been going on, I'm on the next bus home.'

When I come back with the two bottles of beer, Rena snatches hers, takes a long glug and says, 'I don't think you're going to like what I'm about to tell you. It really could have made a huge difference to the last twenty years of your life.'

CHAPTER TWENTY-THREE

THEN

I locked myself into our draughty bathroom, eyed up the minuscule frosted window while I 'cleaned myself up' as per Heather's instructions, and hoped that a small fire somewhere in the building would bring all of this to an end.

Twenty minutes later the banging on the door from my flatmate turned pimp jolted me back to reality. 'Will you hurry up?' she shouted through the door. 'It's time.'

I took a deep breath and opened the door. 'I don't want to do this.'

'And I don't care. You haven't got any choice, so go and get changed into something more appropriate and come and be nice to Gary.'

Heather moved towards the hallway, her tight vest top and short denim shirt showing her bare arms and legs. I grabbed at her hand in desperation. 'Isn't there another way.'

'Yes,' she said, narrowing her eyes. 'You go out and get a job and get me the rent. You do know that you owe me close to two hundred quid. You start tonight, you'll have it paid off in no time. Otherwise, you go back to your room, pack up what you have and leave. Now.'

I dropped her hand as if it were red hot instead of the lump of ice I held in my own clammy fingers. 'Okay,' I said. 'Give me five minutes to get changed.'

'You've got three before I send him to you.'

I struggled to fasten the buttons on my blouse. The quality of the material was probably wasted on Gary, but it was the only thing I had that wasn't skintight or in need of a wash. I'd not had the money to take my washing to the launderette and we certainly didn't have a washing machine. That was a luxury too far. As I shrugged my clothes off and put the cleanish ones on, I tried to tell myself that Gary needn't be as bad as I had him pegged in my head, and it wasn't as if I hadn't had sex before. Neither of the two previous sexual escapades I'd been a part of were particularly memorable, although they hadn't been that bad. The first lad was about as clueless as I was and the second was so drunk, I don't think he probably ever knew what had happened. It was a bit of a dim and distant memory for me, especially after a few pints of snakebite. This surely wouldn't be any worse.

I glanced at myself in the small mirror hanging on the wall – only my head and shoulders were reflected back at me – and I went to join the throng.

The laughter and chat were almost as loud as the stench of testosterone. I pushed open the living room door with a feeling of trepidation and saw Heather sat across the lap of a balding, bloated man of about forty. His hands each squeezed one of her buttocks and as she writhed about making moaning noises – there was no way they represented genuine pleasure – he grinned at her. In the only other seat in the room, a man of around forty plus years of age sat leering at them. He took a swig from a can of supermarket branded lager and shifted in his seat as if getting comfortable for the show. This, I presumed, was Gary.

He wasn't exactly ugly, merely unremarkable. Perhaps that meant he wouldn't give me too much of a hard time. He was getting on a bit, so that was bound to go in my favour. There was always the chance that he had done this so many times, he would make it quick. My stomach flipped over as I saw the empty cans beside the chair and I felt the glimmer of hope that I might be let off the hook this evening.

Then he focused his attention on me. Cold eyes, I remember thinking as I mustered the energy to smile at him.

'So you're the stupid slag who's kept me waiting half the night. Best you get a move on, love, and come and climb aboard.' Gary patted his thigh with the grubby mitt that wasn't gripping a can of cut-price lager. 'Your mate here is giving a floor show that's getting me off. Good for a warm up. You're the main act.'

Heather broke off from grinding the bloater's groin and with a nod of her head, hissed, 'Get on with it.' In response to her brief interlude, Bloater tightened his grip on her backside, which caused her to cry out and him to tell her to, 'Fucking concentrate.'

The last thing I wanted to do was to leave the living room. I absolutely didn't want to have sex with this arsehole, least of all with an audience, but there was safety in numbers. I would rather bump uglies with Gary in the same room as two other people than disappear from their eyesight. It wasn't much of a choice. And it was made up for me.

'I've waited long enough, love,' said Gary as he heaved himself out of the chair, one hand still holding the can. 'Where's your room?'

Before I had a chance to answer, he dragged me from the living room and along the hallway towards the rest of the flat. My door was the first we came to, not that I think that would have made any difference to him. He would have ripped my clothes off whichever room we'd have found ourselves in and forced himself inside me no matter where we were. The only thing I was grateful for was that it was mercifully quick.

Without a doubt, I hadn't wanted to do it, I felt ashamed and hatred towards the man panting and heaving beside me on the mattress. However, I certainly didn't expect what came next. And whatever wrongs I had committed in the past, I most certainly didn't deserve it either.

CHAPTER TWENTY-FOUR

I sit at the table, gripping my beer and watching Rena, wondering what it is she's going to tell me. Would it have stopped Gary – the first of many disgusting men, by the way – who had sex with me, threw me around the room, beat me and forced me to do things that I can't think about even now without having to fight the urge to cry and shake with hysteria. Or is she referring to having to learn very quickly how to safely dispose of a body? Whatever it is, I'm not completely convinced that I want to know the answer. Yet, like watching an accident, I can't seem to look away.

'Once I tell you this, I can't unsay it. You can't pretend that you didn't know.' Rena's eyes lock onto mine. She looks up at me, her forearms resting on her thighs, her fringe covering her forehead, so she has to peer out through her hair. It makes her appear younger, vulnerable. Wait, hang on. She's about to tell me something momentous and I'm starting to have feelings of pity for her. Just how good is this woman?

'Are you playing me?' I ask after a few seconds of silence.

'Absolutely not.' Rena settles back in her chair, so I know this was a deliberate move to get me to lower my guard and it hasn't worked. She's less ashamed now and more down to business. 'I want to know that you're prepared for what I'm about to say.'

I nod, slowly and deliberately.

'Okay, then,' says Rena. 'How well did you know Heather Knight before you moved in with her?'

I shrug. 'I suppose it was a couple of weeks, perhaps a month. She was always hanging around near to where I lived, but in the pubs and bars whenever I went anywhere. I'd see her outside on the pavement smoking and then I'd see her chatting to people, men mostly, and she seemed to be enjoying life. Not a care in the world.'

'And how did you meet her?' Rena takes another swig of her beer and waits for me to answer.

'Oh, I don't know. It was years and years ago.'

'Who initiated the contact?'

'Who initiated the contact?' I repeat. 'That sounds a little police-speak, doesn't it? I don't know.' I think about it, but I really can't seem to recall when or where we first got chatting. 'One minute I saw this girl around and the next, she was someone I'd see and speak to regularly.'

Rena raises a well-plucked eyebrow at me. 'And you never for one second thought that it was staged or arranged by your new best buddy Heather Knight?'

'You're saying that she deliberately targeted me?' It was decades ago but it doesn't stop a feeling creeping up my spine that turns me both hot and cold. 'Why would she do that? What could possibly have been in it for her?'

'Other than someone who was deeply unhappy with their life, prepared to stoop to her level to make ends meet rather than go back home to Mummy and Daddy's, and be her fall guy if it all went tits up? Nah, you're right, Avril, absolutely nothing.'

The use of my current, pretend name doesn't pass me by.

'There must have been a number of girls she could have got on board,' I say. 'She must have singled me out for another reason if what you're saying is correct.' Rena is holding something back, I can tell. Her face is arranged in a perfectly neutral expression; she is working hard at giving nothing away.

At last, she caves at the stare-off.

'Well, yes, she picked you because of your contacts.' She tips the rest of her bottle of beer down her throat and peers around me to get a better look at the bar. I can tell she's about to get up and get another, but I have to know what on earth she's on about.

I grab her arm as she moves to stand up. 'I'll get the beers, just tell me what you mean. What contacts? I didn't and don't have any contacts. I was an eighteen-year-old girl, who had finished her A levels and hadn't even worked at a Saturday job for more than a couple of weeks.'

'Yeah, that's right.' She brushes my hand away, stands and says, 'Woolworth's, wasn't it? Something about the Pick 'n' Mix?'

I'm far too stunned to move or respond. How could Rena have known such an obscure fact? I'm pretty certain I have never told a soul. I hadn't told my mum the reason I was sacked – she assumed I'd stormed out rather than that I was fired – I hadn't told anyone at school and Heather herself didn't know. Even the person who fired me covered up my criminal act. Apparently it was too much of an effort to call the police and get them involved, so the heinous crime of grand theft confectionary was written up as 'unsuitable for role requirements' or some other such tosh.

It doesn't register with me how long Rena is at the bar for, and I'm still reeling from shock when she comes back with the drinks. I do know that she's going to enjoy making me suffer. The smugness is running riot on her face.

What else does this woman know about me?

'I worked in Intel,' says Rena. 'And we knew a lot about you.'

'Me?' I feign surprise. 'Why on earth would Kent Police know all about a Saturday job I was sacked from? There was no reason for me to come to the police's attention at that particular time.'

'Ordinarily, you wouldn't have. Except in this instance, Heather was keeping us very well informed of all you did and everywhere you went.'

'I went to school, lived with my parents and then I moved in with Heather. That's it. That was my life until I got married, and the rest, you already know.'

'Adrian, yes, you've told me about him.' She stops to glug her beer and I try to remember whether I've told her his name, or if it's something else she learnt from a secret file on me. If she knows minute details from my adolescent years, I suppose there's no reason she shouldn't know something as basic as my ex-husband's name.

'If you stop to think about it, the information held by the police may not necessarily be accurate.' She allows that to sink in and as it does, I have a knot of tension in my stomach that's growing by the second.

'Rena, what's this all about?'

'It seems that Heather Knight was a registered police informant.'

My mouth drops open and I stare at her. This can't be true. Yet why would she lie to me?

'Heather was a couple of years older than you and had been on our books since she turned eighteen. It was before I joined Intel but I knew who she was. Her information was always spot on. Who had drugs and where, who the local handlers of nicked stuff were and where their lock-ups were. See, she was smart.

She never got greedy and was paid in small and sporadic amounts, so it never aroused suspicion. And, of course, she was making a pretty good living with the stream of revolting men she welcomed into her humble home. Well, your home too.'

I'm having trouble digesting this. 'I, I don't know what to say. Are you telling me that she didn't need to sleep with those men to make ends meet? What am I saying? That *I* didn't need to do what...'

Rena moves beside me and shuffles me down the bench. I feel her put her arm around me, but I'm too shell-shocked to react.

'Not really,' she says. 'It was never life-changing amounts of money. It would have kept her in chips and vodka, but that was about it. No, she needed other employment.'

The word employment is left hanging between us.

I find my voice and say, 'I just about made enough to cover the rent, let alone food and booze.'

'Yeah, I know.' Rena squeezes my shoulder before dropping her arm and reaching for her drink. 'We kept tabs on her income and it turned out that Heather was what you might call an entrepreneur. You see, it went a bit wrong when we sussed that the flat you were sharing with her wasn't the only place she was renting.'

'What?' I spin on the cheap plastic bench and scrutinise her profile. 'She had another flat? There were nights she didn't come home, but I never thought she had two places.'

'Three to be exact. Each of them had two young girls living there, barely out of school, left home with no or minimum contact with their families, and were earning money on their backs for Heather. She had quite the income. That's where it went a bit belly up for the police. We couldn't be seen to have an informant on our books who was not only working as a prostitute, but was whoring out other girls. We had to cut her loose and that was around the time she upped and left.'

I close my eyes and stay perfectly still. I chance that Rena doesn't know the entire reason that Heather suddenly packed her bags and disappeared. I'm going to have to be very guarded about what I tell her, and find out how much she knows.

CHAPTER TWENTY-FIVE

The rows between Heather and me were almost as violent and fuelled as the beatings I took from the many men she brought home so I could pay my rent. One or two were only there for the sex, yet even they were too much to bear. Craig was particularly troublesome. I think he was actually in love with me. He used to arrive early for his appointment, or date, as he liked to call it. He often brought me flowers and always turned up smartly dressed and smelling of aftershave. I suppose I should have at least found these occasions easier and tolerated them more. Still, I knew where I stood with a good hiding. The punchy ones liked to knock me about a bit – never the face, always the body – and most didn't stay for longer than half an hour or so. Craig's length of visit was another problem. He wanted to stay and chat, ask me all about myself and what a nice girl like me was doing living in such a place. The usual platitudes and waffle. There were times I wanted him to bugger off, still it was preferable to getting a kidney punch or being pushed face down into the mattress while a repugnant man got his kicks in. Figuratively as well as literally.

It was something else that Heather and I argued over. She thought I should encourage Craig, but I thought he was a drip who could only get a woman to have sex with him by paying them. Then she would remind me that was what all the men who frequented our little love nest did, and the arguments would start all over again.

Since my visit to see my mum, I returned to my parents' house on three occasions. Each time it was after another screaming match with Heather, and they were often on the back of a visit from an especially nasty regular of hers who had a fetish for strangulation. 'There must be better ways for us to pay the bills,' I pleaded with her for the hundredth time. 'I can't do this much longer. I'm exhausted and broken.'

Heather would narrow her eyes and reply, 'And what's stopping you from leaving? I'm not forcing you to stay.' The worst thing of all was that she was completely right. This always had me hankering after a reconciliation with my parents, where I'd travel for an hour by bus, walk to their road and stand at the top of the street, too afraid to go to the door in case they slammed it in my face. So I'd come back to the flat again and pretend that I hadn't stormed off, make Heather tea, and we'd carry on as before.

That was until Gary turned up one evening while I was on my way back from the shop. The sound of his drunken voice carried from the living room to the front door.

I jammed my key in the lock and ran towards Heather who was huddled in the corner of the room, wedged in between the sofa and the wall. Her face was a bloody pulp and her hands were shaking as she tried to shield herself from his blows.

Gary had his hairy back exposed to me and I did the only thing I could think of, I jumped on him, my arms encircling his neck. The carrier bag from the corner shop was still in the crook of my arm. The loaf of bread and jar of coffee swinging uselessly in front of his chest as it registered in his pissed-up brain that someone was clinging on to him with their shopping dangling before him.

With one huge, angry shout, he grabbed my arms and flung me across the room towards the armchair. I fell about two feet short and hit the floor, the wind completely knocked out of me. I struggled for breath as all six foot of him loomed over me.

'I'm going to fucking do you in and then your scrubber of a mate,' he spat at me. His eyes were bloodshot and the pupils like pinpricks. Gary had often boasted that he dabbled in all sorts of drugs when alcohol simply didn't do it for him like it once did. There was no reasoning with this man. I was looking at a simple case of hurt him or get hurt.

Gary took a step towards me, leaned forward and grabbed my ankle. I kicked him hard with the other foot, but all that seemed to do was anger him. It certainly wasn't going to stop him pulling me across the carpet towards him. I tried to sit up, which was a futile gesture as he swung a punch to the side of my head. I saw black. I knew that if I passed out, I wouldn't wake up again. Gary was going to kill us both.

I forced myself to look up, willing my eyes to focus on something, on anything. For a fleeting moment, I worried that the force of the blow had caused brain damage or hallucinations. Heather was on her feet, an extra-large jar of Maxwell House coffee raised aloft between her hands. She brought the glass container down with such force, I had to look away. There was a dull thud, loud but unmistakably the noise of something making hard contact with bone. Then Gary dropped to the floor beside me, catching his head on the corner of the table as he fell. I stared into his unseeing eyes. I couldn't be more relieved to see there was no sign of life.

'You've killed him,' I said. 'With the coffee jar.'

'I've saved your life,' said Heather, struggling to stay on her feet, her eyes now swollen shut. 'With the coffee jar.'

They were her last words before she passed out and fell on top of dead, violent Gary.

CHAPTER TWENTY-SIX

I stall for time, not wanting to answer Rena. She asks me twice if I'm okay and then adds, 'I said that as soon as you knew, it would change things. Sorry, I may be guilty of information overload.'

I start to speak but I'm interrupted by my phone. I fumble around in my handbag, angle the screen away from Rena so she can't see who's calling and realise that DC Katie George is calling me again. Bloody hell, I'd forgotten all about our meeting. I see from the time on the display that it's only five o'clock.

'It's the police,' I tell Rena. 'Best you don't make a sound.' She moves back over to her own seat, still watching me like a hawk. I don't know whether Rena will be able to hear what Katie's saying, but I assume that she can, so I stand up and put some distance between us.

'Hi,' I say into my phone. 'Are we still on for later?'

'Yes, hi, Avril. We are. I know it's a little early but how about I come and get you now? I could be with you in about thirty minutes.'

I look over at Rena. 'It's a bit awkward right now as I'm out.

Just been to see a friend over Canterbury way and you know what the buses are like.'

'That's ideal,' says Katie. 'I'm at Canterbury police station. I can meet you at your friend's place.'

I put a hand up to my forehead and rub at the worry lines. 'No, no, I was in Canterbury and now I'm on my way...' I can't say Hill Hole and don't know what else to say that won't have her racing to a made-up destination 'Listen, let me finish my drink and I'll get on the first bus that's Faversham bound.'

'Right.' Katie says the word slowly and deliberately.

'Is there a problem?'

'When you say drink, do you mean alcoholic?'

'Yes, I've had a couple, but I'm almost finished. I promise I won't hold things up any further.'

I hear Katie suck her breath in at the other end of the line before she says, 'It's really not a good idea to take a statement from you if you've been drinking, especially as we were due to record it. I'd be in all sorts of trouble and it's not fair on you.'

'I can hold my drink.' I don't know why I'm trying to insist I'm okay. I don't want to do the bloody statement anyway. 'Although, now I think about it, I haven't eaten and I've had three.'

There's a sigh and she says, 'How about first thing in the morning? I'll pick you up at 8.30 am.'

I know that I can't wiggle out of this one, so I agree. Then I break the news to Rena that I've got to go. I avoid her questions about what the police want to speak to me about as she would know that the police don't take statements from witnesses who have been slinging beer down their neck. 'Katie wants to come over and ask me about something, and I could hardly tell her where I was and who I was enjoying a libation with, could I? Besides, I've got a lot to think about.'

I grab my handbag from the bench, throw my phone inside

and think it's probably a good idea if I use the ladies' before I leave. I scan the room and spot the sign above the door. 'I'll see you soon, no doubt.'

Rena nods at me, her attention already focused on getting another beer, and she walks away. I watch her lean against the counter and strike up a conversation with Sadie before I nip off to the loo.

When I come back out a few minutes later, she's chatting away, seemingly, not a care in the world. I may as well not exist. An hour or so ago, I turned up at her door which she opened with a baseball bat in her hand, chased her down the road as she ran after someone who had thrown a brick at her window and then I absorbed every tiny detail of information she threw at me. Now, she has her back to me, as if she's forgotten I was ever there.

Still, I crave her attention and approval, and it's not merely because she knows so damned much about me.

CHAPTER TWENTY-SEVEN

THEN

I stared at Gary's face with morbid fascination. He was still remarkably ugly, although he was now remarkably dead with it. I wasn't sorry he wouldn't live to see another day or punch another woman in the stomach. My only regret was that he was dead on our living room floor.

'Oh my God, oh my God.' Heather was displaying the telltale signs of a breakdown. That was the last thing we needed. I certainly couldn't hide a body on my own. It was going to be difficult enough to do it as it was.

'Listen,' I said, as I got to my feet. I guided her away from Gary's body and to the other side of the room. When I was satisfied that her back was to him and I had her attention, I said, 'We need to get rid of his body and we need to do it soon.'

'How do we—'

'Leave that to me. All you have to do is keep an eye out when I tell you. I've got to nip out—'

'No! You can't leave me here, not with him over there.' Heather made to turn round, so I forced her out of the room.

'We don't have time for this, you know that. I need to go and get help and there's only one person I can think of who'll help us. You have to stay out of the room and wait for me. Don't move anything and don't let anyone else in except for me. Understand?'

I gripped her shoulders. My fingers digging into her flesh must have focused her as her head snapped up and said, 'Yes, I'll see if we have any bleach or whatever.'

I wasn't entirely convinced she was on board, but I didn't have the time to find out. I grabbed my keys, a jacket and patted my pockets for the couple of coins I had from the shopping and hoped it would be enough to cover the call.

Within five minutes I made it down the urine-soaked communal stairs, across the road to the phone box and was racing back to the flat when I saw one of Heather's regulars leave the kebab shop beneath our flat. He threw his kebab paper in the bin and glanced up at our window. The lurid grin was clear from where I stood waiting to cross the road. There was no way I could let him in the flat, and given the state of Heather when I left, I couldn't be sure she would stop him getting inside.

I ran across the road and stopped in front of him. 'Sorry, but she's not in.' I could smell doner kebab meat, chilli sauce and onion from three feet away.

He belched and said, 'You'll do then, love.'

I had had enough of nauseating men for one evening, particularly those reeking of rancid meat with the manners of a pig. 'No, sorry, I've got someone coming round to see me and he'll be here any minute.'

'Then I'm sure he won't mind joining the queue.' Death Breath took a step towards me and I instinctively moved back. I was about to tell him to sod off when a car pulled up and someone shouted, 'Melissa, get in.'

I recognised Craig's voice and grabbed the door handle. 'Sorry, er, thingy, but I'm spoken for.'

I hadn't managed to close the door before Craig pulled away

and drove to the small car park at the back of the parade of shops. I opened the door to get out but he leaned across and pulled me back towards the seat. His face took on a peculiar appearance in the faint glow of the amber streetlight. A shadow across his nose and cheek made him look eerie, menacing even. All the vile things I'd let him do to me, and here I was fully clothed, feeling especially vulnerable. Perhaps it was the corpse on the floor in my flat.

'I said I'll help you. Only, you have to keep your promise to me.' The weight of his stare made me shudder.

'Yeah, of course. I said I'd do what you ask. Now, please help us.'

I couldn't stay in the car and agree all over again to the sordid details of what I'd agreed to on the phone. I didn't have time for this. If the breath monster still went back up to the flat, all of this would have been for nothing. I might as well have called the police myself. Not that the thought of legging it and leaving Heather to clear up her own mess didn't appeal. I could have walked back out of the flat and both the problem of Heather pimping me out and Gary stuffing every orifice I have with animal, mineral and vegetable would all be things of the past.

I reached the flat door, breathless, sweaty and wondering exactly why I was saving her skinny arse before I realised that Craig wasn't behind me. I couldn't wait in the open-sided walkway in case one of the neighbours who had previously ignored us decided it was time to get to know the real Melissa and Heather and popped out for a chat.

I unlocked the door and was about to close it behind me when Craig made it to the top of the stairs with a large wooden trunk. 'You might have helped me,' he said, an edge to his voice I hadn't heard before.

I covered the distance between us and grabbed one of the

handles and together we dragged it into the flat. The trunk barely fitted through the door and it was heavy.

Once we were inside, heaving and recovering, Heather opened the bathroom door. Her wild eyes fixed on the trunk. 'Are we, are we putting him in there?'

'That's the idea,' said Craig. He opened the trunk to reveal a medium-sized suitcase, a small suitcase and a holdall. He unzipped the holdall, pulled out a box of latex gloves, black electrical tape and a roll of black plastic bags.

'Fucking hell, Craig,' I said. 'Have you done this before?'

He gave me a withering glare. I suddenly felt nervous.

'I hope you don't expect us to cut him into pieces,' said Heather. Her hand flew up to her mouth and she heaved.

'Toilet, now,' I shouted. 'I don't want to clear up vomit as well as everything else.' I shared her sentiments. I hadn't signed up for dismembering a body.

Meanwhile, Craig busied himself lining up his macabre kit in the hallway and I couldn't resist having a peek in at Gary. I saw his body sprawled on the carpet and thought I saw him twitch. My imagination was going into overdrive. I shook my head and as I stepped back into the hallway, I saw a shadow at the front door.

A loud knocking was followed by shouts of 'Heather' from the breath monster. This was the last thing we needed.

I bent down and said in Craig's ear. 'He's not going to go away until I let him in. I'll get Heather to take the punter outside straight into the bedroom while you and I deal with him.' I thumbed in the direction of the living room so he knew exactly who I was referring to. Not that there should have been much doubt. It was, after all, our first cadaver.

'Wait a minute, I'm coming,' I called as Craig and I dragged the trunk and paraphernalia out of the way. 'I've got someone here with me.'

Craig raised an eyebrow at me. 'What?' I mouthed at him.

I had to give him credit – I had called him out of the blue to help me get rid of a body and not only had he raced straight over here, he had some sort of plan and appeared to give little concern to the dead man.

Aware that the imbecile was still banging on the front door and I had to persuade Heather to come out and distract him, I had no choice but to leave Craig and take care of the other crisis before the neighbours called the police.

Without knocking or caring, I barged into the bathroom. She was crouched in the corner, her hands over her head. Every annoyance of the last two months surged through my veins to the point that even the loud knocking noise was blocked out. I wrenched her hands away and pulled her up by her hair. 'Fucking get your shit together, you silly twat,' I said. 'You pulled me into this nightmare and now you're going to do something to get us out of it.' She shook at my words and I wasn't entirely sure it was all getting through to her brain, yet I couldn't seem to care. 'That nasty bastard you keep giving blow jobs to for clearing your tab in the kebab shop is here. I'm going to let him in and bring him in here. You'll keep him busy while me and Craig take care of Gary. Got it?'

Tears rolled down her bloody cheeks and she nodded.

'Got it?' I repeated.

'Yes, I'll do it.'

I jammed her up against the mildew wall. 'It's not a request. Keep him busy until I say so.'

'Of course.' She bit her lip and screwed her eyes up. It didn't stop the tears, and it didn't stop me from hating her with every part of me.

CHAPTER TWENTY-EIGHT

I really need to put some distance between myself and Rena, despite what I realise is turning into an obsession with her. I trudge back through the same streets we walked along an hour or so ago, ensuring I don't lose my way. It's not the most salubrious of areas, although there are few people around. On the bright side, my chances of getting mugged are more limited than they were in the direct vicinity of Rena's flat. Perhaps I should nip back and make sure that the local kids haven't popped her window while we were supping on our beer. I hesitate, not sure whether to let her worry about it and get myself home, or if I should do the decent thing.

I am so busy concerning myself with someone else's meagre belongings that I find myself in a street I don't recognise. A slight panic overtakes me until I glance back and see the road I should have taken. I tut at myself and make a one-hundred-and-eighty turn and make sure I am on the right path.

The second I step into the street, I freeze. A man is walking towards me and if I'm not very much mistaken, it's none other than John Smith. Luck is on my side and he doesn't look up from his mobile phone as he bangs away on the screen.

Whatever it is he's typing, it's making him furious. I glance around and look for somewhere to hide. It's not that I'm scared of him – I can still see the bandage stuck to the top of his head, so as long as I manage to swing my handbag high enough, I'm pretty certain I could dislodge the scab on his scalp. I just don't want him to know I've spotted him, so I dive behind two large industrial size rubbish bins. If he is the observant type, there is a chance he'll glance backwards as he passes me, but I duck down so that my head is lower than the black lid and hope for the best.

My heart sinks as I hear the sound of his footsteps change as he steps from the pavement onto the road. I take a punt about which side of the bin I should edge along. Quite frankly, it's starting to smell so I hope he doesn't stop and make a call.

John starts to say something into his phone and, for a moment, I think he's actually talking to someone, and then I realise that he's leaving a voice note.

'Listen to me, I'm done now, okay? I've had enough being at your beck and call. We're quits now, Rena. So leave me alone.'

I creep out from behind the Biffa bin and stare after him as he stomps away.

What reason could Rena possibly have for getting him to throw a brick at her window and more importantly, why would he be so indebted to her that he wouldn't tell the police who stabbed him in the head?

CHAPTER TWENTY-NINE

THEN

For once, Heather probably got the better deal. It took much effort on my part to persuade Craig that we shouldn't dismember Gary there and then in the living room.

'It'll make moving him easier,' said Craig, sizing him up as he circuited the body, his chin between his thumb and forefinger as if deciding where to place his furniture, rather than dispose of a corpse.

'No,' I said, feeling the beginning of a headache. 'We need to get him in the trunk for starters. The state of Heather, if her friend in there doesn't get what he wants, there's a good chance he'll walk in on us. Besides, we don't own one good blade between us.'

Craig started to say something and rather than give him the opportunity to tell me all about his collection of knives and other pointy paraphernalia, I bent down and picked up the box of latex gloves. 'Here,' I said as I pulled out a pair and handed them to him. 'Let's at least get Gary in the box.'

For some reason, this made Craig laugh. I was getting increasingly concerned about him. I had always found his fixation with me worrying, but I had never had him down as a psycho. When this was over, I had to sever all ties with these people, Craig as much as Heather. It shouldn't be difficult. I planned on getting far away. I already had the hatchings of a plan. It's only that most of them wouldn't be alive to see it through to the bloody and brutal end.

'Are you all right there, Craig?' I asked. His eyes danced at me. He really was getting off on this. Kill him or ditch him? I couldn't decide. At least not until Gary was decomposing far from my hovel of a home.

'Absolutely, Mel.' I had never told him it was acceptable to call me Mel, but to be fair, I had never told any of the losers who had crossed the threadbare threshold it was permissible to do any of the things they did to me. It dawned on me, not for the first time, that men were disgusting creatures. I had read about an animal species that were capable of reproducing despite only being in the presence of females. Surely that could make the evolutionary jump to humans? Unless I needed some heavy furniture lifting (and to make it clear, I'd simply buy lighter stuff), I could get by. Then I remembered that I had sixteen pence to my name and no way of keeping a roof over my head.

In the meantime, I had a man – an actual living, breathing one – to help me shift the dead one.

For now I was grateful for the upper body strength. There would undoubtedly come a time when I feared Craig, but for now, I had to get what I could from him.

'You're staring at me,' said Craig.

'Am I? Sorry, I was just wishing both of us out of this.' I watched his face break into a sickly smile. Was he actually that into me or merely another great big, colossal pervert? In only three months, I had become the world's biggest cynic and hater of most of the human race. I suppose that went with the job.

Craig stepped over Gary and stood in front of me. He put his hand up and caressed my arm. It was an act so tender, it made my flesh crawl. 'What are you doing here, Melissa? You're in amongst all of this hate and turmoil and I can see that you deserve better. When this is all over,' he broke off to wave his fingers at Gary's body, 'perhaps you and me could give things a go. Properly.' That was the point the gentle stroking of my arm became a grip. Despite the icy hand around my heart, I smiled at him, not wanting to show I was scared. I needed to keep my cool.

'I certainly need you,' I said. A dumb grin replaced his earlier smile, giving me valuable thinking time.

'I knew you'd come around.'

Not only were his words sobering, but his finger marks on my bicep were going to remain imprinted for some time to come.

'It's important that we get the situation under control before we plan for our future.' I hadn't worried about throwing up at the thought of Gary morphing into my carpet if we didn't get rid of him. The crap I was coming up with, however, that truly was nauseating. If this man thought I'd let him anywhere near me once we had taken care of business, he was more stupid than I ever gave him credit for. Still, at the very least, I could exploit that lack of brain activity.

I even went as far as fluttering my eyelashes at him. Like the fool he was, he fell for it.

'Whatever you say.' Then he actually leaned forward and kissed me on the forehead. That hit me harder than his fingers digging into my arms.

Once I had taken care of Gary, Craig was next on the list.

CHAPTER THIRTY

I make it back to my Faversham home without any further trouble. It's a lovely part of the day with the sun hours from setting and a cooling breeze to the early evening. It would have been a good time to go to the police station and make a statement, but sometimes life has other plans.

I get inside and shut the door, wondering what the rest of the night will bring, only to be disturbed by the sound of someone knocking as soon as I get as far as the kitchen. I turn and hurry back to the door, expecting to see my young detective friend Katie. Perhaps she changed her mind and is desperate to speak to me after all.

I fling the door open and find Fiona, my next-door neighbour. She is holding a huge bouquet of flowers and has a sombre look on her face that has the perfect blend of *sorry not sorry* about it.

'What's—' I try to say.

Somehow, she frees a hand from the flowers and holds out her palm towards me. 'No, please don't. Whatever it is you're about to say, there are no words. I had no idea.' That's strange as neither do I. She thrusts the monstrous floral arrangement at me and adds, 'You know where we are if you want to talk.'

I resist the urge to shout 'Why don't you fuck off' at this annoying middle-class bore after she brushes away a tear with the hand that isn't presenting me with flowers that I now realise are a funeral sheaf. The arrangement is some eighty centimetres long and forty centimetres wide, all beautifully tied with a frayed straw bow. No doubt this little lot cost somewhere in the region of eighty quid including delivery, whereas the same amount of flowers in a hand-tied bunch would have been less than half the price. What is it with people preying on other's misery? There really is no mercy in this sodding cruel and vile world.

I smile, try to look bereft as I accept the offering and then disappear back into the house. I carry the flowers as if they are volatile explosives and baulk at the thought of who could be sending me these timely reminders.

I place them on the kitchen table and peer at the individual blooms. They are exquisite, yet the mere sight of them chills my blood. It's difficult to understand who would know it's the exact date I took a life and left a man bleeding out on the bare, scorched earth.

I steel myself and open the card. The envelope is adorned with the sombre print of a dove as it majestically swoops across the paper. The rest of the space is taken up with the name I'm currently going by and my address. I dismiss the idea of wearing gloves – as if I'm going to the police with this – and I pull out the card. In handwriting I don't recognise, I see the words *Melissa, you didn't think this had gone away, did you?* ☺ *Happiest of anniversaries.*

My shaking hands can hardly force the card back inside. It's via Interflora so I know my chances of getting anything out of them are remote. Not that I need too long to consider the list of suspects. Top of the list is Heather herself. All I need is to book a visit to her via the handy Gov.UK website, hope that she will accept my request that I drop in to see her, plus enough gumption to actually go through with it.

The thought makes me feel nauseous, yet I know I won't get any answers otherwise. I pick my phone up and start the online application, something that is remarkably easy considering I'm about to enter one of His Majesty's supposedly most secure women's prisons, Holloway.

It comes as quite the shock when, sometime later, I discover that not only did Holloway shut in 2016, but Heather was transferred to East Sutton Park Prison and it's based in Maidstone, about sixteen or seventeen miles from where I am sitting. And it's an open prison with day release for work placements.

I'm so utterly screwed.

CHAPTER THIRTY-ONE

THEN

Craig worried me, Heather worried me, Gary's lump of a dead body worried me. I needed to get through this and out the other side, and then I would start afresh. For now, I helped Craig push, pull and heave the body inside the trunk. We had decided that the easiest way would be to put black bags around his hands, feet and head, tape them up and then try to fold him over. It was something that would have been bad enough without Craig constantly telling me, 'You're doing such a great job, darling,' and 'We're a proper couple of Bonnie and Clydes, sweetheart,' and the one that made me heave, 'We're in this together, babe.'

After some crunching and squeezing, Gary was inside the trunk. Both Craig and I were sweating like total bastards. I had heard him pant before, but this was off the chart. 'I think we need a drink,' I said. 'Only, we don't have any.'

Craig reached into his trouser pocket and pulled out his wallet. With a theatrical flourish, he pulled out a twenty pound note and held it out. I went to take it but he snatched it back. He narrowed his eyes and said, 'I don't usually have to provide the refreshments and pay you for your time.'

'Whatever you want. I'm in your debt for helping us out like this.'

'As long as you know that.' He held the note back out and said, 'Beer, get beer, plus a bottle of wine for you. A sophisticated woman shouldn't drink lager. I don't like to see that.'

I snatched the money and left the room. I wouldn't let him see me cry. It was bad enough having to have sex with these vile creatures – especially when I thought Craig was less of an arsehole than most of them – but being humiliated and forced to feel something akin to gratitude, that was too much.

A woman's cry from Heather's bedroom snapped my attention back to the mess I was in. It sounded as though she was pleading with Death Breath. I took a step towards her room. Then I glanced over at my own bedroom door. I probably had time to run in and grab whatever meagre possessions were worth taking with me, then head off into the night. Never to be seen again. Except, Heather knew where my parents lived and she was bound to share that information with Craig and subsequently the police. If I wasn't here to defend myself and tell them that it was her who'd whacked Gary on the head, who knew what lies she would tell. Craig wouldn't take too kindly to being mugged up like this either.

Unpleasant, albeit not violent, noises were coming from Heather's room. I wasn't up for helping her out again, even if things had taken a turn for the worst. She was most definitely on her own this time. I verged on taking flight for a second too long. The living room door opened and Craig said, 'Why are you still here? I fancy a beer.'

'I, er, was about to grab my jacket.' The thin material of my top felt thinner than air on my torso. I gave an involuntary shiver.

'Wait.' Craig ducked his head back inside and emerged with

his black leather bomber jacket. 'Put this on.' He watched me push my arms inside and leaned forward, grabbing it by the collar. He pulled me to him and kissed me on the mouth.

I froze, completely dumbfounded as to what was going on. Heather had lured me into one dangerous situation, and now here I was in deeper water with someone I could only think of as totally unhinged.

'Now, don't you worry about a thing. I'll be waiting for you when you get back and we can take care of business.' If his words weren't bad enough, the salacious wink was enough to have me hurrying for the exit.

I didn't exactly rush to get to the nearest off-licence and back, yet I made good time all the same. If it wasn't bad enough that I thought Heather would stitch me up as soon as she had the chance, I had no doubt that Craig would too. He was in as deep as I was – more so as I didn't have a burial grab bag – but he was a loose cannon if ever I'd seen one.

I burst back through the door with four cans of 4.8 per cent strength lager and a bottle of room temperature Lambrini. It was about the only one the shop had that didn't require a corkscrew, something that we didn't possess.

I paused at the living room door; two men's voices drifted towards me. This wasn't good at all. I pushed open the door and was greeted with Craig perched atop the lid of the trunk and the other monster on the sofa.

'Where's Heather?' It took me a split second to work out that she wasn't in the room.

'Calm down, love. She's making herself decent.'

This seemed to send Death Breath and Craig into a frenzy of thigh slapping and hoots of laughter.

'I know, Damien. Decent. As if!' said Craig. Never had I hated anyone as much as him at that moment in time. 'Don't just stand there gawping, Melissa. Get us our drinks.'

The second Gary's body was out of here and in the ground, I planned on putting as much distance between myself and this sorry set-up as I could manage.

CHAPTER THIRTY-TWO

I don't know where to turn. I can't ask for Katie's help because she is, at the end of the day, a police officer. I'll have to tell her everything, including my visit to Rena's and how John Smith was leaving her a message on the phone. Clearly I can't trust Rena either and the only other person who might be able to shed some light on things, is Heather. If Heather is incarcerated at His Majesty's pleasure on a part-time *how about a trip to the museum or a course at the local college in basket-weaving* type of way, then it's most likely her behind this. Ordinarily, I would rule her straight out. As my options are increasingly limited, I start my online application to visit her at East Sutton Park Prison.

Within seconds, I have trouble believing that I'm being so stupid. If it's an open prison and she is free to come and go, I set about tracking her down through other means. It takes me some time to find local businesses near the prison that offer work placements, but where do I start? I'd much prefer the element of surprise, even if any of the companies I find actually confirm that a forty-nine-year-old woman who goes by the name Heather Knight works for them.

I sit back on the sofa, phone in my hand, unsure how I'm ever going to find her before she does me some serious harm. I keep reminding myself that what happened wasn't all my fault – in fact, it was very much Heather's doing. It was her who introduced Gary to me, made me have sex with him to pay the rent, and it was Heather who smashed the back of his head in.

I try to block out the rest of the story – it's too unpalatable. There was more to Heather than I knew at the time, and since Rena's revelation that she was some sort of police grass who, for all intents and purposes, groomed me, there is no doubt more to her now. I need to prepare myself for meeting her and plan exactly what I'm going to get out of this.

I push myself up from the sofa and wander into the kitchen. I know I'm out of wine, but I'll see what else I can find to drink. Worst comes to worst, I'll put the kettle on.

I just need to keep my mind busy.

CHAPTER THIRTY-THREE

The last thing Rena can afford is a new car. However, the importance of moving about with ease hasn't passed her by. She grips the keys to her Renault Capture in her fist and pictures Avril traipsing to the bus stop and waiting an undetermined number of minutes for her three pound ride into town. Avril might have resigned herself to public transport, but it won't do for her. It's too unreliable for a start.

It's hardly her dream car – it's probably *no one's* dream car – but as long as she isn't expected to be the getaway driver, it'll have to do for now.

On the plus side, she has enviable bartering skills and its purchase didn't completely wipe out the money she'd managed to put away. Her negotiations mean that she burnt another source and used another favour. She has somewhere to sleep, money for food and a full tank of petrol, what more could a dismissed police detective and ex-con ask for from life?

Well, revenge for a start.

Rena opens the driver's door, takes off her beige, cotton utility jacket and throws it on the passenger seat. Then she slides in and drives out of the used car dealers, a smile on her lips. It shouldn't take long at all to get where she needs to be and to set the next part of the plan into action.

At the next left junction, Rena pauses to give way and glances down at her jacket pocket. A spool of red ribbon poking out of the top turns her smile into a grin. It's taken a long time to get all the pieces in place, but one thing she absolutely has had at her disposal was time. There was very little else to do in prison, apart from go to the gym, read and plot. Being the achiever she is, she frequently combined her activities.

Next on her list is John Smith. She shakes her head at the audacity of the man. They are quits when she tells him so.

Thirty minutes and a Kent'ish twelve miles later, Rena pulls to a stop outside a large, detached house in Ospringe, a small village not far from Faversham itself. She runs an eye over the façade. An impressive four-bedroom home, complete with a well-maintained garden fence running along the neat lawns mirrored either side of the footpath.

She can't see John's Peugeot; he's unlikely to be anywhere else. Like her, his options are limited. From previous visits, she knows he parks it at the back of the property, next to his dad's Lexus. With her focus on the front of the house, Rena calls his mobile number. There's movement in the living room window. 'Gotcha,' she says to herself as she waits for John to answer.

'Rena, this is it. We're done——'

'No, we are not, John. I suggest that you come out here now and get in the car with me. If not, well, I'll guess that at least one of your parents are home and probably won't like me knocking on the door and telling them what their son's been up to. Just an assumption.'

There's a sigh and then he says, 'Give me five minutes and I'll be out.'

'You've got two or I'll come to you.'

In less than ninety seconds, John opens the door to the Renault Capture and gets in.

'Is this your car?' he asks.

'Don't fucking start. You've already annoyed me.'

With that, she pulls away and drives towards Avril's house.

CHAPTER THIRTY-FOUR

I did as I was told and fetched the drinks for the men. Apparently, it was acceptable for me to drink Lambrini. *Well, that's just swell, Craig, thank you so much,* I thought as I poured myself and Heather a glass of something that tasted like a street dog with a urine infection had passed. I handed Heather her UTI specimen and watched her expression – not the one when she dared to take a sip, as that was similar to my own gurning – but as she tried to hold the glass to her swollen lips.

I moved away and sat back down on the floor. Craig clocked me looking at the trunk and smiled at me. He had one foot resting on his other knee as he sat on Gary's makeshift coffin. He was loving every single minute as he held court, Damien guffawing at his pathetic jokes. Christ, this fool thought he was in charge and that my surreptitious glances at the trunk were because I was frightened. I was lamenting that the size of the box meant I couldn't squeeze Craig and Damien in there too. Even if it had the capacity to hold a trio of spunk-filled wasters, that would have thrown up the next problem of how Heather and I would get it down the stairs.

At that moment, Heather didn't look capable of getting

herself down the stairs, so quite how Craig and I would fare on our own was concerning. The way the bonding exercise was going between the misogynists, I was gripped by a new fear that Craig might try to enlist Damien's assistance. With every fibre, I regretted calling him. Everything about this caused a cold sweat to trickle down my spine.

Once the beer was gone, Damien decided his time was up and he had better places to be. He stood up, belched and stuck his hand in his jeans pocket. He pulled out a wedge of ten pound notes and with one eye closed, presumably to focus, he peeled off four notes and leant towards Heather. She barely had time to look up – and would have struggled moving her bruised neck at any speed – when Craig was on his feet.

'Leave that with me, mate,' said Craig, as he reached towards the cash. 'You know what these girls are like. They never eat properly without someone making sure they don't splurge it on Lambrini and Rothmans.'

What new hell was this? I opened my mouth to object, yet something made me realise this wasn't the time. If we didn't break ourselves out of this, Heather and I would be beholden to this man forever. No matter how long it took, Craig was going to get what was coming to him. I could play the long game.

In the meantime, I decided to make nice and let him think it was going his way. I opened the door for Damien and avoided eye contact with anyone in the room. One thing at a time.

I walked back into the living room and saw Craig with his hand under Heather's chin, gently turning her face left and right. 'That's not too bad, Hev. I've seen worse.'

Hev? Who was this man? And why on earth had I let him infiltrate our lives? Oh, yeah. I stared at the corner of the room.

'It's all right, doll. I'll get it taken care of.' Craig's attention was now on me. Not a situation I wanted to be in, but nothing in several weeks had gone right, so I shouldn't be surprised.

Without another word, he left the room. I kneeled in front of Heather. 'We have to get away from here,' I whispered, frantically listening out for any signs that Craig was about to come back. Her eyes searched mine for reassurance that I had some sort of a plan, an exit strategy that would make all of this a terrible memory and not the living nightmare that it was. She opened her mouth, couldn't quite form the words, and then the tears came.

'We go to the police,' I said, my voice barely audible above my own hammering heart. 'We tell them he was going to kill me so you had to do it. It was him or me.'

'I, I... What about Craig?' For the first time, she seemed to wake up and sense there might be a way out of this.

'We'll take care of that when we need to.'

'But didn't you call him?'

I didn't get to answer her before Craig put in a reappearance. In one hand he had Heather's denim jacket and in the other, a navy blue scarf from my bedroom. He held it inches from my face and said, 'Remember this?' I closed my eyes and shuddered. I recalled the details of one particularly hideous night when I let him tie me up very clearly. It was the first and last time. I'd been meaning to throw it away. Now I watched him drape it around Heather's throat. 'There, no one will see a thing. Help her into her jacket, Melissa, and I'll drop you off.'

'Drop us where?' I said as I got to my feet before doing as I was told to get Heather's arms in her tatty jacket.

'I know a pub not far from here,' said Craig, sizing up the trunk. 'Give me the keys to the flat, I'll make sure you're out of the way and then come back and take care of our little problem.'

'Who are you going to get to help you?' I said, feeling my legs turn to jelly. Sooner or later I knew that shock would kick in; I suppose the time had come.

'Not for you to worry about, sweet cheeks.' He held out his hand. 'Keys?'

Once he dropped us at the pub, I would call the police. This had gone far enough. I expected to get arrested, spend some time at the police station. I knew I stood a fair chance of going to prison, but at this rate, it would be better than Craig calling the shots.

I fished in my pocket for the single key and dropped it into his palm.

'Come on,' he said and led us from the flat to his car. Meekly, we followed like lambs to the slaughter.

CHAPTER THIRTY-FIVE

It doesn't take long for me to find the bottle of vodka in the fridge. I originally went on the hunt for milk, but this is an absolute treat. I know that I hadn't put it there, so if I dabbled at the bookies, I would put my money on Rena letting herself into my house at some point and leaving it there. I have no idea when she would have done it, but it is abundantly clear to me that she may well have dropped by from time to time whenever she fancied and I would have no way of knowing.

'The sun is over the yard arm,' I mutter as I pour myself a glass of neat vodka. 'Cheers,' I add, for absolutely no reason and down it in one. It burns. I find myself scanning the garden for weasels, then red ribbons. The vodka on top of the beers means I am dangerously close to being drunk, and with that went all caution to the wind. I open the back door and sit on the step.

I probably should check that no one is waiting in the undergrowth for me, or lurking in the shed, but I'm tired. I've been worn out for years. It started when I left home, moved in with Heather and my life went awry. I've been deceiving myself that running from my past was how it had to be. It really has to stop. It's time I met this head on and dealt with the fallout.

Banging on the front door jars me back to my predicament. With a heavy heart, I get to my feet and wander through the house to let whoever it is inside. Friend or foe, I'm past caring.

I fling the door open. Rena stands shoulder to shoulder with John Smith. He glances down at his feet, she smiles with the reassurance of the criminally insane and I doubt my ability to accept my fate without question. If it comes to it, I'll fight these bastards to the death.

'Avril,' says Rena, her voice as smooth as John's domed head. 'We owe you an explanation. Can we come in?' She's already got a size seven knee-high black boot over the threshold.

I pull a face, turn and walk back to the kitchen. I can hear them behind me, and a click as the front door shuts.

Once we get to the kitchen, I hold the dwindling vodka bottle by its neck and ask, 'I suppose that you put this in my fridge? Exactly when and where do you keep getting this booze from, especially the one in the middle of the night?'

Rena goes to the cupboard and gets out another two glasses, pours one for John, which he wordlessly takes, and grips the other to her chest. I top up my own and then I wait for the revelation I am sure will come.

'Yes, I put the bottle in your fridge.' Rena takes a tentative sip. 'I thought about putting it in the freezer instead, but with your track record of poor eating, I wasn't sure you'd ever look in there.' Something about her tone has me on full alert.

'I eat just fine.' I don't know why I need to defend myself from her criticism. A memory is pushing itself to the forefront of my mind. The last person who chose to pass judgement on my nutritional intake was Craig. I clutch the corner of the draining board.

'It doesn't take any form of detective training to see the takeaway wrappers and microwave dinner boxes stacking up for me to work out that scurvy is probably only a moon cycle or two away.' Rena smirks at me. John stares at his glass but still says nothing.

'What do you and *John Smith* want? Give me answers or I want you both out of my house.' The vodka has worked its magic in my bloodstream.

'My name really is John Smith,' says John Smith. He looks at Rena for encouragement as a child looks at a parent. She nods and he continues. 'When you saw me on the pavement the other day, Rena and I had had a disagreement, and I'd told her to drop me off and I'd walk back into town. I decided to take a shortcut through some fields, got ensnared on some brambles and used a penknife to get myself out.' He finishes his vodka and gives the smallest of gasps as it hits his stomach.

After a woefully long time, I fill the silence by asking, 'Then you *fell* on your own penknife, which happened to get embedded in your head, you pulled it out and made your way back to the pavement where I found you?'

'That's pretty much the sum total,' says John. He puts the glass on the kitchen table and wipes his hands on the legs of his jeans. They are a faded black and he has his taupe polo shirt tucked in at the waistband. He is truly uninspiring. If I had to use one word to describe him, it would be wet.

'I then drove back to find him,' said Rena, reaching for the vodka, 'saw you were helping him and left you to it.'

'Why did you pretend that you didn't know each other and why did John lob a brick at your window?' These two are telling lies like there is no tomorrow, only I can't figure out why.

Rena shoots John a sideways glance, widens her eyes at me and says, 'Without giving too much away, you had enough to contend with, what with your house being broken into and then your neighbour getting murdered. I thought that you could do without more subterfuge. Look, we're coming clean now. John was angry with me for leaving him and so tried to smash my window in retaliation. We've sorted that bit out.' Now Rena full-on glares at John.

Why are they feeding me such rubbish? Are they trying to detract from a bigger picture?

'I got the impression that something was off with you when you left earlier,' says Rena, launching a full-on charm offensive as she flutters her eyelashes and gives me a coy smile. 'I wanted to make sure you were okay, and as John came round to apologise and offer to pay for any damage to the window, I thought the best thing would be for me to let you know. Clear the air, that sort of thing.' The corner of her eye twitches. Is that a sign that she's lying? Or is the fact she's lying actually a sign that she's lying.

Something catches Rena's attention and she takes a step towards the rear window. 'There's someone in your garden.' I turn and look at where she's pointing. Nigel is striding towards us, his hands in his corduroy trousers, causing a slight bunching up to the navy blazer he has seen fit to pair them with.

'It's my neighbour.' I find myself inexplicably happy to see him, especially as there doesn't appear to be room in his pockets for both his hands and his weasel.

'Hi, Nigel,' I call out with more gusto than I intended. I don't want him to realise how pleased I am to see him, and neither do I want to give the game away with my other unexpected guests either. Sadly, I fail to play my cards close to my chest and all three eye me warily.

'Has Willy been this way?' asks Nigel. He stands on the step, peering into the kitchen, his focus initially on me, then Rena before he gives a long hard stare at John. 'Do I know you?'

'No, no, I'm pretty sure that we've never met,' says John. I notice that his cheeks are tinged pink and his tongue darts out to moisten his lips. He makes me think of an embarrassed lizard.

'And who the hell is Willy?' says Rena, not so much of the

playful smile now, more a furrowed brow and, if I'm not mistaken, bewilderment.

'Er, Willy is Nigel's weasel,' I say, beside myself to have such insightful knowledge to pass around. This vodka is good stuff. I should probably eat something before long.

'A weasel!' John looks as if he's about to leap onto the nearest chair. He folds his arms across his chest and scans the floor. 'Aren't weasels dangerous?'

'What's the matter with you?' asks Nigel. 'Weasels are partial to mouse brains – it's their favourite. Do you have mouse brains?'

This strikes me as the funniest thing I've ever heard and I laugh like a drain. This vodka really does have a kick to it.

'I think you're having some sort of an episode, Avril,' says Nigel. 'We've spoken about this, haven't we? Do you need to come over for a coffee again?'

The alcohol is good stuff, but I know I've never set foot in Nigel's house before, let alone been inside for a coffee. This is akin to neighbourly concern. That in itself makes me nervous.

Everyone notices the shaking hand I extend towards the draining board when I put my glass down. 'Actually, Nigel, that does sound like a good idea.' I turn my attention to the other two. 'If you don't mind, I think Nigel and I need one of our chats.'

'What if the weasel comes back?' says John. He runs his hands down the front of his trousers as if checking for a stowaway.

'As long as you don't provoke him or get between him and a rabbit, I'd say you were quite safe,' says Nigel. 'Let's go.' He flicks his fingers at them in a get out motion.

Rena practically slams her glass down beside John's.

'I'll talk to you later,' says Rena as she makes her way back to the front door. Nigel raises an eyebrow at her tone, but remains silent, his hands back in his pockets. John scurries after Rena and I hear the door slam.

'Do you want me to check they've gone and aren't hiding in the bathtub?' says Nigel. 'Why don't you trust them?' There's more to Nigel than a modest beard, a tiny carnivorous pet and the dress sense of landed gentry.

I gawp at him before I get myself together to form actual words. 'What makes you think that I don't?'

'Apart from it being written all over your face, I watched them pull up outside. They were rowing and there was certainly something bullish about that young woman's attitude towards the lad. She has something over him, mark my words, and so I worry that either the same is true of you, or she's about to make you beholden to her for something.' He steps towards me and locks his eyes onto mine. 'Tell me I've got it all wrong and I'll bugger off now.'

If I am such an open book to my neighbour and new best friend, then he must be able to read surprise as it rampages all over my face. I'm also a bit taken aback that he swore. Somehow, I think it's beneath him.

'Is the offer of a coffee at yours a genuine one?' I pull a weak smile at him.

Nigel gives the curtest of nods. 'Of course. We'll go through the gaps in the fences.'

I lock the back door and follow him to the loose panel in my fence and across next door's garden to his own place.

This is the first time I realise that the gardens as so easily accessible. If it hadn't been for the last few days, I may have wondered how Nigel managed to gain access to my property so easily. Meaning that, if he can come and go, so can anyone else.

CHAPTER THIRTY-SIX

THEN

Craig tried to make small talk with us on the way to the 'safe house', as he kept calling it. The excitement of the situation was bringing out even more outlandish behaviour in him. I thought that if he winked at me one more time, I was going to lean across from the front passenger seat and poke his eye clean out of his skull. Each time he did his Popeye impression, he followed it by calling me 'Babe' or 'Sweetheart' or the ever nauseating 'Chick'. I shuddered that I'd had sex with this oxygen thief, even if it was for money.

As much as to break into his running commentary on how great this was going to be, us all working together and him being able to take care of me properly, I chanced a question. 'Where are we going, Craig. It's getting so late.'

'I told ya, darling, it's somewhere safe, init?'

And why he had started talking like this was a total mystery. He told me he had a boring office job in a bank and now he was attempting to talk like some sort of gangster instead of a pen-pusher.

I feigned sleep for the rest of the journey and pretended to wake up as we slowed and turned into the car park of a pub. I wasn't entirely sure where we were, but I had seen a sign for Ashford some miles back. If I had to guess, I would have said we were somewhere between Ashford and the Kent coast, although exactly where, I had no idea.

There were a couple of lights on at the rear of the Hare and Hatchet, shining on a virtually empty car park. A white transit van was parked in the far corner against a high wooden fence which ran from the furthest corner of the pub to the boundary and covered all three sides of the tarmacked area. No sooner had Craig pulled the car to a stop at the rear entrance, someone appeared from the shadows. I craned my neck to see them push the metal barrier across the entrance of the car park into place before walking towards us. He reached my door and opened it, letting the cold inside.

'So, this must be the Melissa I've heard so much about.' His smooth, pale skin accentuated his green eyes. The hood of his jacket hid his hair and gave no indication whether he was solid and well built, fat or skinny. Everything about his demeanour gave him an air of authority and under different circumstances, I just might have been very attracted to this man.

'Dylan,' said Craig, his face now next to mine and his hand on my thigh, 'thanks for helping us out here. We'll get these two inside and take care of business, yeah?'

'It's okay, Craig,' I said. 'You can say it in front of me and Heather. Not only were we there, but I called you, remember?'

A short laugh rang out from Dylan, then he said, 'She's got a point, Digger.' Craig's fingers dug into my flesh and I felt him bristle beside me.

'So, you both want me to keep repeating what we're about to do? That doesn't sound very sensible to me. Shall we get indoors where we can talk.' Craig removed his hand, turned off the ignition and got out of the car.

'Oh, someone's in a bad mood,' said Dylan. I was warming

to him, but then again, I'd thought Craig was okay when I first met him. Perhaps this one was just as bad and we were walking into an even worse set-up. Still, this scenario was definitely borne out of necessity. I needed to think of a way out of this.

I heard the sound of the rear car door opening behind me. I had completely forgotten that Heather was even there. Would my escape plan involve her? I think I would be entirely forgiven for leaving her behind. It wasn't as if she had brought much to the party, other than prostitution, misery and murder.

'We've got you a couple of rooms made up, ladies,' said Dylan over his shoulder. We followed him the short distance to the door which turned out to lead to the kitchen, and shuffled inside after him.

The kitchen was huge, every shiny surface spotless and metal rack upon metal rack of crockery, pots and pans. The rows of knives stuck to metallic strips grabbed my attention and I wondered if they planned on bringing Gary's body here and carving him up. I made a note to avoid the meat pies and claim to be vegetarian if anyone offered me food. I fantasised that we would be out of here by daylight, yet the gnawing feeling in my stomach told me different. Craig's words about taking care of me had unsettled me no end, and I didn't figure that he would let me out of his sight for long.

The harsh overhead lights were bringing on a headache and all I wanted to do was sleep.

'This way, girls,' said Dylan. We obediently trotted along after him, across to the main bar. Again, it was a spacious area; ten tables laid with place settings and another lounge area with something like fifteen tables of various sizes, chairs tucked neatly under them.

Dylan showed us to a table, lifted the flap at one end of the bar and said, 'Brandies all round, I think. It's good for shock.'

He lifted a glass to the optics, added two measures to it and then repeated it with another three glasses. Heather and I sat side by side, watching him as if it was some sort of floor show. Craig stood at the bar, propping himself up by his elbow, his other hand hung awkwardly at his side. In Dylan's presence, it was almost as if he didn't quite know how to handle himself. It was fascinating, yet a little worrying in equal measures. I had seen how Craig could behave when he had to, so this put me on high alert.

My mind went into overdrive as Dylan clinked three of the glasses together and carried them over. He placed them down and slid one across, gave me a look that melted me and sat down. He made a point of leaning in towards me and said, 'I hope both you and your friend will be comfortable here. We run a good pub, and don't as a matter of course let the rooms, but you two are an exception. A happy exception, but nevertheless, an exception.'

Craig didn't react.

I picked up my drink and took a tentative sip. My throat felt like it was on fire. I was used to cheap vodka and sometimes gin. Neat brandy was a whole different league. I tried not to splutter. I knew how juvenile that would make me seem, even without my pasty skin, and complete look of being clueless as to what was happening.

I blinked back tears. The sudden need to cry was a direct result of the drink that threatened to put in a reappearance. Although, I suppose it was more a build-up of weeks of living day to day, punter to punter, wondering how I had managed to spectacularly fuck everything up, and now I was helping to hide a body. The sound of Craig dragging over a chair and sitting directly opposite brought me back to the present.

'Anyone else here?' he asked Dylan.

'No, bruv, just us four.'

Had I heard correctly? Were these two related or was it a

figure of speech? I studied Craig's waspish face. It had always seemed to be too small for his body and his lips were so thin, they gave him a mean appearance even when he had been nice to me. I suppose they had similar shaped chins, but that was about it. I could simply ask, yet I didn't want to draw attention to myself. I was hoping to slip away as they went off to take care of Gary. The quieter I kept, the less chance there was of them recalling I was even here.

'That won't work.' Craig gripped his brandy, his knuckles white as he held the glass and downed it in one. 'We need someone here while we're out, in case of any problems.' He glanced in my direction as he spoke. I couldn't interpret whether this was a veiled threat or if he was under the illusion he was doing me some sort of favour.

'Relax,' said Dylan. 'You always worry too much. Besides, Kenny'll be here soon.'

Craig's wafer-thin lips formed a tiny 'O' and he narrowed his eyes. 'You asked Kenny to help us out? Are you insane? Of all the people you could have called, you contacted *him*?'

'He's fine, he's a different person these days.' Dylan had a smile playing around the edges of his mouth. 'It's only natural that you should be wary of our big brother. After all, you still owe him two grand. And he'd like it back.'

That was when I knew I wasn't getting away from Craig any time soon.

CHAPTER THIRTY-SEVEN

Nigel's house is homely and welcoming. The wall between the kitchen and the living room has been knocked through, making it seem much larger than the downstairs of my cottage. It's also lighter and airier, and the furnishings are a mixture of older, undoubtedly expensive pieces, interspersed with modern lamps, throws and framed prints on the walls. He catches me looking as he makes for the coffee pod machine which sits atop a work surface that is either granite or quartz. It's not my area of expertise. It cost a fair bit, of that I am sure.

'What were you expecting?' he asks, mug in one hand. 'You look surprised that I don't live in some sort of mausoleum. Regular coffee or would you prefer to choose?' He indicates a wooden box with several varieties inside.

'Regular is fine, thank you.' I walk over to a bookcase and see a large metal cage on the floor. It's tucked next to one of two large armchairs.

'That's Willy in there,' he calls over the noise of the machine gasping hot water into the mug.

'He wasn't lost after all?' I crouch down and watch Willy as he looks at me and backs into the corner.

'No, twice in such a short space of time would be ridiculous.' Nigel takes a step towards me and adds, 'I wouldn't get too close, if I were you.'

I immediately stand up and back away. 'Can he get me through the bars?'

Nigel indicates that I sit in the chair furthest from the cage, which I happily take.

'Mmm, he has been known to pick the lock and get out but weasels can attack humans if they feel threatened. It's unlikely; chances are they'll run away, only he can't as he's in a cage.' Nigel holds out my drink.

'He's done what? He picked the lock?' I take the coffee and am immediately comforted by the aroma.

'When I say "picked the lock", you know what I mean?' says Nigel, on his way back to fetch his own drink and a dainty sugar bowl with tongs. He settles into the chair at right angles to mine and drums the fingers of his left hand on his leg. He balances his other on the arm of the chair, mug of coffee level with his face. 'So, tell me about yourself.'

The sudden change of topic and his easy manner of speaking take me off-guard.

'I, er, well, I've been here nearly five weeks now and I'm renting the cottage after my marriage broke down. That's about it.'

Nigel isn't buying it for one minute. I've displeased him in some way. The change in expression is miniscule, but it's there all right. The finger drumming intensifies. Then he smiles and says, 'I see. How long were you married?'

'Fifteen years.' I take a sip.

'Any children?'

'No.' I don't expand on that and he doesn't push it.

'How long are you staying for?'

'I haven't really decided and I have no plans.' Sat here,

another human being showing more interest in me than anyone else has for many years, unless they had something to gain, I realise how utterly sad and pathetic my life has been. I refuse to let this man see me cry, at least, that's what I told myself until the tears were running down my face, falling onto my cheap Matalan T-shirt.

Nigel is across the room like lightning. He puts an arm around me and flourishes a black silk handkerchief in front of my red, puffy eyes. I hold in a laugh at this. He's being kind but obviously he has a silk hankie and not a box of tissues like everyone else. 'Keep it. I've dozens more.'

This really does make me laugh and suddenly we are sharing a great joke and guffawing like old friends. This is the last way I expected my day to go.

It's a complete treat.

CHAPTER THIRTY-EIGHT

THEN

Our first night at the Hare and Hatchet was nowhere as miserable as I thought it was going to be. The four of us sat in the bar as we waited on the arrival of Kenny, the big brother who Craig clearly would have preferred to be out of the picture. It was fun watching him squirm, and listening to Dylan's constant put downs. I probably shouldn't have enjoyed it as much as I did, but I had little else going on, and it served him right for calling me babe, darling, sweet cheeks, chick and the other ridiculous names.

Two brandies later, car headlights lit up the bay windows, followed by the sound of a car pulling up at the front of the building. I looked at Heather in mild surprise as I distinctly heard two voices, one male and one female, as they noisily made their way to the main door. Before Dylan had a chance to get up, there was a loud banging and the man – Kenny presumably – called out, 'Fucking let us in then.'

Dylan unlocked the bolts and threw open the door. 'You bastard, Ken. You might have given me a second to get up. Why are you making so much noise?'

Kenny was six foot of solid muscle. His brown suede jacket

was unbuttoned, showing a white, round-necked T-shirt and dark blue jeans. His hair was a similar style and colour to Craig's, only, Kenny's suited him. He was also just about the ugliest man I had ever seen. His skin was pockmarked, his nose was bent as if it had been broken, set and then rebroken, and he had cauliflowers for ears. He stood in front of Dylan, hands by his sides, his fists clenched.

'You old wanker,' said Kenny and then smiled revealing almost perfect teeth, were it not for one of the front ones being solid gold. He opened his arms wide and the two manhandled each other for several seconds in a bear hug. This was followed by much back slapping and shouts of, 'It's bloody good to see you.' 'Been a long time, bro,' and other indulgent comments. Craig, meanwhile, sat and bided his time until it was his turn.

'And what's this little testicle been up to?' said Kenny. He took a couple of strides towards our table, Dylan frantically locking the doors behind him. Craig stood up, arms out, only his greeting wasn't the same as his brother's. Instead of an embrace, Kenny punched him in the stomach, causing Craig to double over. Kenny's next move was to put him in a headlock and spin him round to face us. With a grin, Kenny stuck a finger up each of Craig's nostrils and pulled upwards until his brother was standing on tiptoes.

'All right, girls?' Kenny said to me and Heather. 'Heard you two got into a spot of bother. It'll be a pleasure to help you both out, especially as this skid mark already owes me. I'll stick it on his tab.' With that, he let go of Craig, who crumpled before our eyes. 'Get up, you wanker,' said Kenny.

It was only then that I got a good look at the woman who had walked in with the more unhinged of the three brothers. She was your typical brassy tart: tight leopard-print top paired with a mid-thigh length black leather skirt, black patent stilettos and long blonde hair. She was pretty in a cheap way, and I guessed that she was younger than she looked. From appearance alone, I thought she was in her early thirties, but she was probably nearer to twenty-five.

'Hello, Pearl,' said Dylan, leaning in for a kiss. 'You're as beautiful as ever, I see.'

Pearl gave the sort of deep and throaty laugh that only the heaviest of smokers could usually manage. 'You're as slick as your brother is disturbed.' Her voice was actually lovely and would have beaten Kathleen Turner to first place in a honey-drenched tones competition. She glided across the somewhat worn carpet and inspected Heather and me.

'This is Melissa,' said Dylan, as he pointed at me. I gave a small nod. I didn't want to speak; compared to Pearl I would sound like I had just inhaled a balloon full of helium. 'And this is Heather.' He smiled and his face softened when he said her name. Interesting.

'You two aren't going to give me any crap, are you?' said Pearl, one hand on her hip and the other outstretched to point an immaculate red nail back and forth between us.

We both shook our heads.

'Then, how about a drink?' said Pearl.

'Good idea.' Dylan thumbed in the direction of the bar. 'Melissa, do the honours. Get Pearl anything she wants and the three of us will be back when we're done.' He aimed his next remark at the clichéd gangster's moll. 'You won't get any trouble out of these two, and if they do play up, you know what to do.'

Heather and I exchanged worried glances. I remembered that I was supposed to be fetching Pearl a drink and didn't want to displease my angsty babysitter. She could certainly take me in a fight, of that I had no doubt. I got up and made my way to the bar, awaiting my orders. I was careful to sidestep the brothers Grimm.

'See you soon, gorgeous,' said Kenny. He grabbed her backside with both hands and squeezed. He was quite the catch.

Pearl watched as the three of them walked back through the pub to the kitchen, and presumably the car park. Dylan and Kenny went first, side by side, with Craig trailing along behind. I would have felt sorry for him if he wasn't such a gonad.

We heard the sound of the back door being locked. Instantly, Pearl ordered a drink from me and sat on a bar stool scrutinising my every move while she gave me instructions on how to fix her the perfect martini. She encouraged me to make some cocktails for myself and Heather, again, under her watchful eye. Still, it passed the time, we didn't have to pay for the drinks and it wasn't the most terrible part of my evening. And it turned out that Pearl was good fun. Heather even crept over and joined us at the bar.

Soon the three of us were lined up with cocktails in front of us, giggling like we were old friends. Only we weren't. There was still the heavily made-up peroxide elephant in the room who apparently knew what to do if we played her up.

Eventually curiosity got the better of me and with the help of some gin, tequila, vodka, a little rum and splash of triple sec, I said, 'Pearl, how did you and Kenny meet?'

There was an awkward silence – perhaps I imagined it – and then she said, 'It was a few years ago. I've never looked back.' She swirled the remnants of her drink and said, 'It was the day my fortune changed. There's never a dull moment.' Her tone was flat, her words on the way to their own execution.

Unsure whether to add a follow-up question or leave it there, I was about to say something else, perhaps it would have been a little foolish, when headlights illuminated the pub and the sound of a diesel van pulling up outside stopped me.

'It's about time you got back behind the bar and poured a

few pints, love,' said Pearl. 'Two Stellas and an ale. Then, us ladies need to make ourselves scarce.'

By the time the three of them had made their entrance, Pearl was hurrying us through the bar and upstairs to the staff quarters. Her hand on my shoulder stopped any chance of me dawdling and overhearing exactly how they had got rid of Gary. I was going to have to listen at plenty of keyholes to find out the details. After all, my future depended on it.

When we reached the landing, Pearl flicked on a light switch. The décor was old-fashioned, yet still a vast improvement on Heather's flat. That already felt like a lifetime ago. The carpet was hardwearing, although clean, and the magnolia walls had one or two scuff marks on them, but were otherwise in good condition.

There were four doors, all closed, all with keys in the locks on the outside. For some reason, that made the hairs on the back of my neck stand up. No one likes being locked inside a room.

'This one,' said Pearl, and pointed to the one at the end of the hallway. Heather pushed the door open and felt for the light switch. It was a modest room, high ceiling, same carpet and walls painted in the same colour as the stairs and hallway. Against the far wall there were two single beds separated by a small cabinet and a table under the window with a hairbrush, deodorant and a couple of other toiletries I couldn't quite make out from across the room.

'You can share for tonight,' said Pearl. 'Over there are a few bits to tide you over, girls' stuff, you know. That door there leads to a shower and toilet. You'll find whatever you need for now either in the cabinet or in the wardrobe.'

Wardrobe was a bit of a stretch. It was an alcove with a couple of dressing gowns on hangers and a low shelf with what looked like T-shirts and underwear neatly folded.

'I don't understand,' said Heather. 'You didn't even know

that we were coming until an hour or so ago. How have you managed to get everything ready in time?'

Pearl's throaty laugh echoed around the room. 'Oh, Heather. You two aren't the first and you won't be the last. 'Night.'

With that, she stepped back into the corridor and locked us inside.

CHAPTER THIRTY-NINE

I convince myself that I am not scared of Rena. She makes a habit of surprising me, but surely she would have killed me by now if she were that way inclined. It doesn't stop me leaving Nigel's house and going home to check that every door and window is bolted. Nor does it stop me lying awake for some hours before I finally fall asleep.

Even then, I have a broken night. Every creak and noise wakes me, every perceivable change in temperature I imagine a door silently swinging open somewhere and Rena slithering inside my home.

The alarm on my mobile phone intrudes into a fitful sleep at 7.30 am and I get ready for DC Katie George's arrival feeling groggy and exhausted. My eyes feel as though I have grit in them and my skin looks grey. 'What a state,' I mutter to myself at my reflection in the bathroom mirror.

Twenty minutes later I am showered, dressed and drinking my first coffee of the day. I fight the urge to scan the tree for red ribbons, except the pull is too great. The branches contain only leaves and a couple of sparrows. My tormentor has let me off. I know that I should eat something, even though food is the last thing that I want. I get to my feet and gingerly open the bread bin. I can't recall when I last looked in here, so I hope that the mould hasn't reached danger levels. I'm surprised to see a sliced brown loaf, its use by date still days away. I didn't buy that, I know I didn't. It is unusual tactics for someone trying to scare me by getting my shopping. I had a conversation with Nigel about my lack of transport and being reliant on buses. Perhaps he bought it for me but I've no idea how he would have got inside the house. I hold it up and examine it. It hasn't been opened, that much is clear, and I don't even know how someone would go about poisoning a sliced Hovis. If they went to that much trouble, perhaps I should just eat the poxy thing. My stomach is rumbling, so if I eat enough of it, it should be mercifully quick. Yet I can't bring myself to eat anything. I throw the bread back inside the bin and put the lid on.

Time for another coffee before Katie gets here and I spend the rest of the morning trying to avoid answering her and telling her anything near to the truth. She is going to ask me endless questions and I am going to squirm and cover what I've been up to for the last few days with my new best friend/murderer/disgraced police officer/ex-con. The combination of my nerves, two coffees on an empty stomach and a lack of sleep, is making me feel very queasy.

Right on time, there's a knock at the door. A fresh-faced Katie stands on the edge of the property, car keys in one hand and mobile in the other. For a moment, I think that I could have Katie's life if I hadn't monumentally fucked everything up. If only I had turned a different corner and avoided Heather Knight, I could have become someone decent with a future.

'Are you okay, Avril?' she asks, worry taking over her

features. 'You seem miles away.' Today she is wearing a knee-length grey skirt and jacket, a white cotton blouse and while her footwear can't be described as elegant, her shoes are nowhere near as vile as the brogues she wore when we first met.

'I didn't sleep very well,' I said. 'Nothing to worry about. Shall we get going?'

I lock up and follow her to the police car, an unremarkable Ford Focus that made me feel good for each and every taxpayer in the county of Kent.

Katie waits as I click my seatbelt into place, she starts the engine, and despite the completely empty country road, indicates and pulls away from the kerb like an octogenarian with a cataract. Impatiently I glance at my watch. Not that I have anywhere else to be, but this is going to take some time.

We chat about life in Kent and make small talk about the amount of new houses springing up in Faversham and the surrounding area, Katie telling me that she plans on buying a place with her boyfriend in the new year as soon as they have the deposit together. I almost envy her life and the promise that it holds, then I figure that she deserves to be happy.

Katie picks up speed along the derestricted stretch of road, although when I glance over at the speedometer, she is going at a steady fifty miles an hour. I spot sheep and cows through the hedgerows and on the gentle slopes of the fields on either side of us. It's a beautiful day.

As I look back at Katie to say something witty about cows and flatulence, I see a car hurtling towards us from a side road. I open my mouth to shout, to warn Katie, but it's too late. There is a bang, horrendous screeching of metal tearing and then the car spins and all goes black.

CHAPTER FORTY

THEN

'Heather.' I waited for her to answer me across the darkness. I could hear her breathing as we lay on our beds. It felt very lights out in the dorm, apart from the three amigos downstairs, at least one of whom was a colossal pervert. Perhaps it was a family trait – that would answer a few questions I had. 'Are you awake?'

'Melissa, please. I'm really trying to hold it together and the only chance I've got of stopping myself from going insane, is by getting some rest and hoping I don't have nightmares.'

'It's been an ordeal. You should probably talk about it.'

I heard her turn over. Her voice was clearer now, so I suppose she was now facing me in the pitch black. 'If I could go back and stop what happened, I would. Gary was a total bastard, but I'll have to live with what I've done. Not to mention, you and I will now have to face the music. It's what we get for involving Craig.'

'Hang on a minute – what other options did we have? I couldn't get rid of the body on my own and you were catatonic. Who else was I supposed to call?'

There was movement from her side of the room and a rustle of bedsheets. From the change in her voice, Heather was now sitting upright. 'You actually thought it was a good idea to trust Creepy Craig? He's a disgusting bastard. Depraved doesn't even cover it.'

Panic washed over me. 'What? It was you that told me he was one of the better ones and that I wouldn't have any issues with him.'

'You wouldn't, love, not all the time you did exactly what he wanted. He ever tie you up?'

I clutched the sheet to my chest. 'Once, yes.'

'Oh, that's right, with the scarf he put around my throat.' She gave a deep breath and said, 'Well, next time, wait until he breaks out the red ribbon. You should never have called him. There's something very wrong with him.'

CHAPTER FORTY-ONE

I wake up feeling as though I've been hit by a bus. I try to turn my head and hear a voice say, 'She's awake. Avril, Avril.' I notice that it's no longer light outside and wonder if I've lost a day or two. I remember I was in a car accident and I've no idea where I am. I can only hope I'm in a hospital ward. My eyes are so heavy I'm having trouble keeping them open and everything hurts like hell. Even my skin feels like it's on fire. I try to look down at my arms. Perhaps the car caught fire and I've been burned. I make it as far as the bare unscared flesh on my left arm. I don't have the energy to lift my arm, but I see a needle poking out of the back of my hand.

I try to say something but the words won't form, let alone come out. I see the blue hospital curtain part and a nurse appears as well as someone I recognise but can't place.

My breathing is rapid and if I could manage to make any noise, I think that now would be the time I started to scream. What happened? Where's Katie? What happened to the driver of the other car? Only no sound comes out when I breathe. I don't even think I manage to pant, although I know I'm hyperventilating.

'Avril,' says the nurse, 'I'm Jenna, your nurse. I've been here with you for most of the time you've been asleep. Try to breathe slowly and take your time. You're in the Medical Assessment Unit at the William Harvey Hospital in Ashford.'

'When can I talk to her?' says the woman with the sternest expression I have seen in a long time. I think it's the jowls that do it. I have a memory of this larger than life character talking to Katie on the road outside my house when Joan's body was found. She is Katie's detective inspector. This can't be good.

'Wh...' is about as far as I get before my croaking voice gives out and my throat feels as though I've been swallowing razor blades.

Nurse Jenna frowns. 'It's not a good idea at the moment as she's only just woken up. She'll be a bit disorientated.' Then she turns her attention back to me. 'The doctor will be along to see you soon. She can answer any questions you have.'

I take it as a cop-out from Jenna. Surely if I am that seriously hurt, I wouldn't even be awake with a police officer wanting to have a word with me. The thing is, I want to talk to her. I need to find out what's happened to Katie and who the hell tried to kill us both.

Then I start to cry.

Jenna gently takes my hand – the one without the needle poking out of it – and sits beside me on the bed. 'We don't have any next of kin details for you, Avril. Is there a partner or someone we can call?'

That's the thing, isn't it? I'm truly alone.

I want to speak to the police officer. All I can manage is to whisper, 'Katie?' and wait for her response.

'Do you want to talk to me, Avril?' The police officer takes a step closer and I nod.

Jenna gives my hand a squeeze and says, 'If you're sure, I'll give you five minutes.' She gets up and her shoes squeak on the lino as she disappears behind the curtain.

'I'm Detective Inspector Louise Pengully.' Her accent is a local one with a tone that means business, although she does have a kind face. I hadn't been able to appreciate that the last time I saw her. 'Can you remember what happened?'

I try to swallow and manage to say, 'So quick,' and follow it with a barely imperceptible shake of my head. It's then I realise that I was trying to lean forward, so I allow my head to fall back against the pillow. I feel wiped out.

'A blue Peugeot came from a side turning and drove into the driver's side of your car,' says Louise. 'The driver was nowhere to be found by the time witnesses arrived and the police turned up. Do you know anyone with a blue Peugeot 207?'

My head feels as though it's going to split in two. I am not even sure that I know what a 207 looks like, and have so few acquaintances, I doubt I could help her anyway. I give another miniscule shake of my head and hear her sigh.

'Okay. I'll let you get some rest.' Louise makes a move, but I can't let her go, not without finding out about Katie. I grab uselessly at the air, clawing for her attention. She stops, half in and half out of the chair. It's obvious what I'm trying to ask; she won't make it easy for me. 'I think you should wait until the doctor's been and we'll talk again then. I'm under orders from the nurse not to overdo it.'

Louise attempts a smile which doesn't make it all the way across her mouth, let alone to her eyes, and then she's up and walking away. I watch her as she too disappears behind the curtain.

I sink further back into the pillow and cry myself to sleep.

CHAPTER FORTY-TWO

THEN

I had to hand it to Craig and his brothers – they broke us in gently. To begin with, we were told that we could work behind the bar to pay for our keep. I had nowhere else to go and neither did Heather. She allowed Dylan to arrange clearing out the flat, bringing the few personal possessions we both had to the pub and handing back the keys. It struck me as odd that she'd acquiesced without a murmur. Even though her life had been governed by whoever was paying her the most to have sex with her, at least she had enjoyed some sort of freedom with the choice of packing her belongings and disappearing if the mood took her. Now, she seemed resigned to the fact she was going to share a room with me and pull pints to make ends meet. Whereas I had other plans.

I enjoyed working behind the bar. The punters were mostly friendly and many bought us drinks. We weren't allowed to drink alcohol while we were working and we couldn't keep the money, but once a week when the place shut early, Dylan was happy to let us drink our tips and play pool until the early hours. It wasn't the high life, yet I felt better than I had in a long time.

Then, one afternoon, I had the breakthrough I was waiting

for. Two of the regulars came in and stood at the bar, ordered their usual two pints and two toasted sandwiches of the day – they never cared what it was – and carried on talking about the local story that had dominated the lunchtime news.

'Yeah, he was found out in the woods near Blean,' said Lager Top. 'Apparently he'd been there a while and my sister-in-law, the one who lives next door to the PCSO, said he was only found because it looked like some sort of wild animal had started to dig him up.'

'Any idea who he was?' said Pint of Guest Ale.

I made out that the drip trays right in front of the two men needed my undivided attention.

'No, he's a bit of a mess, what with all the chewing and death, so I suppose it's going to be DNA and missing person enquiries, that sort of thing.'

'Could be drugs?'

'Melissa,' shouted Dylan from the bottom of the stairs. I hadn't seen or heard him come down. His eyes were wide and he was still buttoning up his shirt, his hair still damp from the shower. 'I'm going out. Hold the fort until Craig and Kenny get here in an hour. You can do that?'

'Yeah, course. Where's Heather?'

'Upstairs. She's not feeling too good. Don't disturb her.'

With that, he was gone and Lager Top and Pint of Guest Ale had taken their sandwiches to the far side of the bar, well outside of my earshot.

As I poured the next round for Thursday's ever busying lunchtime crowd, it made me wonder, not for the first time, exactly how far I would get if I emptied the till and ran out of the door. Usually at least Dylan was in the bar, mostly Kenny too during the day, and Craig in the evenings. At weekends we often had the pleasure of Pearl's company too. The only other people here regularly were a waitress called Anne who was very good friends with Dylan and the two in the kitchen. The chef and his assistant always kept themselves to themselves and I wasn't about to start trusting people I had hardly exchanged a word with. Heather wasn't even here. Could I risk it? What if I snatched fistfuls of notes and legged it? Most people didn't watch what the bar staff were doing if they weren't in the middle of fixing their drinks.

After I poured my next customer's order, I took their twenty pound note to the till and keyed in the drinks, totalled the amount and opened the drawer. There was at least £150 in cash, not including what was in the till at the far end of the counter. I put the twenty pound note under the clip with the other two, counted out the change and gave it back to the customer with a smile.

I hesitated, my hand on the money.

I looked towards the door and daylight beyond. It had been days since I'd left this place. We weren't even allowed to go to the shops in case we didn't come back. This was my chance.

Then the door opened and Craig stood in the doorway. The sun illuminated him from behind so I couldn't see his features, but I knew that standing here with my hand in the till wasn't going to make him smile any time soon. I slammed the drawer shut and grabbed a cloth to wipe down the countertops, my appearance at nonchalance no doubt looking as unconvincing as it felt.

Craig was still breathing heavily when he leaned over the bar, his baby soft cheeks turned towards me. 'Got here as fast as I could,' he said. 'It was my turn to pick our little sister up from school, but she's with her dad now. A pint when you're ready.'

'Of course,' I said and picked up a glass. I hoped he couldn't see that my hand was trembling as I held it under the tap.

That had been my one and only chance in seven weeks and I had blown it. I didn't know when I'd get another.

CHAPTER FORTY-THREE

Over the next day, between the CT scan, multiple X-rays and the never-ending observations they keep me under, everyone avoids answering my questions about Katie, so I know that it's not going to be good news. Jenna's squeaky shoes herald her arrival in the late afternoon and she tells me that I've got a visitor. 'It the DI, she's back again to ask you some more questions.' She gives me a thin smile, tops up my water cup and pulls back the curtain in a flourish to reveal a grim-faced Louise Pengully.

'Avril, how are you feeling?' she asks. She pulls out a chair and sits down, without giving me a chance to answer. Her tablet balanced on her knee shows me she is poised for business. This is happening then.

'I feel like I've been hit by a car.' My attempt at humour is not well received. 'Please, tell me about Katie.'

Louise pauses, glances up at me from her tablet and takes a deep breath. 'She's alive—'

I gasp. 'Oh, thank fuck. Can I see her?'

This is met with a firm shake of her head. 'Absolutely not. She was rushed into theatre straight after she got here. She had internal injuries and internal bleeding and besides, she's in Intensive Care. I'm not at liberty to discuss her condition in detail with you, but what I will say is that it's a miracle that she's still with us. And that you got off so lightly with concussion.'

The last sentence is spoken with a hint of resentment. *None taken*, I think, yet don't dare to say it. This woman is clearly the classic bark is worse than her bite sort and the tic dancing around her left eye and the constant shifting in her seat tells me that she is clearly distressed and worried about her colleague.

'Listen, if there is *anything* I can tell you that will help find who did this, you know that I will.' This was probably the longest sentence I've uttered since being in the car with Katie, moments before the crash. All over again I find myself crying.

Louise leans over and pats my arm. It's a kind gesture and makes the tears come faster until I'm a snotty mess. She's there with the tissues and that makes it worse.

Eventually I stop blubbing and say, 'I'm sorry. I'll keep it together, I promise. I genuinely like Katie and I want to help. The only thing is, all I remember was chatting to her and then I glanced over at her, and, well, saw something looming towards us. I didn't see the driver and as much as I try, my mind is a total blank.'

I finish talking and despite being exhausted at having said so much, I feel enlivened. I meant every word. I am struggling to picture any of what happened and I couldn't describe the driver or any other details. Louise has yet to ask me if I have any suspicions about who could have done this. Now that's a different matter.

Would Rena or her worn-down sidekick have done this? I am failing to see what they would gain by putting us both in the hospital, but then again, Rena seems to be unravelling in front of me. It must be something really serious for her to act with such desperation.

'Is there anything at all you can tell us?' says Louise. She jiggles her foot up and down and forgets to blink. 'Anything?'

Her eyes plead with me to tell her more, but then I would have to come clean about Rena visiting me and that I lied to Katie about when I had last spoken to the disgraced former officer. That, naturally, would come back to me and I want to keep my powder dry for as long as possible. If Rena or John Smith are behind this, it puts me in danger too. For now, I would have to play that down.

'It was early in the morning, so maybe someone who was still half-cut from the night before? No insurance? Whoever it was panicked? Or maybe it was someone else that Katie was investigating?'

'We have a team working on every possibility.' Louise shuts the cover of her tablet. I sense we are almost done here. 'There's a chance you're right and it's a horrible accident, nothing more. That's why I've decided that the uniformed police officer, who's been sitting outside the entrance to this part of the ward, no longer needs to stay and keep tabs on anyone who comes and goes to your bedside.'

'I, I—' I try to sit up and peer around the wafer-thin curtain towards the corridor.

'It's okay.' Louise all but puts a hand on my chest to push me back on the bed. 'You probably weren't even aware there has been one. It was to make sure that if you or Katie had been targeted, no one was going to sneak back in the night and finish you off. You can't tell me anything of any use, and we haven't got anywhere with our enquiries. The Peugeot was reported stolen, so that's where it's taken us – a terrible accident.'

'Whose car was it?'

As soon as the words leave my lips, I know that I have made a mistake. I try to keep my expression neutral, and probably fail.

'Why?' Her eyes narrow and the tic is back.

I start to shrug and realise that it hurts too much. 'Wondered if it was someone local or further afield. You know, like someone using the car for burgling houses or whatever it is that criminals do with stolen motors.'

I should stop talking now. What drugs have they got me on?

She hesitates. 'We'll talk more later. When they send you home, you can come and speak to one of my officers at the police station.'

Before she leaves, Louise pulls out a business card from the inside of the tablet cover and places it on the locker next to my bed.

'Get some rest.'

CHAPTER FORTY-FOUR

THEN

Things started to change in the pub after Gary's body was found. As hard as I tried to eavesdrop, I only managed to pick anything up from the local news, and that was the usual generic spiel. Police had confirmed that the body of a thirty-two-year-old man (Christ, I thought he was in his early forties), had been found in woods being prepared for the reintroduction of bison and had been named as Gary Lumley, adored father of three and cherished by his wife and family. A couple of photos of him flashed up on the TV in the corner of the bar above the pool table. One of him with his arm around a woman, presumably his wife, and another with a small child on his lap.

Craig caught me staring across at the lunchtime news item and waved his hand in front of my face. 'The beer is about to spill,' he said crossly before he stomped over to switch off the television. He had a point – there was Tennent's Extra all over the floor.

I shook myself out of it and carried on serving customers. All the while I kept a watch on Craig as he marched back across the carpet that was getting stickier by the day. The place was starting to look a bit grubby. The cleaner had quit, stock was running low and Dylan seemed more and more absent as the weeks went by. Heather was often in our room, pale and clammy and I most certainly had cabin fever. Everyone seemed tense, Craig more so than most.

I waited until the last punter was across the threshold and we were closing up for the afternoon. Craig was mooching around in the cellar, changing a barrel of beer with such concentration, it was as if he had never done it before. Something I knew he had done hundreds of times.

'Are you okay?' I asked.

'Of course I'm not bloody well okay.' He snapped the pipe back into place on the top of the lager keg and glared at me. 'You've seen the news. We could go to prison.'

I wasn't sure what to say to this. Obviously we could go to prison. Heather had smashed someone over the head and Craig and his brothers had got rid of the body. I wasn't exactly in the clear either. 'What should we do?' I took a step towards him. I needed to find out as much as I could about their set-up and any other side hustles they were running and get myself some sort of a plan.

We were within touching distance, so I did the only thing I could think of – I put my hand up to his cheek. Instantly his hand flew up and gripped mine. He stepped closer and whispered, 'It's about time I made you pay me back for helping you. Up until now Dylan has been very strict about his policy of not messing with the merchandise, but he's not here, is he?'

He squeezed harder until I gasped at the pain. 'You're hurting me, Craig,' I said as I tried to take my hand back.

He didn't seem to hear me, or didn't care that I'd even spoken. 'I've always liked you, Melissa. I think about you all the time. You know that you drive me completely crazy, don't you?' Then he let go of me and ran both hands through my hair, a smile twitched at the corner of his mouth. I could see from his glazed eyes that he was somewhere else entirely, and wherever that was, it was far from here.

I knew that no one would hear me scream. The cellar was a number of steps down from the bar and besides, all the customers had gone home. The only other person in the entire building was Heather, and whatever was wrong with her was unlikely to make her wander down here at three o'clock in the afternoon. I had no chance of fighting him off, so I would have to try something else.

'Hey, it's really cold down here,' I said. 'How about we go upstairs? Sit in the bar or something.'

Craig let go of my hair and started to run his fingers up and down my arms, alternating between slow and caressing and occasionally digging his fingers into my flesh. I tried not to react, but I was starting to panic. It wasn't the first time I had been alone with a man and forced to do stuff I really didn't want to do. This time, though, I knew I was in the company of someone who was more than capable of getting rid of a body. Somewhat badly as it turned out, yet nonetheless, this person helped hide a corpse.

'Where is everyone?' Dylan shouted from the bar. Craig put a finger to my lips and pulled me close to him, his other hand on the back of my neck.

By this time, I was shaking. All I wanted at that moment was for Dylan to come running down the stairs and at least I would be safe for a brief while.

'I know you like my brother,' said Craig as he traced my lips with his finger. 'I've seen you making eyes at him when you don't think I'm watching. Except, I'm always watching you, Melissa. One day you'll tell me that you love me. It can't end any other way.' With that he forced my face up to his and kissed me.

Craig had me in a vice-like grip and all I could hear was my heart hammering and the blood pounding in my ears. And then Dylan thudded into the cellar and said, 'What the fuck are you two doing down here? Didn't you hear me calling?'

I took two or three rapid breaths, anything to fill my lungs, other than the sickly aftershave Craig had doused himself with, and tried to steady myself.

Craig laughed and said, 'There I go sweeping her off her feet. We were, you know, busy, bruv. We had no chance of knowing you were back, did we, Melly?'

Melly? He really was a psycho.

'Well, put her down. I need her for this evening. I've a job for you.'

'For me?' I said and pointed at myself in case anyone was in any doubt.

'Yeah,' said Dylan, his green eyes sparkling. 'You two have been here some time now and have taken advantage of my good and generous nature. You didn't think it was going to be all pulling pints, playing pool and free keep, surely?'

I looked from one to the other, a new horror gripping me. Dylan's expression gave nothing away, while Craig's resembled a watered-down version of my own. 'But me and Heather have got jobs. We work here for you.' My feet took me a step backwards, the back of my legs pressed against a cardboard box of pint glasses.

'That's really cute,' said Dylan. 'We helped you, risked a lot to get involved, despite my dozy little brother thinking with his dick – as usual – and now it's payback time.'

'What do you want us to do?' I hadn't wanted to ask the question because I had an inkling what the answer was going to be. The next part I wasn't prepared for.

'Not an "us", love, not just yet.' Dylan crossed his arms and towered over me. 'Heather has, shall we say, other fish to fry at the moment. You're flying solo, but a seasoned old lag like you is bound to get the hang of it.'

If the situation hadn't been so awful, I might have found Craig's next actions amusing. He stepped in front of me, pushed me out of the way and poked his finger into his brother's chest. 'She'll go when she's good and ready.'

Dylan raised his eyebrows and stared at the finger between his pec muscles as if a heavy fly had landed there. Then he pitched forwards and spoke very slowly, enunciating every syllable. 'I strongly suggest that you remove your digit before I snap it in half.' Craig's head moved back, followed by his hand.

'Now, we'll try again, shall we?' said Dylan. 'Melissa, go upstairs and get ready. There are clothes on your bed. We leave at seven o'clock and we go out the back door, not through the bar. Understand?'

I nodded, Craig remained motionless.

'Digger? Understood?' said Dylan.

'Yeah, yeah,' said Craig. 'Leave it with me, Dylan.'

Dylan's footsteps reverberated up the stairs to the bar and then as he ascended the staircase to the bedrooms. I heard Craig sniff and instinctively I put out a hand to his shoulder. I was about to ask him if he was all right – not that I really cared – when he slapped my hand away and said, 'You heard the man. It's time to get ready. Enough of the freeloading.'

My God, what happened to these brothers to make them like this? What sort of a family did they come from?

CHAPTER FORTY-FIVE

It is two days before I'm discharged from hospital. In the end, out of pure desperation, I call my soon to be ex-husband Adrian and ask him to pick me up and take me home. Once he finishes his lecture down the phone on how not to get rammed by random strangers through no fault of your own, he sashays his way to the ward and escorts me to the car park. He insists that I wait by the entrance on the bench reserved for those wishing to smoke themselves to death, despite the sign telling them to do it elsewhere.

The Mazda MX5 edges across the waiting zone and the world's most careful driver pulls up. He leaps from the car and minces towards me. It is the first time that I wonder if he is actually gay. I had never before realised how camp he is and perhaps that was what had attracted me to him.

These are the things that crowd my head once I find myself not only alone, but with nothing to do and no means of getting out of the house. I was advised to take it easy and recuperate. That is all well and good, except I have very little means of making sure I've even got the essentials in, let alone taking it easy.

Once my soon to be ex-husband leaves my house, I set about checking the cupboard and fridge for any means of sustenance. Unsurprisingly, there's sod all. I toy with the idea of a takeaway, then I realise that I don't have any cash and the last time I tried to pay by credit card online, I was met with a website unfit for purpose that sent me in endless circles until I gave up and made a Pot Noodle.

Then a thought struck me – Nigel, I bet he's got food.

He may only live a couple of doors away, yet it still takes me ages to get there. Once at his door, I bang with as much vigour as I can muster and pray he answers. His Toyota is on his driveway, so I guess that he's home. It doesn't mean that he wants visitors. Would I open the door to a random knocking at seven o'clock on a Friday night? Hardly.

To my astonishment, he flings open the door. 'Dear girl, you look like death warmed up. What happened?'

What is it with this man that makes me want to cry? My bottom lip wobbles and my cheeks are wringing wet.

'For pity's sake, come in.' He puts a steady hand on my arm and leads me inside to the comfort of his home.

Once I'm back in the same chair, he assures me that Willy is safely tucked up and urges me to tell him what he can do to help. The kindness of his words almost set me off again, but I refrain from crying and try my best to explain.

'I think it's all my fault, you see,' I manage to say after several tissues are passed my way – I notice that the silk hankies aren't being handed out left, right and centre. 'If Katie hadn't been driving me to the police station, we wouldn't have been rammed.'

Nigel examines his fingernails for a couple of seconds and then harrumphs. Until this point, I didn't even know that humans actually made this sound. I am tempted to smile, but

I've too much on my mind to enjoy myself. Katie may actually die. And it will all be my fault.

After several moments, Nigel settles back in his armchair and says, 'Why are you blaming yourself? You couldn't possibly have known what would happen, could you?'

He's completely correct. There is no way I could have known, and still, I feel so guilty. I struggle to find the words to explain how I'm feeling without telling all to Nigel. Then again, perhaps I should tell him everything. It would be the only time I have ever been completely honest with another human being. Up until this point, I've lied to everyone I've ever been in contact with. But can I really trust this man with his insane purple trousers, cravat and blazer combo? Where does this man shop? The eighteenth century?

I rest my head against the back of the chair. 'My name's not really Avril.' For the briefest of moments, I'm not entirely sure whether I said that out loud. Perhaps I only breathed out and imagined I spoke. Then Nigel breaks into my thoughts.

'What is your name?' His voice is as smooth as his silk hankies.

'It's Melissa. Melissa Collins.' I stay where I am, head back, eyes closed. If I treat this as a therapy session, I can pretend that afterwards, Nigel will be bound by a code to keep my dirty secrets and not tell the police. Or Rena. Or anyone else who comes to find me.

To fill the silence, and not wanting to stop now in case I lose my nerve, I carry on pouring out my heart.

'I had a very normal upbringing. Boring, but normal. I took it for granted. It all started so well – parents, nice home, little sister to torment and play with. Then it took a tumble.'

I catch my breath. I can't believe I'm telling another living person this. After so long, all those years of thinking I should keep it all in, here I am regurgitating my life to someone I've only spoken to on a handful of occasions.

I sit forwards, my arms resting on my thighs. 'She was a wonderful kid: kind, funny, she lit up any room she walked into. Then when she was thirteen, she became ill. Leukaemia claimed her and there was nothing we could do. Nothing except sit and watch her fade away. It was hard on us all, my mum the most. I suppose it would hit any mother like a physical blow, yet mine seemed to take it personally and started to resent me and the fact that I was the healthy one.'

'I'm sure that's—'

I put my hand up to stop him. I've heard this before from counsellors, from the few friends I had at school at the time, from other members of the family, but I know how I'd felt, how my mum had made me feel. Like the second-best daughter had made it out alive.

'She'd have been happier if I'd died,' I say through gritted teeth. 'I overheard her once. After my sister's death, she had a friend round for moral support and to drink tea and be a shoulder to cry on. My mum didn't know that I had come home early from the shops. I heard the two of them in the kitchen. They were sitting at the table, the door was ajar, and as I walked through the front door, I heard my mum crying – which was nothing new – and then she said, she said...' I look at up the ceiling. There's a crack running the width of the room. I focus on its path from the coving to the light cluster in the centre to resist the temptation of glancing at Nigel.

'My mum said, "I wish it had been Melissa and not Natalie. I would find the whole thing so much easier."'

Nigel gasps. Credit to him, he then coughs to make it appear as if he isn't appalled that a mother would say such a thing. Composure regained, he says, 'I'm sure that you didn't hear her properly, or she was referring to something else, such as, erm, such as, well, I don't know. Perhaps one of you inherited your grandmother's chin?'

If I can't smile at that, what can I smile at?

'Anyhow, from that moment on, I really didn't care for my parents, or anything they had to say. My dad ignored me from the day of Natalie's diagnosis, so I guess he felt the same.' I feel exhausted all of a sudden and then remember that I've only just come out of hospital and I am supposed to be at home taking things easy.

'Where are my manners?' says Nigel. 'I haven't even offered you a drink. How about something to eat?'

My stomach rumbles. It's been about six hours since I had a warm, curly NHS cheese sandwich. 'Well, I wouldn't say no to a little something.' I give him a pathetic look and hope it's done the trick.

'Are you on all sorts of medication?' Nigel stands up and gestures towards a wine rack. 'I have a lovely Pinot Grigio in the fridge or I can uncork a red.'

'I had planned on co-codamol and the scrapings from a jar of Branston pickle, but I prefer your offer. The Pinot would be lovely.'

'You stay where you are, I'll get you a glass and then make us something to eat.' He winks at me – I like it. It makes me feel as though we're co-conspirators. 'We can have a little late supper on lap trays. How about that? Then you can finish telling me why you're pretending to be someone else, and then I'll escort you home.'

I am powerless to resist, so I sit back, and wait for my wine and supper.

CHAPTER FORTY-SIX

THEN

I got out of the pub cellar in record time and rushed up the stairs to the bedroom I shared with Heather. When I opened the door, I expected to see Heather lying on her bed, eyes closed and pretending to be asleep. Instead, the room was empty. Her clothes were also gone from the hanging space in the alcove. I ran to the bathroom and saw that her stuff had also been removed. I was about to turn and go back down to the bar and demand that someone explain, when a door further along the corridor opened and she stepped out.

Heather was wearing a pair of midnight blue pyjamas, the bottoms skimming the carpet and her sleeves pulled down over her hands. She didn't look as pale as the last time I saw her, but she still didn't appear to be the picture of health.

'Heather.' I stopped in my tracks and waited for her to speak.

'Dylan thought it was time that I had my own room.'

I noticed that it was about her and not about neither of us having to share. Only, something stopped me from speaking my mind. I had never been completely certain that I could trust this woman, but now she was sleeping in the daytime, in brand-new pyjamas and she had a room of her own without anyone bothering to tell me.

'What's going on? I had no idea you'd taken your stuff and left me.'

Heather pointed at the door behind her. 'I'm in here. It's what, six feet away?' With her sleeves over her fingers, she seemed childish. Everything about her said young and vulnerable. And I suppose that she was, we both were. Men had been taking advantage of us and we had continued to let them. I knew it had to stop. The only problem was, I didn't know how.

'Why are we being split up?' There was a tone to my voice that I hadn't intended, yet it seemed to jolt her into the here and now. Her eyes widened and she crossed her arms.

'We aren't a couple, Melissa. It's about time that you started to stand on your own two feet and give me some distance. Dylan has done this for both of us, so stop complaining.'

I took a step nearer. 'I can't believe what I'm hearing from you. It was you that dragged me into this in the first place, destroyed any chance I had of normality, and then you smashed someone's head in and I had to take care of it.'

Heather snorted with laughter. 'Really? You had to take care of it? I think you'll find it was Dylan, Craig and Kenny.'

'And only because *I* called Craig. How good is your memory?' By this time, I was within an arm's reach of her. 'What exactly is the matter with you? You look bloody awful.' I had worried for some time that Heather might have been on drugs. There were dark circles under her eyes and now that I was up close, I could see that her skin was blotchy.

A noise behind her startled me, although not as much as the sight of Dylan coming out of her bedroom. I stood with my mouth open, glancing from one to the other, understanding what was going on, while not wanting to accept it. He stood behind her and placed a hand on each of her shoulders.

'Melissa, you're supposed to be getting ready.' He leaned towards Heather's ear and said in a stage whisper, 'And I've told you to stay in bed.' He gave me a grin that drained my spirit and felt the need to add, 'What with you in your condition.'

'Are you preg...' I couldn't even bring myself to finish the sentence. Now it was so obvious, I couldn't believe how stupid I had been. That first night, Dylan staring at me, all the while watched by Heather. She had well and truly made her move as soon as she saw an opportunity to get herself out of the mess she'd made. The mess, I don't need to remind myself, that she created for both of us. All this time, she had been having sex with Dylan and I hadn't noticed a thing. This woman really did have the morals of a polecat.

I stood in the corridor and gave them both a slow handclap. 'You've excelled yourself there, Hev. I have to hand it to you, you have played an absolute blinder.'

It took two seconds for Dylan to step around her and pin me up against the wall with one hand. 'Now, you mouthy little slag, get in there, get ready and be downstairs by seven. If you didn't have to go to work, I'd give you a reminder of what happens when you step out of line.' He grabbed my face with the hand that wasn't crushing my windpipe and squeezed my cheeks together. 'And fucking smile when you're out tonight. Mess this up and it's the end of the line for you.' Spittle hit my skin and it was all I could do to keep from crying.

CHAPTER FORTY-SEVEN

THEN

I got myself dressed up like a dog's dinner, as per Dylan's directions, and made sure that I went through the kitchen to the back door. Craig was waiting for me in his car. He flashed the headlights at me across the car park and I walked as quickly as I could in the ridiculous three-inch high-heeled shoes that men thought women should wear. I got into the car with some difficulty and shut the door without a word.

'You look terrific,' said Craig. He leaned across and kissed my cheek. 'There's no need to be nervous; I'll be there the whole time. This is only an escort service, nothing too difficult for someone with your talents.'

I glanced down at my 'talents' which were squeezed into a dress that was as tight as it was short. I could have balanced a tray of drinks on my boobs and knew that if I attempted to bend over in any way, everyone behind me was going to see straight up my Chatham Pocket.

'I picked out the shoes,' said Shit For Brains.

'Oh,' I said. 'I didn't know that.'

Craig made a nodding motion that I presumed meant that he thought he had done a good thing. He really was a moron.

Sadly for me, he was a moron who was in charge of my future if I didn't handle this right.

'Where are we going?' I said, aware he was about to salivate all over me as he stared at my bare legs.

'Don't you worry, princess, it's for me to worry about. All you have to do is carry on looking luscious.'

He drove us out of the car park and onto the road. The traffic was building up considering it was outside of most people's commute. I thought about grabbing the wheel and driving us into another vehicle, but what if I accidentally caused someone's death. What if I survived but I wasn't able to talk or move? Craig might claim I was his beloved and take me home. I would be at his mercy. The thought of a bed bath from this lustful lunatic made me shiver.

'If you're cold, I can turn up the heater,' said Craig. His paper cut thin bottom lip stuck out when he was being sincere. I fought the urge to grab it and pull it over his head.

'Thanks, but I'm okay. Someone just walked over my grave.'

Craig suddenly braked and after a honk from the driver of the car that almost drove into the back of us, he pulled over. 'Do not ever say that.' His expression put me on edge. Why that was such a trigger for him, I had no idea.

'It's a saying,' I said. 'I'm sorry if it bothers you. I didn't mean anything by it.'

He pursed his lips and raised his eyebrows at me. 'I won't hear any such nonsense about your grave. You know that I don't want to take you to this party, don't you?'

As I opened my mouth to speak, he shushed me (by the way, women love that as much they love men picking out their shoes and clothes) and moved a little closer to me. His hand was in my hair, then his mouth was on my cheek.

'I'm besotted with you, Melissa,' he said. 'The day you called me to help you was the best day of my life.' He broke off the hair stroking to try his luck with my breasts. 'I'd do anything for you.'

'Then let's get away from all this,' I said.

The reaction was instant. His head jerked backwards. A total transformation took hold of him. 'No, we need to go to the party. It's Dylan's orders. You have absolutely no idea what'll happen if we don't get you there on time.'

Craig put the car in gear and pulled out into the traffic, scarcely checking the road was clear. He remained stony faced the entire fifteen-minute journey to a cul-de-sac where he drove to the end and parked in front of a large, detached property that was both equally unique and vulgar. It was a two-storey house with a large, open, front garden and a tall fence either side adjoining the walls. It gave it an air of being both secure and welcoming. The only problem was that there were a series of statues across the lawn, one of which was a large plastic giraffe, and the façade of the building was painted a shade of pink that would have made Barbie say, 'Don't take the piss.' There was also a fountain by the front door adorned with flashing lights. I dreaded to think what was going on inside.

'You want me to go inside that house?' I said. 'Who lives here?'

'That's not important. You only have to do what you're told, and I'll take care of the rest.'

Craig was talking to me as if we were strangers. In some ways we were, despite knowing one another for what felt like a lifetime, yet was only something like six months. He had a weak jaw; there was nothing impressive about his profile. Being white hot angry clearly brought out the best in him – it was the most alive I had ever seen him look. It suited him, and that was scary. Crazy seemed to run in the family.

For now, at least, I needed him on side. I had no idea what I was walking into.

'Craig,' I said as I put a hand on his arm. He looked surprised. 'I'm sorry if I've upset you. I know that you only ever want what's best for me and I don't think that I've ever told you how grateful I am.' I trailed my fingers up and down his bicep. I hated myself for it, but I was running out of options here.

He leaned across, ran his tongue up and down my cleavage and reached for the glove compartment. His fingers grasped around something and with a flourish, he held a spool of red ribbon in my eye line.

'When we get home,' he said, 'Heather's in her own room now, so we can have some fun. Come on, let's get this out of the way.' He fondled the ribbon. 'Think of this as the warm-up act. The main event will be just the two of us.'

CHAPTER FORTY-EIGHT

Nigel returns to top up the wine glasses and brings knives and forks. 'I thought I had a bottle of Grey Goose vodka somewhere,' he says as he puts a set of cutlery on the arm of my chair. 'I was going to offer you a vodka and tonic, but I must have drunk it. Perhaps I'm losing my memory.'

I fiddle with the fork prongs to avoid looking at him. He's clearly very astute, so I wouldn't be at all surprised if he had seen the bottle in my kitchen. It seems that Rena has paid him a night-time visit too. That makes me madder than the thought of her creeping back into my home under the cover of darkness. Nigel has been extraordinarily kind to me, and I know it's not because of the reasons men have historically wanted to gain my approval or win me over.

I watch his retreating back as he goes to the kitchen to fetch my *supper*. I've never had supper before. Even my parents called it tea or dinner. I like it.

Nigel hands me a tray with a dinner plate half-filled with green salad and a beautifully light and fluffy omelette covering the other half. As he goes to get his own, he calls out, 'Usually I would add a little spice and fold some cheese in, but you said you'd had a cheese sandwich at the hospital.'

It makes me smile that he's remembered this detail.

He comes back with his own tray and sits down. 'Too much cheese can be hard to digest,' he adds as he picks up his knife and fork. 'You don't look as if you need anything else to stop you getting a good night's rest.

'I've always slept well. I can't imagine what it's like to have insomnia.' Nigel continues to chat away while I eat. From time to time, he takes bites of his food but carries on talking. I suppose that he is trying to give me time to enjoy my own meal without feeling that I should explain myself.

I savour every morsel and after a short while, I put my knife and fork down.

When Nigel finishes his last mouthful, he gets up and takes the tray, and once again replenishes our glasses.

'Now,' he says, purple-clad legs crossed, 'tell me what's brought you to Faversham.'

He won't let me get away with half a story, so I pick up from where I was earlier. 'My mum's words really hurt me. I didn't feel at the time as though it was something I could tackle, so I became a typical moody teenager, rebellious, a little out of control, I suppose. I ignored my parents. I mean, why would I want to talk to a mum who thought that her life would have been better if I'd have died, plus a father giving me the cold shoulder.

'Then there was my great aunt, Ivy, she was the best. She lived in Faversham, not far from here. Me and my sister used to go and stay with her occasionally in the holidays. I think it got a bit much for Auntie Ivy in the last couple of years, what with two young girls running around. I loved the area, the countryside, and it was nice to get out of the suburbs, so when my marriage disintegrated, I came to the one place I had happy memories of.'

'That wasn't your parents or anywhere you lived after leaving home?' Nigel takes a sip of his wine while he waits for me to answer.

'My parents' house, you know the answer to.' I take a swig from my own glass. 'After that, let's say, my next couple of sets of digs were not the most salubrious. I shared with a so-called friend for a while and that did not end well.'

'Where's your former housemate now?' His question touches a nerve.

'The answer to that is one I'd like to know myself,' I say, and drain my glass. Nigel is across with the bottle and fills it before I can pretend to object.

'Cheers.' I wave my glass at him and he nods. 'Her name was Heather. She was a bit older than me and lived a somewhat unorthodox life. At the time, it appealed to me. I had my entire life ahead of me and I made a decision that's had ramifications for me for the last twenty plus years. We got into trouble, a lot of trouble, with one thing and another and I'm not proud to say, I ran away and left her to face the music.'

'Hence the change of name?' I notice that Nigel doesn't replenish his own wine. I suppose that he feels the need to stay one step ahead if he has to pick me up from the pavement on my way home.

'It is the reason I now use Avril Benham instead of Melissa Collins.' Again, I pause, unsure whether I can put my faith in someone I barely know. 'A terrible thing happened, and Heather killed someone.' I look at Nigel for a reaction, but there isn't one. 'She was trying to protect me from a man who was attacking me. If she hadn't hit him, I don't doubt that I'd have died that night.'

I squeeze my eyes shut, but it does little to stop the hideous memory that refuses to leave me in peace. Up until Gary's death, I could have walked away, I could have got myself out of the flat, even if I hadn't returned to my parents, I would have made a life for myself and it would have been significantly better than this one.

'It was self-defence,' says Nigel. 'Surely the police could see that.'

I give a bitter laugh. 'No, not us, we didn't go to the police.' This is the first time Nigel makes any kind of negative reaction. I have to hand it to him, it's a fleeting look of bewilderment; still it was there. 'That's right, we thought we could take care of it ourselves and that led us to even more torment.'

CHAPTER FORTY-NINE

THEN

My initiation ceremony at the house where style and good taste went to die, could have been worse. I was mainly there to sit on seedy men's laps and pour them champagne. Several did run their nicotine-stained dirty digits up and down my legs and one lurid old bastard tried to stick his fingers under the hem of my dress. As the hem was barely covering my crotch, his intentions were very clear. I pushed him away with a smile and said that I had to go to the bathroom.

I all but galloped along the corridor until I found the third door on the left and went inside. I locked myself into a very plush downstairs toilet decorated with fancy tiles and a pile of hand towels next to a sparkling handbasin. I was just about to congratulate the house owner on managing a tasteful loo, even if it didn't extend to the rest of the monstrosity, when someone knocked on the door.

On the verge of telling them to go away, a voice said, 'Melissa, let me in. It's Dylan.'

I rushed to the door and put my ear up against it. 'Why are you here?' I said. I needed to make sure it was him before I let anyone in. I didn't trust any of these old geezers in a room full of other perverts, so being in a toilet with one was something I wanted to avoid at all costs.

'I have to make sure that Craig is handling everything okay, now open up.'

There was no one else I could think of who would know both of the brothers' names, and besides, it did sound like Dylan's voice. I unlocked the door and opened it an inch.

Dylan pushed against it, knocking me clean out of the way. He stepped inside and closed it behind him. I heard the lock click back into place. 'What are you playing at?' he said.

'Me?' I asked with a tone to match my astonishment. 'I was using the bathroom and you knocked on the door. You could have been anyone.'

Dylan's expression couldn't have been any more obvious. His eyes lingered on my breasts. 'I picked out the dress,' he said.

What was it with these penis-for-brains men and their obsession with dressing up women like cheap whores? I wondered if I had time to whip off one of my shoes and ram the heel into one of his beautiful green eyes.

'I've seen the way you look at me, Melissa. I'm not blind.' He reached out a hand and pushed my hair back from my shoulder. He played with a strand of hair, his fingers teasing out the curl at the end. 'I knew that you'd look exceptional in that dress. I know I'm not wrong.'

By now he had me pinned up against the wall. At nineteen years old (yep, I'd had a birthday while at the Hare and Hatchet and no one had even noticed) I had a dismal understanding of what was coming next. I couldn't say that I accepted what was about to happen, but what good would fighting it do? There was only so many times I could tolerate having my throat squeezed and my windpipe feeling as though it was about to be crushed before I blacked out for the last time. I tried to turn my face away, but Dylan was having none of that either.

He held my face with one hand while he undid his zipper with the other.

There was one bonus of not being allowed to wear any underwear – I had no clothing to adjust when he was done.

Dylan leant against me, panting and smiling, obviously pleased with his work.

When he had regained his composure, he pulled his trousers up, washed his hands and said, 'Get yourself cleaned up and get back out there. And not a word about this to Heather.'

I locked the door behind him, sank to my knees and cried.

This was never going to happen again. If I couldn't get away from these people, I would have to think of another way to deal with them.

CHAPTER FIFTY

I wake up with a start, unsure where I am. Initially I start to panic when I think that someone must have restrained me in some way. It takes a second or two for me to realise where I am and my fear fades away. I must have fallen asleep in Nigel's armchair.

I shake myself free from the woollen blanket he must have mummified me in and allow my eyes to adjust to the slow light from a corner lamp. The curtains are drawn so I've no idea what time it is and I don't have my watch on. There is a freshness to the air, so I guess that it's the early part of the morning where even the birds don't quite fancy facing the day. I can't hear a thing. I see a piece of paper on the floor a couple of feet in front of me.

I pick it up and take it over to the corner lamp.

> *Young lady,*
> *Please feel free to help yourself to tea, coffee, etc.,*
> *and if you wake early and want to take yourself to bed,*

I have made up the spare bed in the back bedroom.
Don't go home until I awake – I don't think you should
be by yourself until you're feeling a little stronger. You
had a nasty accident.
Nigel

I hold the note to my chest. He cares more about my well-being than my ex-husband of fifteen years. It doesn't escape my notice that he added in a reference to the accident causing my weakened state so I didn't mistake it for him meaning the half of the sorry story I told him. If only my mental health could be fixed like my physical health. I doubt my mind will ever recover.

There is a noise from the cage in the corner of the room. Bloody hell, I'd forgotten all about the weasel. At least he is in his cage and it's reassuring to know that Nigel doesn't sleep with the bloody thing. Another weirdo in my life is something I can do without.

I pour myself a glass of water in the kitchen. The display on the microwave clock tells me it's 4.38 am and I think that I probably should go home, despite Nigel's suggestion to curl up in his spare room. As tempting as it is, I have to face the music some time.

I go back to the living room and find my shoes, phone and keys and can't resist a peep outside in the street. I almost jump out of my skin when a shadow crosses the window. I hold my breath and hear movement outside. Was that a person? It was far too large to be a fox and unless the bison have escaped and made their way up from Canterbury, there is nothing else in the English countryside that could possibly throw a shadow of that size and height.

I strain to make out any sort of noise and the poxy weasel

decides that this is the perfect moment to start thumping about in his cage. I can hear someone outside, I'm absolutely sure what I can hear is them moving along the front of the house in the direction of mine. I hesitate about whether to try and confront them. That would be incredibly stupid, or to call the police, who are unlikely to get here before they have disappeared into the countryside, or if I should make a lot of noise and turn lights on.

I decide that my best plan is to do nothing. If this is Rena or her friend John lurking about, I shouldn't bring attention to Nigel's door. None of this is his fault. For once, I should do the decent thing and not use those who have only tried to help me.

I crawl over to the lamp, switch it off and eke back the curtain. I peer through the two-inch gap, one eye searching out the intruders I know are outside. I still can't hear anything, but then I smell it – smoke.

'No, no,' I say, looking round for my phone. I have to wake Nigel up and let the rest of the neighbours know. I dial 999 and tell the operator I need the fire service. My legs won't work and I don't think I can make it to the top of the stairs without passing out. I shout up the stairs to Nigel and almost instantly I hear movement.

He appears in silk pyjamas – obviously – and I think he's wearing a smoking jacket over the top. I don't have time to take it in before I shout, 'Fire!' at him.

The operator is asking me where the fire is and is anyone trapped inside. I have no idea so without thinking and despite Nigel's voice booming out telling me to stay where I am, I rush out into the street.

There's a flicker of flames at my living room window. The curtains are on fire. What absolute new hell is this. I feel my knees start to buckle and watch as the heartbeat of red slowly devours the front room.

Nigel appears beside me, puts one arm around me to stop me from falling and takes the phone from me with his other hand. I can hear him speaking to the operator, but I take no notice of what he says.

I stand dumbly and wait for the sound of sirens.

CHAPTER FIFTY-ONE

It's a few moments before Rena completely gets to grips with what's happened. Her mind can't fully take on the facts that are being crammed inside it. Avril wasn't at home and the fire was put out before it spread too far. It really shouldn't have come to this, and yet she couldn't see any other way. Things are about to explode and if she had any time, not to mention money and a passport, she would be out of the country quicker than anyone could say double-crossed.

Rena had to spend the night in her nasty flat. Sometimes it was best to be at home with an alibi rather than charging around all over the country. It would be easier to prove where she was for starters. Secondly, she was tired, so a night in her own bed wouldn't be the worst of things.

Only, she couldn't find sleep. It was always one step ahead of her. Even in prison she had always slept well, although she had less on her mind then. Everything that happened from here on was personal and she knew who was going to pay for it. It wouldn't be her; it would be the bitch that had cost her everything.

Rena glances across at the broken window as she waits for her coffee to brew. This had all been that sodding woman's fault and she would make sure she knew the true meaning of suffering by the time Rena was done with her.

225

CHAPTER FIFTY-TWO

I watched the season change from winter to spring and then waited for the promise of summer. Heather was waddling around by this time, patting her stomach and being a smug cow about everything. Dylan didn't exactly fawn over her, but he did fret if he thought she was overdoing things. The closer it got to her due date, the more the pair of them got on my nerves. I was expected to carry on my escorting duties, dressed up like a dog's dinner, tottering around on impossible heels, and being nice to disgusting men. The only mercy was that I was only having sex with about one in ten of them who rubbed my thighs and dribbled on my breasts. All in the name of keeping a roof over my head.

That said, I couldn't have got away if I'd have wanted to. Any time I did leave the pub, it was either to be driven to a gathering of the sexually depraved, or walked around by Craig or Dylan.

One afternoon I was in my room flicking through a magazine when I heard Heather cry out from her room across the hall. At first, I wondered if it was Dylan trying his luck with his pregnant hostage. Then something in the urgency of her crying hit home. This was a different sort of sound.

I ran across the hallway and burst into her room. There she was on her bed, dressing gown open and her hands between her legs. She held them out towards me.

'Shit,' I said at the sight of blood on her hands. 'I'll get help. Don't panic, I'm sure it'll be fine.' I really didn't think it would be fine, but there was little point in letting her know that.

I took the stairs two at a time and found Debbie, the new barmaid, leaning against the bar braying with Pearl. They both raised an over-plucked eyebrow at me.

'Dylan,' I said. 'Is he here? It's Heather, there's something wrong with her.'

'Stay here,' said Pearl, getting to her feet. 'Debbie, keep tabs on the pub. I'll go and make sure she's all right.'

Debbie, all five foot three and seventeen stone of her, moved to the other end of the counter where two of the regular late afternoon punters were waiting for their swift pint on the way back to their middle-class suburban homes. As soon as she was twenty feet or so away, I scanned the bar and focused on the late afternoon watery sunshine visible through the window.

For once I had on jeans and a sweatshirt and I had my knock-off Adidas trainers on, bought for me from Folkestone market by Craig. I had never tried running in them, but even in my slut shoes, I knew I could outrun Debbie.

A surreptitious glance in her direction and I ambled to the edge of the bar where Pearl had left the countertop up and the waist high door pinned back in her hurry to get to Heather. It was now or never.

I raced across the pub, threw open the door and ran for my life.

CHAPTER FIFTY-THREE

THEN

I ran and ran until my lungs felt as if they would burst. I tore through the streets, trying to get myself as far from the pub as possible. I had no idea where I was going and couldn't get my bearings. Craig had driven me most of the places I had been in the last four or five months and as much as I had tried to pay attention, I was still clueless. One thing I did see on a road sign was the word Faversham.

I stopped and ducked into the doorway of some flats to get my breath back. I stood panting and scanned the streets. It was fairly busy with late afternoon shoppers, mums dragging their children home from school and commuters making a bid for freedom before the rush hour kicked in. I waited for a car to draw up and Dylan or Kenny or some other crazy person to pull up and drag me inside and take me back to my prison.

I looked at the faces of those wandering up and down the road and wondered if anyone would help me if I asked them. Would the police take me seriously if I said I had been kept against my will and made to sleep with men and act as an escort? Similar thoughts had crowded my mind since the very first moment Craig took us from the flat to the pub. Only, since the day we'd stuffed Gary inside a trunk, I had been raped, beaten and attacked without the supposed freedom of walking away. Dylan had made it very clear to me on multiple occasions that Heather and I were his girls, and we weren't going anywhere without his say so.

I felt like collapsing on the spot and sobbing until someone helped me. Then I remembered that seldom had anyone come to my rescue and the last time I had asked for assistance, that came in the form of Craig.

Wallowing in my own misery was not going to get me out of this. I needed to get a grip and take action. I put my hand in my pocket and found a couple of coins. I had found them down the back of a sofa in the pub when I was having a late-night drink with Craig and he had me pinned down. As soon as he got up to clean himself up, I felt between the seat and the back where I had heard his change fall. There was at least four pounds and that should be enough to get me away from here.

The best plan I had was to catch a bus to Faversham and hope that worked out. The first problem I had was knowing where the bus stop was. Once I figured out the route, the next part was to hide near the bus stop somewhere so that anyone driving or walking by wouldn't see me.

Once I regained what little composure I had, I asked a couple of people to direct me to where I needed to be and then hung around in a nearby charity shop until I saw the bus approaching.

I got on, paid the driver and tried to make myself invisible. I was petrified and exhilarated at the same time. I sat on the back seat of the double-decker bus, hardly able to believe my luck at getting away. Then I started to doubt myself. Perhaps they hadn't really kept me against my will all that time. What if I had imagined it and I was free to go at any time? That couldn't have been a thing, surely? Why would I stay with someone who was forcing me to do the things I'd been doing for no pay and just to stay in a room and avoid being on the streets?

Wasn't that what I'd done when I had lived with Heather in our flat?

No, no, this was definitely different. Naturally, things were frequently unpleasant – I wouldn't pretend otherwise – but we had some choice over who we let into the flat and who we did what with. At least, I thought we did. Perhaps I was wrong.

The bus rattled on, stopping at places I didn't recognise and hadn't heard of. Passengers got on and off, but most of it was a blur. I tried to make sense of whether I had felt any better about living in our tiny, grotty flat than I had living in the room above the pub. It had got to the stage where I couldn't differentiate the two. Both events had become one long continuous nightmare.

It was only once the bus got anywhere near to Faversham that I stopped to wonder how Heather was. Perhaps she had lost the baby. That made me shiver and I wrapped my arms around myself for warmth. I hadn't even had time to grab a jacket. Now the adrenaline had worn off, I was feeling the drop in temperature. It was also getting dark outside and I had no idea if my great auntie Ivy was even still alive, let alone living in her modest cottage.

I knew the way from the town centre. As soon as the bus drew up by the train station, I got ready to get off – and I was aware of the looks the two women by the door were giving me – still I smiled politely and thanked the driver as I jumped off.

It took me about another hour to reach Auntie Ivy's cottage. I lost my way a couple of times, and as it was getting dark, I was amazed that I'd managed to find my way at all. I turned a corner and there it was. It was as I remembered: standard roses sat proud either side of the door and the cottage garden filled the space from the wall all the way to the neat wooden fence and gate that opened onto the pavement. The plants and shrubs weren't as full of colour as they had been when I was last here, but this time of year meant it was bursting with promise. The eternal hope of spring.

There was also a light on in the kitchen.

I stopped for a second and relished the moment. I had made it and she was going to be there to comfort me and make me a hot chocolate, just like she used to when I sought refuge here after Natalie died. This would make it all go away.

My weary feet dragged me along the pavement towards the gate. I was a stone's throw away when I saw a figure at the window. My mum's face was illuminated by the overhead strip lighting as she stood at the kitchen sink.

The elation I had felt at making it here was replaced by a feeling of dread. If my mum was here, there were only a couple of reasons. One had to be that either Ivy had passed away or Ivy needed permanent care. It had been on the cards for some time, and I hadn't wanted to do it, I hadn't wanted to give up my teenage years and my early adulthood to tend to her every need. Yet, somehow, I had given myself over to taking care of the needs of strangers for a tenner here and a bottle of vodka there.

I shrank back into the shadows so that my mum didn't see me. Not that she ever did.

I had nowhere else to go; this was the last place of safety for me. I waited until she moved away from the window and I stole through the gate and round to the back garden.

Little had changed in the garden. It had always been a bit of a wilderness. It was a wildlife garden before such things were trendy, mainly because Auntie Ivy liked the mess and the hidey-holes for badgers, hedgehogs, bats and frogs.

I tucked myself away beneath the dining room window. I sat

on the ground, my arms around my knees to keep out the evening chill that was threatening to make my teeth chatter, and listened to my mum talk down to Auntie Ivy.

'Really, Ivy, I've told you about leaving the downstairs windows open.' My mum's voice sounded like a donkey's bray, unless that was merely my interpretation. 'Anyone can get in here while you're asleep or even when you're watching the television. Neither Gerry nor I can keep coming over here, you know. We're both very busy.'

It made me angry to hear her talk like this, but I hadn't wanted to take care of the old lady either, so I wasn't in a position to criticise. It didn't stop my blood from boiling as I sat on the concrete wishing my backside wasn't numb.

'You really are going to have to come home with us this evening until we get something more permanent sorted out.'

There were protestations from Ivy, and these were immediately shut down by my mum who insisted she was going to go upstairs and pack a bag.

As soon as I was sure that she had made herself scarce, I stood up, massaged the feeling back in my posterior and stared through the window. Auntie Ivy sat with a glum look on her saggy lined face and put a lace hankie up to the corner of her eye. I tapped gently on the pane and then she looked over, momentarily confused, but her expression turning to one of happiness on seeing me.

I put a finger up to my lips and then blew her a kiss.

She looked elated to see me and tried to get out of the chair. I wildly gestured for her to stay where she was. Noises of her moving around were bound to alert my mum to something being amiss and I couldn't stand another row. I glanced up to see whether I could detect signs of my mum in the bedroom packing Auntie Ivy's battered beige suitcase, the sort that evacuees carried to places they had never heard of. Auntie Ivy refused to part with it, as tiny and impractical as it was.

Panic gripped me when I peered back through the dining room window and couldn't spot Auntie Ivy. Then I saw her bending over trying to retrieve her handbag from the floor.

'No, Auntie Ivy,' I mouthed, afraid to speak out loud. I shook my head but she wouldn't look up.

She grabbed her purse and opened the catch with arthritic fingers and grabbed a bundle of notes. She gave me a cheeky grin and with her free hand, put her crooked forefinger up against her lips. Then, with my heart in my mouth, I watched her shuffle across the carpet towards me.

'Sit back down,' I hissed at her. Nothing was going to stop her. She reached the window and with momentous effort reached up to the open top window and dropped the bundle of notes.

They fluttered down and I picked up the four twenty pound notes and the four ten pound notes.

'Pension day, love,' she said, locking eyes with me. The only problem was this tiny journey had expended all of her energy. Her worn out fingers were still gripping the top of the window, leaving her literally hanging by one frail eighty-six-year-old arm.

From the other side of the window, I tried to jump up and catch hold of her fingers as they slipped from my grip and she tumbled to the floor.

Auntie Ivy landed heavily on her right hip and cried out in pain.

I wanted to stay and help, I really did.

Only I didn't.

CHAPTER FIFTY-FOUR

I watch the fire engines arrive, firefighters charge around and put out the flames. Mercifully no one is hurt and the damage is mostly kept to the front room. Nigel stands shoulder to shoulder with me – he cuts quite the figure in his navy silk pyjamas and smoking jacket, at least, that's what I think it is. Even the chief firefighter seems to listen to him intently and while insistent that we stand well clear, checks in with us sporadically.

Of course the police arrive and I have mixed emotions at the sight of DI Louise Pengully. She has a particularly busy dress on with birds, parrots and all sorts of leafy plants adorning it. It's hideous; it suits her.

Despite my gut reaction to seeing her berating DC Katie George on this very same pavement only days ago, I have warmed to the detective inspector. She cares and that's a rare quality.

Her face seems carved out of stone as she thuds towards us from the unmarked car that she screeched up in. I take a step backwards, sure that I am about to get a bollocking for allowing someone to set fire to my home.

'Oh, my good grief, Avril.' Louise's eyes crease at the corners as she frowns. 'Either you are extremely unlucky or someone has it in for you.' She puts a hand out and her fingers linger on my forearm. It's a very tender gesture, one that threatens to make me cry since I first realised I had lost the deposit on my rental.

'I think, officer,' says Nigel, angling himself so that he is closer to me than Louise, 'Avril has had the worst time and perhaps a cup of Earl Grey or similar in my living room would suffice for now. There can't be any need for a full statement from her at this moment in time. She was, after all, asleep at my house in the armchair when she woke and realised that something was amiss and called the emergency services.'

Louise hesitates. She looks towards his home and then back at mine. 'That's a good call. First brief account now and you can make an appointment with one of my detective constables for the morning. We can even visit you at Mr...'

'Spencer-Churchill,' said Nigel.

Obviously.

'One of my officers can speak to you at Mr Spencer-Churchill's house,' says Louise, 'providing that's okay with you, sir.'

Nigel gives a small bow and waves his arm in the direction of his home. 'Why don't we go there now. I'm not used to parading in my night-time attire, so I would be more comfortable inside, if that's permitted.'

I have to hand it to him, he's charming and it works. Louise trots up his garden path, followed by myself and Nigel who has a satisfied look on his face.

Once we reach his front door Nigel says,' Oh, inspector, I think that officer is trying to get your attention.' The red-haired detective with the West Country accent who came to see me with Katie on the day of my burglary is looking in our direction. 'He waved at you,' says Nigel.

Louise turns towards him and in one fluid movement, Nigel opens the door, ushers me inside and shuts us inside his house. 'I think you've had enough for one day. Get yourself up to the spare room and I'll let you know when it's clear.'

I'm too tired to argue so I climb the stairs, steal into the room and lay down on the bed. I'm enveloped by the crisp white duvet cover as my head sinks into the pillow and I struggle to keep myself awake. The noise in the street is a welcome distraction. I don't know that I actually want to drift off before I at least get an explanation from Nigel as to why he's being so chivalrous. I don't owe him anything and yet he's got my back. I'm not used to such acts of kindness and I need to make sure that I'm not being played.

A rapping at the front door jolts me back to hyper alert. Nigel tells Louise in no uncertain terms that she can't speak to me right now. 'The poor thing is wiped out and has gone to bed.' He gives her instructions to send someone much later in the morning and he'll make sure that I'm ready by 11 am at the latest. She tries to insist that it should be earlier, but he's having none of it.

I hear the door close with a tiny bit more force than is probably necessary and for several minutes, I enjoy the peace and solitude.

I doubt it will take Rena long to find me – that's if she wasn't watching the whole thing unfold from a nearby vantage point. I know I need to get away from here to keep myself safe, and to protect Nigel from being swept up in it all. That thought gives me a start. I am actually concerned for someone other than myself. Well, that hasn't happened in a long time.

Then there's a gentle tapping at the door and Nigel says, 'Avril, are you still awake? I've made you a drink. I can leave it out here if you'd prefer.'

'I won't be a second,' I say, reluctantly getting up from the bed. It's the most comfortable bed I've laid on since the start of my acrimonious break-up, and I most certainly didn't want to ever find myself sleeping on that mattress again.

Nigel stands at the top of the stairs with a tray in his hand. On it are two mugs, two glasses and a bottle of rum. 'Now, I don't want to presume, old girl, but I'm happy to join you for a nip of rum and a hot chocolate, or I can take mine back downstairs. Whatever makes you feel more comfortable.'

'The last person who made me hot chocolate was my great auntie Ivy,' I say. 'I never got any booze in mine though.' I feel sad talking about her, although not actually guilty, which I suppose I should. Time to atone?

Nigel stands there like an overly attentive night porter. I don't have the heart to turn him away.

'Please,' I say and open the door to allow him in.

He walks to the dressing table, puts the tray down and pours two generous tots of rum. He hands me one. 'Now, help yourself to the chocolate. It is hot and I'll sit here.'

He tucks himself into a tub chair wedged between the dressing table and the wardrobe and holds the glass under his nose. He inhales and then takes a sip.

'I can't thank you enough,' I say and take a sip of my own. It's been years since I've drunk rum. A few days ago, I would have found it hysterical that 'Uncle Albert' had a bottle of dark rum, now I can't believe I live so close to this man and I've been such a twat about him.

'Happy to help.' He takes another sip and emits a sound of satisfaction.

'I have to ask why you're being so kind to me,' I ask, 'especially when I haven't exactly been the friendliest of neighbours.'

He considers my question. 'I'll explain why if you finish

your story of how you came to end up in Faversham after you and your flatmate ran away from a dead body.'

To stall for time, I get up and exchange my empty glass for the mug of chocolate.

When I'm settled back on the bed, pillows propped up behind me, I carry on my tale of wasted lives. 'It was worse than that: we didn't only leg it, I called someone to take care of the problem, and he called someone else who helped him get rid of the body.'

'Ah,' says Nigel.

'Ah, indeed.' The chocolate is comforting and stirs up memories, mostly pleasant. 'The problem with doing someone a favour is that they often ask for something in return.'

'And what did these people ask for in return?' asks Nigel.

I let out a long, slow breath. 'We had to... live under their roof for a while and repay the debt.' The noise in the street suddenly subsides, as if most of the emergency services have gone quiet to hear my confession.

'It's not as if that way of living was new to me or Heather,' I say, determined that I am not going to cry over what I did to survive. 'Except, we were forced to do what they wanted, when they wanted and who they wanted us to do it with.'

'And before that it was different?' Nigel has a great way of asking me questions in the most nonchalant manner.

'I suppose so. It wasn't lots better, to be fair, although my memory has tried to convince me over the years that it was.' I yawn and Nigel stifles one of his own.

'How did you finally get away?' he asks.

'I ran. I had the opportunity, one I passed up the first time around after Gary–'

'Gary?' Nigel tops up his glass and then mine.

'The one we... Heather killed.' I take a greedy gulp.

'And what happened to Heather?' asks Nigel.

'I have to say, you're certainly to the point with the questions. What did you say you did for a living?'

'I didn't.'

'I left Heather behind.' It's probably the first time I say those particular words out loud. 'It doesn't make me feel bad, even now, especially in light of what I recently found out about her.' I anticipate another question from Nigel at this point, but when one isn't forthcoming, I feel obliged to fill the silence. 'I had the chance to get away from a miserable, often violent, situation, and I took it. She'd have done the same. Besides, it was spur of the moment.' I hear myself and I recognise an attempt at justifying my actions from twenty years ago. Still Nigel says nothing.

'I think about Heather a lot and now I think she's back and responsible for some of what's been happening.'

This time he does have a question. 'Don't you think it's more likely to be your brunette friend and her sidekick?'

'You may be right but there's a couple of other things that only Heather would know about.' I yawn again.

Nigel stands up and takes the mug from me. 'I think you should get some sleep. I can only hold DI Pengully at arm's length for so long. She'll be here at eleven on the dot, I've no doubt. Good night, Avril.'

I close my eyes and sleep rushes to greet me before Nigel closes the door.

CHAPTER FIFTY-FIVE

THEN

It wasn't the first time I had run away, and even at the time, I knew it wouldn't be the last. I backed away into the shadows and sought refuge behind the safety of a tree. From a distance of twenty feet or so I could hear Auntie Ivy's cries for help as she lay in agony on the floor. If I could hear her, why couldn't my mum? I wrestled with my conscience. The easiest thing to do was to pound on the front door and shout, or I could alert one of the neighbours, or I could run to the phone box on the corner and phone for an ambulance. What did I do? Absolutely nothing.

It was about ten minutes before my mum came wandering into the room, her face instantly switching from indifference to full alert. I had to hand it to her, she took control of the situation and within only minutes, blue lights were filling the sky like the bat signal. I tracked the eerie glow above the rooftops as it heralded the ambulance's journey along the street and came to a stop the other side of Auntie Ivy's cottage.

What I had done so far in my life was despicable, only not as low as waiting until the paramedics took my great aunt away, my mum beside her, clutching her hand, and then breaking into her cottage.

I caused minimum damage, and I made a promise that one day I would have enough money to come back, repay her the £120 she had given me and reimburse her for the window I'd smashed.

I was dog-tired, and I needed somewhere to rest.

The next day, I helped myself to whatever food I could find, which wasn't much. A lot of it was months out of date and she had some sort of horrible long-life milk in the fridge. Why didn't she buy regular fresh cow's milk like everyone else?

Then I had a nose through her letters and private correspondence. She hadn't paid her electricity bill, her gas bill or council tax. Then I saw her shopping receipt. The amount of food Auntie Ivy bought was pitiful. I took the notes back out of my pocket and spread them on the table. I should leave this money for her. She needed it more than I did. Only, why wasn't my mum taking more interest and better care of her? She was an old lady of almost ninety years of age. Surely someone should have been looking out for her.

Under the guise of trying to find something that might help Auntie Ivy, I started going through her drawers and cupboards. I promised myself that if I found a stash of money, I wouldn't shove it in my pocket along with the rest of her cash. Deep down, I thought that was highly unlikely when she had so many outstanding utilities bills.

An hour or so later, when I'd eaten the last of the bread, used up the scrape of butter and enjoyed all four of the Jammy Dodgers in the biscuit barrel, I came across a last will and testament.

My greedy eyes scanned the pages until I got to the part where she said who was to get her house and belongings. It took me three goes at reading it before the words sank in. I got her cottage and everything in it.

This was news, big news. I had somewhere to call my own. My own home. I didn't have to share it with anyone.

I never had to worry about living with vermin ever again.

CHAPTER FIFTY-SIX

I am vaguely aware of a knocking sound, followed swiftly by voices and footsteps crossing the threshold of Nigel's oak floorboards towards his kitchen. I sit up with a jolt and rub my forehead. Everything still feels a bit fuzzy, although it's difficult to distinguish whether it's the rum, interrupted sleep or being knocked unconscious in a car accident. Then I remember that Louise Pengully is probably downstairs, with Nigel being his usual charming self and making her tea.

I gingerly get out of bed and spot a note that has been pushed under my door. It's from Nigel telling me that there are clean towels in the top drawer of the dresser and there are some of his daughter's clothes in the wardrobe, and to take whatever fits. I smile at the last line that informs me he is, 'beside myself that I don't have any spare ladies' unmentionables, but that is probably for the best.' His handwriting is exactly as I would expect; he writes with an ink pen and it's flowing and florid.

I set about making myself decent, put on a pair of three-quarter length purple trousers (perhaps they dress alike for Father's Day) and an oversized white T-Shirt.

They stop talking when I enter the living room. Louise has taken the chair I previously made myself very comfortable in and Nigel is in his usual place. 'Good morning, Avril,' says Nigel, getting up and gesturing I should have his seat. 'I'll make you a tea and then I'll leave you to it. Things to do in the garden and Willy likes the fresh air. He's out there now, having a whale of a time, or should I say weasel of a time.'

I laugh because it's polite. Louise doesn't, as she probably doesn't have a clue what he's talking about.

'How are you feeling?' she asks, getting the preliminaries out of the way.

'I'm okay. Please let me know how Katie's doing. I can't stop thinking about her.'

Louise gives a tight smile and says, 'She's still in Intensive Care. Her spleen was ruptured, which is what caused the internal bleeding and meant she had to undergo hours of surgery.' I give a small gasp and put my hands over my face. Louise continues. 'She's getting the best care. She's in a coma, but it's an induced one until the swelling on her brain has reduced and she's in a more stable condition.'

'Tell me that she's not going to die,' I say through my fingers.

'Katie isn't out of the woods yet, but she's a lot tougher than she looks, that one. I'll let you know if anything changes in the next few days.'

Nigel brings my tea and silently glides out of the room.

There is then a shift in Louise's demeanour and a tiny change in her posture which I take to mean that it's now down to business. I brace myself.

'So, Avril. Anything you want to tell me first off?'

I push out my bottom lip and shake my head.

'I know a fair bit about you, your real name for example.'

I think I've stopped breathing. It was inevitable. Sooner or later, my past was bound to catch up with me.

'I really wish you'd have told us earlier, Melissa.' Louise is staring at me, but it's not a withering look she's throwing my way. No, she seems concerned. Perhaps she is more ally than enemy after all. 'We could have kept you safe, you know.'

Louise settles back in her chair and gives a sigh. Then she waits for me to speak.

I fiddle with a lock of my hair; a habit I thought I had grown out of right before I left home. 'I'd pretended to be someone else for almost twenty years, so I couldn't see the harm in carrying on.'

'You probably would have been okay, if it wasn't for Rena Hargreaves,' says Louise. 'She would have found you no matter where you were or what you called yourself.'

'Why?' I say. 'This is what I don't understand. What does Rena want with me?'

'Pure and simple revenge,' says Louise.

'For what?' I say. 'What have I ever done to her? Until a week or so ago, I hadn't even heard of her, let alone met her.'

'When you contacted the police about Gary Lumley's body, as you know, we made several arrests.' Louise tilts her head to one side and says, 'Kenny and Dylan Caulfield and Heather Knight.'

I nod like there's no tomorrow. 'I know. I gave their names to the police during one the endless stream of interviews. *And* I was there at the trial. Where are you going with this, Louise?'

The detective inspector seems mildly surprised at my use of her first name, but she continues. 'We never caught Craig and we didn't suspect anyone else's involvement.'

I shrug. 'As far as I know, there was no one else.'

'What we didn't know and hadn't realised, much to the police's shame, was that there was another family member on the periphery. Rena Hargreaves is half-sister to the Caulfield brothers, and she shared a cell with Heather Knight when Heather moved from Holloway to HMP Bronzefield.'

All I can find to say is, 'I'm so fucked.'

CHAPTER FIFTY-SEVEN

THEN

After the trial the police took great pains to make sure that I kept away from Kent and encouraged me to learn all about my new identity. It was still an extremely lonely existence. I'd had little to lose. Even so, the adjustment was something else. I hadn't had many friends over the years and the few relatives I had were either dead or wanted nothing to do with me. The feeling was mutual. The crippling isolation gave me panic attacks and I wondered if this is what my life would always be like.

They first sent me to Skegness. The unforgiving winter got me down, while I liked the feel of the place and its seaside attitude. I managed to find a job in a pub – I knew how to pour a pint and chat to the punters – and it was reasonably well paid. Harold, the landlord of the Jolly Sailor, didn't ask too many questions either. He was particularly impressed with my beer barrel changing knowledge, and the fact that I could make a cocktail. There wasn't much call for a Gin Fizz or a White Russian in off-season Skeggy, but he was a total pisshead. He used to get me to make him a cocktail of the day to mark the end of a successful lunchtime shift and another at the start and end of the evening session. He paid me straight out of the till and often slipped me an extra tenner for locking up when he was three sheets to the wind and had to take himself off to bed early.

For the first time ever, I was having a great time. Nothing could spoil it.

Then someone walked in the door and I felt my world about to come crashing down.

Craig Caulfield pushed open the saloon bar door and headed straight towards me. Luck hadn't totally abandoned me: the gents' toilets were immediately to the left of the entrance and he ducked inside before taking much notice of anything else in the pub. This coupled with Harold being sober for once and putting in a stint behind the bar, saved me.

'Oh, gawd,' I said. 'I'm really sorry, Harold, but I've got a bit of a woman's problem. I need to nip out and, well, you know…'

He looked ashen at the thought and propelled me towards the pegs where my coat and bag were hanging. 'Take as long as you need. No, forget that – be back before the late afternoon rush.'

With the promise that I would be as quick as I could, I ran through the public bar and out onto the street.

It was a bitter, biting January day in Skegness, and the pub was only a short distance from the seafront. It was nippy on calm winter days; today's sea was full of angry promise. I wrapped my coat around me and hoped that Craig wasn't stopping for more than one drink. I didn't want to stand spying through the window – too risky – although I needed to know if he was meeting anyone and what had brought him to Skegness. It seemed a bit of a coincidence, especially in mid-January, one of the most unlikely times to visit an English seaside resort. Especially when both of your brothers were in prison, along with one of the two women you were making your living from, and the other one had given evidence against your family and then been relocated by the police.

I stood to the side of the window and tried to see what Craig was doing and whether he was talking to anyone. He had his back to me and the only other person I could see was Harold. I had to stand on tiptoes to see above the lower frosted part of the window. Harold shook his head at something Craig said and shrugged.

That was the point that Craig started to turn away from the bar and straight into my eyeline. I panicked, unsure whether to run. Harold looked directly into my wide-eyed stare and shouted something at Craig. At that moment, someone came out of the pub and through the open door I heard Harold say, 'You've used the toilet. They're for paying customers.'

Craig turned back to the bar and slapped some coins down. That was all I saw before I legged it along the road and into a newsagents. I waited until my heart had stopped going like the clappers and the man behind the counter was on the cusp of asking me if I was going to buy the woman's magazine I had been holding for five minutes, and I went back to the pub.

'Not sure what that was about,' said Harold when I got back. He made a meal of polishing a pint glass and inspecting it for smears and finger marks to avoid making eye contact. 'All I'll say is that someone was in here asking for a Melissa Collins – never heard of her, obviously. Only that fella had a photograph of someone who I swear could have passed for your double. I want no trouble in my boozer. I didn't stand for it in London and I won't stand for it here.'

'Course not, Harold.' I smoothed down my hair that had been blown about by the breeze as I rushed around hiding and spying on my past. 'The last few months have been great. I can be gone once we close up tonight.'

I stepped towards the bar where two people were waiting to be served.

Harold put his hand out to stop me. 'You have a job here for as long as you want one, Avril. Do what's best for you.'

I called my police liaison officer that evening. I was gone by midnight, my last view of Skegness was through the passenger window as I was driven away.

CHAPTER FIFTY-EIGHT

My options are limited, so I do the only thing I can think of – I run away. It's not only to save my own skin this time, but because I won't be able to live with myself if Nigel gets hurt. He has been magnificent, asking for nothing and keeping me safe. It crossed my mind on more than one occasion that perhaps he had an ulterior motive, but what exactly that was likely to be, I couldn't say.

I daren't risk going back to my own cottage, not that I have all that much there anyway. Rena knows about that, so I have to assume Heather also has the address. Plus, it's far too close to Nigel's home. There's somewhere much better where I'll find a change of clothes, some emergency supplies and a little cash.

I've checked the journey from Nigel's to my great aunt Ivy's cottage on my phone, so I'm reasonably confident I won't get lost as I stumble through the forests and fields that lie between the two properties. No one else knows about this place, so I'll be safe until I can come up with a plan.

I peek outside and it's pitch black – or as Auntie Ivy used to say, 'Black as Newgate's Knocker'. I can't stop to think about how I let her down too, this is no time for self-flagellation.

I pack what I can into my pockets, take a torch hanging by the back door and a bottle of water from the fridge and silently let myself out of Nigel's front door.

It is peaceful and I can't hear a sound.

I move out of the shadows and across the road and step into the field opposite. I expect a few slips and falls on my way, but the first twenty minutes goes well. The moon's glow adequately prevents me from landing face down until I reach the edge of the woods.

Nocturnal creatures are moving through the undergrowth, their movement given away by scratching and crunching noises. Some fall silent as I pass, some don't care I'm among them. Could be worse – it's England so nothing is going to chew my face off or drag me into a nearby river and feed me to its family. The only predators I have to worry about are the human kind.

Sporadically I take my phone out and check I'm still going the correct way. I don't want to repeatedly use it and light myself up if I am being followed, and I need to avoid running the battery too low. A fox eyes me warily and a few small mammals nip in front of me. As long as one doesn't decide to run up my trouser leg, I can deal with it. I am still relieved when I make it to the other side and see a road up ahead.

I've planned that I can get away with walking along tarmac for a mile or two. I'll see a vehicle long before its lights illuminate me, and this time in the morning, I don't expect many to pass along here.

I navigate another two fields, a copse and a cluster of cottages before I see my destination. I should stop thinking about it as great auntie Ivy's cottage, as it's mine, all mine. I would have liked the chance for a proper goodbye with her, rather than her dropping her pension money out of the window and falling to the floor. At least my mum was with her in the hospital and she didn't die alone.

I bide my time as I get closer. The neighbours have seen me come and go over the years, checking on the place and making sure nothing leaks or is about to explode. They have no idea that I was also using this as storage for an emergency grab kit. I had managed to carve out a new life for myself with Adrian, the boring bastard, always fearful I would have to take flight again.

I take my usual route along the side of the cottage to where I have left a key. The plastic section at the end of the dining room windowsill pops out easily enough and I poke my finger into the opening to retrieve the single key.

I could hear a pin drop, and one more check around the garden satisfies me that there are no spying eyes.

Within seconds I'm inside, drawing the blackout curtains as I go from room to room guided by the light from my phone. I trudge upstairs to the bedroom I have kitted out over the years for a restful night's sleep on the run. I hoped I would never have to use it, but ever since the police drove me from Skegness to Coventry, I vowed to be master of my own destiny if the need to relocate arose again. The cottage has served as a bolthole for me on days when I need to remind myself who I really am and to cherish the feeling that hardly another soul knows about my chequered past.

It was easier than I thought it would be to keep this place a secret from Adrian. There is no mortgage to take care of and the bills are all registered here so I take care of paying them and no one is any the wiser. I am not the naïve kid I once was, so as well as an escape kit here, I have another one at my rental, including my passport. Fortunately I know not to put all my eggs in one basket, as my chances of returning there for a while have been scuppered thanks to Rena and Heather. I never want to be in the position again where I run off into the street with only the clothes on my back and a few coins in my pocket. No, there's been a lot of water under the bridge since that day.

Once I make sure the place is secure and there is no way anyone is going to surprise me in the night, I take myself off to bed and fall into a deep and exhausted sleep.

CHAPTER FIFTY-NINE

I don't sleep as well as I would have liked. The bed is comfy enough yet I wake and I'm totally unrested. It's as if I feel more tired for having slept. That sensation of it being a very broken night without recalling why.

I sit up in bed and listen. There are no signs that anything is wrong; the door is locked from the inside. It doesn't stop me from getting dressed as fast as possible and picking up the old-fashioned metal clothes press Auntie Ivy used to wedge her bedroom door open with. I always figured that a handy household object would fit handsomely with the police's idea of self-defence.

The floorboards creak predictably as I move towards the door. I unlock it and fling it open, peering into the gloom of the early morning on the landing. There is only one tiny window above the stairs letting in any light. The curtains and blinds downstairs are reassuringly closed and I can't feel any draughts. So far, so good.

I open the bathroom door, check behind the shower curtain, walk to the second box bedroom and find that empty too.

The staircase moans a little under my weight, but I'm soon

downstairs and to my relief, the kitchen, tiny living room and dining room are empty. Or, at least, they are empty of people.

There on the worktop next to the kettle are the pair of baby booties from my larder behind the loose panel.

I freeze. I hold my breath, don't dare to move.

The only sound is the gentle hum of the fridge in the corner and a ticking of the wall clock.

Are they still here?

I thought that I had been so very clever, yet it seems it was wasted. Now, I'm completely isolated and no one knows I'm here. Other than my tormentors.

'Avril.' I know it's Rena even without turning round, still my feet do their duty and move so that I'm facing her.

She raises an eyebrow at what I'm holding. 'Are you going to iron me to death?' she asks, mirth all over her face.

At least she's unarmed.

'How did you find the boots?' I say, my free hand thumbing in their direction.

'Nice touch, don't you think?' She puts her hands on her hips. Today's assassin outfit is a pair of knee-length black shorts over a pair of black tights, lace-up ankle boots and a button up cotton jacket complete with a round collar. There is something pirate-like about her clothes. Under other circumstances, I might have asked her if she was going to make me walk the plank. Now is probably not the right time.

Rena grins at me. 'I sent John to fetch them. I thought you'd like them back.'

'What exactly is your hold over that poor sod?'

The maniacal beaming comes to a stop. 'You wouldn't feel any sympathy towards him if you knew his past. Want to know how I met dear John?' Rena doesn't give me time to answer. 'He was one of the prison officers who was supposed to take care of me when I was banged up. You'd be hard put to meet such a morally corrupt and despicable soul. He took mobile phones into prison for us, drugs, you name it, John smuggled it in. Mind you, the mobile phone he got me came in handy when I filmed him having sex with my cellmate.'

My mouth drops open at this. 'And your roomie being...'

Rena claps. 'First prize, Avril. You *are* paying attention. That's right, none other than Heather Knight.'

She takes a step towards me and I take one back.

'I like to treat life like a game of chess. You know, be a couple of moves in front of your opponent, and Heather was able to help me out with that.' Rena reaches for the metal iron and takes it from me. I had forgotten I was still holding it. She drops it in the sink behind me and grabs a lock of my hair.

While she fiddles with the end of it, I try to think of something to say that will bide me more time, and not provoke her. There is a madness in her eyes I haven't seen before. I've watched her take charge and wear a mask of anger, but never insanity.

'Was going to prison part of your plan?' I ask, instantly regretting my choice of question. She narrows her eyes and frowns. 'I only say that because it seems unlikely that you didn't know Heather was in prison before you were sent down.'

'No, you stupid bitch, going to prison wasn't something I planned.' Rena tugs on my hair, forcing my head around so that she's hissing directly into my ear. 'Only I know how to make the most of the opportunity. It seemed that Heather couldn't wait to tell me all about you and how you'd left her high and dry. With a baby too.'

This prompts her to let go of my hair and walk over to where the baby booties lie beside the kettle.

She holds them up and says, 'They're very pretty. Why have you kept them?'

'I honestly couldn't say.' I'm trying to think fast, except all that I manage to say are truths. 'It got to me that Heather was pregnant and I know that she gave birth in prison. I bought them to send her, but I bottled it. I, I, kept them as a reminder of the shameful things I've done.'

'Do you know what happened to the baby?' she asks. 'Gregory, by the way.'

I shake my head. 'I've wondered all these years, but the police wouldn't tell me and I didn't know how else to find out.'

Rena puts the boots back down and selects a knife from the block next to the sink. She examines the blade and says, 'He died. Hours after she gave birth to him, he died. Complications, you see. If Heather hadn't gone into labour on the wing, and say, she had never been in prison in the first place, he probably would have lived.'

She tests the tip with the pad of her index finger. As she sucks the blood from her fingertip, she stares at me. 'Of course, you understand that he was my nephew.'

'Listen, Rena, I'm sorry, I'm so sorry.' I want to cry. I really am begging her forgiveness and I'm absolutely terrified.

'Now you need to tell me where it is?' she says.

'What? Where what is? I don't know what you're talking about.' I'm full of snot and bordering on hysterics. She is unhinged and armed.

She lunges forwards and brings the knife down. It slices straight through my flesh and I fall to the ground.

CHAPTER SIXTY

I cry out, mostly in pain, but partly in fear. I watch Rena's hand pull back as she raises the knife again and all I can do is shield myself with my hands and close my eyes. Perhaps it won't be so bad and she'll do it quickly.

I hear noises and shouting. I expect Heather and John to come barrelling through the door so that they can help carve me into pieces. The stab wound in my upper arm is screaming agony and I'm losing blood, so the sight of my mum and Nigel rushing towards me must be a hallucination.

Then my mum jumps on Rena's back. Mum's Margaret Thatcher imitation pearls bounce up and down and she claws at Rena's face. In an unprecedented move – for my mum – she bites her ear. I'm fairly certain that I heard mum growl too.

The two of them crash into the kitchen table. Nigel uses both hands to push Rena to the floor and as she lands, he stamps on the hand holding the knife.

I start to pant with the pain and battle to stay conscious. I manage to keep my eyes open long enough to witness Nigel get Rena in a headlock, watch my mum kick her in the ribs and get wrestled to the floor by a police officer. There are now three officers in uniform as well as DI Louise Pengully and the West Country ginger whose name escapes me as I finally succumb to the pain and curl up in a ball.

I hear shouts around me as someone tries to stop the blood pumping out of my arm and my mum demanding that the police officers restraining her let go.

I get what I've wanted for over two decades – my mum cradling me in her arms and telling me it's all going to be all right.

CHAPTER SIXTY-ONE

I'm back in the hospital, same one, different ward. It's nice to have my mum fussing over me, and although we've barely exchanged a meaningful word since I woke up from surgery, I'm glad she's here.

Nigel arrives with a bunch of flowers. He's impeccably dressed as ever. His blazer is British racing green, the rest of his outfit is black. I see that the silk hanky has made a comeback.

'Dear girl,' he says and places the flowers on the table beside my bed. 'How are you feeling?' He leans over and kisses my cheek.

'Like I've been stabbed.'

My mum sits down and holds my hand, the one with the cannula. 'You've been told to take it easy, so not too much chatting with your friend.'

Nigel bows his head and pulls a chair up on the other side of me. 'If it hadn't been for your mother, we would not have found you in time.'

'Were it not for Nigel, I wouldn't have known that you were in trouble.' She gives my hand the tiniest of squeezes as she speaks. Her face is impassive, but the gesture means the world.

'You jumped on her back.' Despite everything, the image of my mum with her immaculate, yet age-worn less-than-thick mane of hair, writhing on Rena makes me laugh.

'I would do anything for you,' she says. She concentrates hard on the back of my hand. 'I can't believe that you disappeared like that. The police wouldn't tell me where you'd gone after the trial. They said you were an adult and it was safer for everyone if I didn't know.'

Nigel clears his throat. My mum and I latch onto the sound and centre our attention on him.

'I traced you through your birth name Melissa Collins,' he says, crossing his legs and pinching the pleats of his trousers. 'As soon as I contacted your mother, she told me that the one place you were bound to return to was the cottage left to you by your aunt. She knew that you went there occasionally.'

I stare at her. She's back to studying the freckles on my hand. 'You knew I sometimes stayed there?'

My mum sighs. 'I knew that you didn't want to see me, so I avoided any chance of bumping into you. The neighbours told me you dropped in every six months or so. At least I knew you were alive.' Her voice is charged with emotion.

I have endless questions, unfortunately I don't have the energy to match, so I contemplate feigning sleep. That really would be out of order, but much more of this intensity, and it'll happen for real.

'I can't stop for long,' says Nigel. 'I have to visit my father. Can I drop you anywhere, Mrs Collins?'

'Christina, please,' she says. 'Melissa's father will be here soon to pick me up and he'd like to drop by and say hello, if that's acceptable.'

I nod as vigorously as circumstances allow. 'Course, it is.'

I hear heavy footsteps in the corridor outside my small room. I know that this is serious as a police officer has been sitting outside the door since I got back from theatre and now Louise Pengully stands in the doorway, worry etched into her face.

My mum stands up and gives a tight smile at Louise. 'I'll get some water for the flowers and let you have a chat, love.'

Nigel kisses me on the cheek again and escorts my mum into the corridor.

'Okay if I sit down?' Louise is already in Nigel's recently vacated seat before I can answer. 'I'm sure you're fed up with everyone asking how you are, so I'll skip straight to it – why did you run off in the night? It was bloody dangerous, you could have been killed.'

I lean back into the pillows. 'I didn't want Nigel to get involved. He's an old man. He could have got hurt.'

Louise taps her fingers on the moveable bedside tabletop. 'Do you know that he's a retired army vet?'

I scratch my head. 'He said something about shooting horses once so that makes sense.'

'Not that sort of vet! A veteran. He was in the army for over forty years. He retired as a major, worked in intelligence and stayed well beyond his tour of duty. How do you think he located your parents so quickly?'

'I assumed it was a Google search.'

'I don't know if you're trying to be funny, glib or you really are this thick-skinned, but you're lucky he's on your side and got to you as quickly as he did. Rena would have killed you, no doubt about it.'

We sit in silence for about a minute. Louise cracks first. 'We searched your house and found a couple of spools of red ribbon, the same kind that we found in Joan Fielding's house. The ends are a mechanical fit with one of the spools.'

'Meaning?'

'Meaning,' she says as the finger tapping gets faster, 'that someone used a pair of pinking shears to cut the ribbon and then left the shears and reel of ribbon in your house, the rest at Joan's. Rena was going to implicate you in Joan's murder and take you down with her.'

'She didn't do a very good job. For a start, you haven't arrested me and she left her fingerprints on the knife used to stab Joan.'

Louise considers this for a second. 'She's been interviewed and admitted to killing Joan, so exactly why she'd want to drag you down with her, but then confess, will probably be something that we'll never get to the bottom of. Leaving her fingerprints behind is too much of a basic error for her, so it's as if she wanted to get caught.'

Or wanted to give me a very clear message.

Even though I'm on some pretty good drugs, I know that this was all about tormenting me to the point of madness. The condolence card, the bereavement flowers, coming home to my door wide open and her running through my home with a knife. Rena is all about revenge and settling scores.

She's not the only one.

CHAPTER SIXTY-TWO

I'm surprised that she agrees to see me in prison, and I'm even more surprised when I find myself in the visiting area waiting for her to be brought up from the wing. I thought a hundred times that I would change my mind and flee in horror at having to face her. Everyone told me it was a bad idea, but I had to know, I had to put things to rest.

I sit with my hands folded in my lap, willing myself not to fidget or pull expressions that would give away my nervousness.

I look towards the guards at the back of the room who are escorting prisoners across to see their nearest and dearest, or in my case, main prosecution witness.

I stand up.

'You came,' said Rena. She looks tired but strangely rested and at peace.

'I wasn't sure you'd see me.' I sit back down and she takes the seat opposite me at the table for four.

'I won't lie, I've little else to do in here.' She looks towards the barred windows. 'And plenty of years to do it in.'

'Why did you do it, Rena? I sat through the whole of your

trial and didn't once hear you give a plausible explanation for why you murdered that woman in her bed?'

Rena tucks her hair behind her ears. The left one has a small chunk missing at the top. I try not to stare at my mum's handiwork.

'I needed to get your attention,' she says. 'That idiot John Smith wasn't supposed to flail about on the pavement right in front of you. He was another one who couldn't follow simple instructions. He was supposed to burgle your house and then keep lookout.

'Being burgled didn't really seem to spook you, so when I saw that old woman a few doors away, I couldn't believe my luck.' She leans across the table, gives me a long, slow wink and blows me a kiss. 'If you hadn't got my heart racing, I might not have found the strength to kill her. You've a lot to answer to.'

Suddenly I don't want to be here. I don't want to be responsible for anyone else's death. I've enough blood on my hands. I start to get up.

'Wait, Avril or Melissa, or whatever you prefer to be called. Because of you my brother Kenny hanged himself in his cell and Dylan got into a fight days after being released and got himself kicked to death. My baby nephew died and I have no idea what happened to Craig.'

I blink rapidly at the sound of his name.

'And I know that you had something to do with his disappearance.' There is a sharper, more accusatory tone to her voice. 'I asked you where it is, I won't give you the satisfaction of asking again.'

'I don't know what you mean.' I'm indignant that she is talking nonsense, yet Rena isn't falling for it.

She throws her arms wide open. 'What am I going to do to you in here? At least let me know one way or another. Have you got it or not?'

I stand up, weigh up how long it will take me to get to the exit before she can attack me, and I say, 'Yes, I have it.'

Then I rush to safety and away from her reach.

CHAPTER SIXTY-THREE

There is one more thing that I have to take care of and this one is extra special.

I sit in my X4, the new car smell still hanging on in there, and watch the front door. I've already been here four times and I know from a little bit of research by Nigel that there are three people officially registered as living here, although one is currently staying at her boyfriend's.

Nigel said it was the last favour he was going to do for me, but smiled as he told me that he hadn't been operational in the army after his active career came to an end, so it was 'absolutely marvellous to be doing something akin to the Army Intelligence Corp days all over again'. I still don't know exactly what he did or how he managed to find the answers so fast, but I repaid him with a crate of wine and a bottle of the most expensive port I could find.

At last, I see the front door open and a young girl of about twenty-five comes out with a backpack and turns in the direction of the town centre. That left only one other person inside.

I get out of the car and go to the boot. I love my new car, especially its spacious boot.

I grab the suitcase by the handle and manoeuvre it to the ground. Once I've locked the car – it's new, it's mine and the neighbourhood is rough as hell – I wheel it towards number eighty-three.

There's no gate. If it turns hostile, my getaway is that much quicker.

I push the case as far towards the front door as it will go, bang on the knocker and then move back six or seven feet.

Heather Knight opens the door. Her face has aged, unsurprisingly, and she's put on weight.

'Your hair suits you shorter,' I say.

She doesn't move and there isn't much of a response.

'That's for you.' I point at the case.

'After everything you took from me, you bring me your dirty washing?'

'Heather, there's no point in me telling you how sorry I am for everything that happened. No words will make anything okay.' I point down at the case again. 'Keep it safe and make sure no one else knows you've got it. It's a lot of money.'

She gives me a searching look, the first reaction.

Heather bends down and grabs at the zip.

'Not here! You need to take it inside.' I glance up and down the street. I didn't know if the wisest thing to do was bring it to her, but I didn't know what else to do with it.

I help her lift it over the step.

'It's used notes and small denominations, but don't flash it around—' We lock eyes and I let go of the handle. 'You'll manage, I'm sure.'

I turn to leave.

'Mel, where did it come from?'

'Let's call it payback from an old acquaintance who sadly is no longer with us.'

I get back in my car and drive to Faversham where the rest of my life is in front of me. That's more than I can say for Craig Caulfield.

***

Twenty months ago

'You had better not be stringing me along, Melissa.' Craig had agreed to meet me, albeit on the insistence that it was somewhere far from anyone or anything else.

'Why would I do that?' There was a neediness to my tone and I didn't like it. I didn't want him to see that even after all this time, I was still scared of him. 'We're in this together.' Although it sickened me to do it, I touched his arm and ran my fingers up and down his bicep. 'We make a good team, so why would I jeopardise that?'

'I worry that you're getting the idea you can go off and do what you want again, like you did last time?' He stared at me, his weak chin wobbling.

'Hey, how much better are we together?' I didn't want to keep up this pretence, but I wasn't entirely sure where the money was kept. I had a good idea, but that wouldn't be enough for me to flee and do it properly this time. I had paid my dues for grassing up the Caulfield family and Heather. I had spent the next two years working in pubs, moving from bedsit to bedsit wherever the police put me. Then I had the good fortune to meet a man so boring and predictable, he was never going to suspect anything I did when he was off at endless meetings and work events. He never questioned the history I wrote for myself either.

'I'm sorry about Dylan, I really am.' I felt him flinch as I said his brother's name. 'He didn't deserve to die, but he's gone and it's time that we started to move on.'

'Move on! Most of my family are dead because of you.' He grabbed my arms and pinned them to my sides. It didn't escape my notice that he leered at my breasts as he held me tight.

'Hey, listen to me. They are dead because Heather killed a man and you were decent enough to help us. That's why they're not here. I've been living a lie for so long, all I want to do is start afresh with you.' I took advantage of his lessening grip on my arms and put a hand up to stroke his face. 'You know that all I want to do is be with you. Only…'

I pulled off my best rueful look and started to cry – right on cue.

'Hey, babe. Don't get upset. It won't be long now, I promise.'

The simpering sap smoothed down my hair and chucked me under the chin. No, Craig, you total sad wanker, just no.

'How long?' I pleaded with him.

With a flourish, he pulled a key from his pocket. 'Remember the lock-up I told you about?'

'Er, not really.' My eyes smiled up at him.

'Oh, Melly, you don't listen. Typical woman!'

Not the chin chucking again, Craig. You really are asking to die.

'The lock-up in Ham Street behind the garage and MOT place.'

'Oh, course.' I rolled my eyes for good effect. 'What am I like?'

'Gorgeous, that's what you're like.'

This was the moment he thought it was a good idea to run a hand down my back and towards my arse. The only problem was that I couldn't let him do that because I had a pair of secateurs in my jean's pocket.

I reached towards them and in one deft movement, had them in my hand and straight through his eye before he even realised what had happened.

I watched him die, uncurled his fingers wrapped around the key and went off to reclaim what was rightfully mine.

THE END

EAST RISE SERIES

Mercy Killing

Buried Secrets

Lost Lives

Don't Trust Him

ACKNOWLEDGEMENTS

A huge thank you from me to everyone who has helped with Twisted Lies. Since joining the Bloodhound kennel, I've been made to feel so welcome, and can't begin to describe the support and enthusiasm from each member of the team. Huge thanks to Betsy Reavley and Fred Freeman for their unwavering support of this novel. Lexi Curtis and her astounding social media graphics. Hannah Deuce for her second to none marketing skills. Shirley Khan, thank you, thank you, thank you. Your editorial skill and sharpness have been invaluable. Maria Lee for proofreading and pointing out things I somehow missed – again! Tara Lyons for all her behind-the-scenes production wonders and editorial support, and just about anything else. I'm indebted to each of you.

Massive thanks to Joanna Swainson, my agent, and her superb team at Hardman & Swainson for championing this novel.

Caroline Leighton has once again helped me out with her medical expertise and knowledge of injuries and hospital treatment. I hope you know how grateful I am for your insight and assistance. Any mistakes or liberties for artistic licence are down to me and not Caroline's amazing medical background.

Matt Johnson, friend, author, ex-soldier, retired police officer, thank you. As was no doubt clear from our conversation, I have no experience or knowledge of the military. Thank you for trying to explain it to me. Please forgive any howling errors!

And to each and every reader or listener, whether you buy, download or borrow from a library, thank you. It's greatly appreciated.

ABOUT THE AUTHOR

Lisa Cutts retired as a detective sergeant after twenty-five years with Kent police, having spent most of that time investigating murders for a living. She worked within the Serious Crime Directorate for most of her police career, including thirteen years within the Major Crime Department and eighteen months with the Professional Standards Department.

As well as having nine crime fiction books published, Lisa's short story, *Waiting,* was included in the anthology *To Serve, Protect and Write.* All fifteen authors featured worked for law enforcement across the United States, the United Kingdom, Canada and Australia. Lisa is the author of the DC Nina Foster books, *Never Forget* and *Remember, Remember. Never Forgot* was longlisted for the Waverton Good Read Award 2013 and the winner of the Killer Nashville Silver Falchion Award 2014 for Best Thriller. She has written four books in the East Rise Incident Room series, *Mercy Killing, Buried Secrets, Lost Lives* and *Don't Trust Him.* The last three to be published were cozy crime books set in Kent, *Murder at the Gardens* being the latest release.

Her latest book, *Street Hearts: An Extraordinary Story of Saving Street Dogs,* was the result of a chance meeting at a library event in Kent. This forged a friendship with Emma and Anthony Smith who had moved from Yorkshire to Bulgaria for a relaxed retirement. Instead, they 'accidently' rescued and rehomed over 1400 dogs. *Street Hearts: An Extraordinary Story of Saving Street Dogs* tells the story of Emma and Anthony's battle to tackle the problem and is published on 29th August 2024.

Lisa also writes a monthly column, *Behind the Tape*, for *Writing Magazine* answering police procedural questions from other writers. She is the patron of Murderous Medway, which takes place across the Medway towns.

As well as taking part in a number of panels at fiction and crime fiction festivals and being on BBC Radio 4's Open Book, Lisa has twice appeared on *This Morning* to chat about TV crime dramas *Broadchurch* and *Line of Duty*.

Facebook: https://www.facebook.com/lisa.cutts.505/

X: @LisaCuttsAuthor

Instagram: lisa_cutts

A NOTE FROM THE PUBLISHER

Thank you for reading this book. If you enjoyed it please do consider leaving a review on Amazon to help others find it too.

We hate typos. All of our books have been rigorously edited and proofread, but sometimes mistakes do slip through. If you have spotted a typo, please do let us know and we can get it amended within hours.

info@bloodhoundbooks.com